ALEXIS MAREE

KINGS OF HELL
ADRIK

By Alexis Maree

I0639718

1

THE KINGS OF HELL
ADRIK

Cover by Alexis Maree | Edits by Fluffy Fox Publishing | Proofreading done by Adrianne Normanton
© 2023 by Alexis Maree

CONTENT WARNING

This book contains scenes of dark natures that may trigger some readers – e.g; torture, graphic sexual scenes, and coarse language. Not all possible triggers have been mentioned. By reading further, you, as the reader, are continuing with the understanding that this book has darker tones and that not all possible triggers may have been mentioned. The author and any who contributed to this work cannot and will not be held accountable for a reader's actions, reactions, or state of mind after reading this book.

OTHER BOOKS BY ME

<u>ALEXIS MAREE</u>
THE KINGS OF HELL SERIES:
The Kings of Hell - Cole

<u>T. MAREE</u>
THE LEAH REYNOLDS SERIES:
Sins in the Silence
Sins of a Daughter
Sins of the Past
Sins of the Enemy
Sins of the Forbidden
Sins of the Blood

STANDALONES
Falling for the Mountain Man
Colorful

<u>LUNA MAREE</u>

L'Amour Island
Her Sir & Sire

THE KINGS OF HELL
ADRIK

This book is dedicated to all of you who read my books and who fell in love with Cole & Mika enough to give Adrik & Cali a chance.

THE KINGS OF HELL
ADRIK

First and foremost, I'd like to thank my friends and family.
You never stop me from chasing my dreams, you support me in my every endeavor, and you don't make me feel bad for the hours I spend at my laptop.
You make chasing my author-dreams worth it!

I'd like to thank Adrianne for being my alpha reader, for helping me find mistakes, plot holes, and for listening to me whine and complain when my characters aren't co-operating.
Thank you for loving my characters as much as I do!

To my ARC team who have been beyond useful in being my cheer squad and for catching those frustrating little errors that slip so many rounds of editing.

Also, thank you to Rochelle Simas at *Fluffy Fox Publishing* for keeping me on as a client and for editing all my manuscripts. One day I'll stop sending you drafts with sentences that start with "but". One day... ☺

THE PROPHECY OF THE NINE

From the first to the last, the Brothers Nine will fall...

The first will face death and prevail,
The second shall follow her blood trail.

The third will endure his deal of time,
The fourth need only await his sign.

The fifth will betray his woman of binding,
The sixth will save she he must be finding.

The seventh will take her to keep her safe,
The eighth will have to rely on Faith.

The ninth alone is left to find,
She who was taken, now hidden by design.

From first to the last, the Brothers Nine must fall,
Or chaos reigns, and they will destroy it all.

Bound to the Second

THE KINGS OF HELL
ADRIK

PROLOGUE

Long story short, there is a celestial war that has been raging since the beginning of time.

Angels vs. Demons.

Light vs. Dark.

Good vs. Evil.

For eons there was nothing but bloodshed and pain, and then humans emerged, and with them, souls. This became the new currency and thus the wars dwindled. No, they didn't stop, but the intensity of them fell way back, and both sides became overly busy with the production of Demons and Angels. In essence, the era of an arms race began. Each side found they could turn souls into Angels and Demons, therefore, increasing the supply of warriors available for battle. This would go on for centuries before the discovery of Witches.

Witches are neither good nor bad. They do not play for either team, and their souls are recycled over time to keep their species alive. They are technically human with human lifespans, but they have the ability to use magic and heal. This is not just an ability, but a calling; a need as basic as breathing for them. Primarily, they heal Angels and Demons, as they are drawn to the beings in pain. They also heal humans, but the urge to heal them is far less than what it is to heal a celestial. They work for neither team, but are there simply to help keep the balance.

That was until someone—no one is quite sure who started it—began collecting an army of Witches.

Not a lot can kill an Archangel, nothing except a Demon Blade.

And the same worked in reverse, nothing but an Angel Blade would kill a King of Hell. So, when Witches were found to possess the ability to heal such wounds, they became highly sought after, and the hunt for Witches ensued, resulting in their race being entirely wiped out.

Or, that's what everyone thought…

Tired of being persecuted by humans and hunted by Angels and Demons—the very beings they were born to heal—Witches went into hiding to protect themselves and their future generations.

Until one day, a Demon King found a Witch, and their existence was exposed.

Now, Angels and Demons alike are on the hunt once again, determined to have the only thing that could save their enemies, and keep it from them at all costs.

One Witch has been found and is now protected.

Will there be more?

CHAPTER ONE
ADRIK

I was bored.

The second circle of Hell—my circle of Hell—was running fine, and I loved that things were going so smoothly. Unfortunately, that left me sitting around twiddling my thumbs.

And you know what they say about idle hands...

I stepped out of my room and into the hallway that was lined with nine doors; each leading to the private realms of each King of Hell. My brothers and I, all nine of us, each held dominion over different levels.

Cole was the ruler of the first circle, and lately had been a royal pain in everyone's ass. Not because he wasn't doing his job—he was—but everyone was tired of seeing that sickeningly smug, overly happy grin on his face. Yes, we all understood he found his mate, Tomika, and now they're fucking like rabbits every chance they get. Honestly, if I had to look at one more *come fuck me* expression on either of their faces, I was going to be sick.

Then there was me, King of the second circle of hell. I, like my other brothers, had not yet found my mate. None of us had even thought it was possible; none of us even knew we were destined for mates. Granted, we probably should have known—our mother Lilith had pestered us for centuries to read the Old Books and learn about ourselves—but who wanted to read dusty old books when there was so much else to do?

After seeing no one in the hall worth talking to, I wrapped myself in shadow and teleported myself onto the surface. The hunt for

Witches was back on, and in my case, I was looking for my mate. Anyway, we all forgot about the books until Mika came along, and in her attempt to rid herself of The Mark which Cole had put on her, she'd come across the prophecy. A prophecy which, if it was to be believed, meant each of us had a mate out there, and that we would each find her in order from first to last. This meant I should be next as Cole had already found his. None of us knew how long it would take to find them or what would happen if we somehow missed our window. We had no way of knowing if our mates would be human, a Witch like Mika, a Demon, or some other mix. All I knew was that if I found her, I would have to follow her blood trail. That was the clue left to me in the prophecy. I'd have my mate after I followed her blood trail. After me, was Malik, followed by Harkyn and Tamas. That brought us to the last four. Donovan, or Nova as we called him, ran the sixth circle of Hell. He was in and out of here most days, as he was on a mission to find Mika's twin sister who she'd been separated from since they were young girls.

Following Donovan was Cassius, Devlin, and then… Corvin. You know, I love all my brothers. I would die in an instant if it meant I could save even one of them. But Corvin… well, I'm a King of Hell and the guy makes me nervous. Not in a *"will he come to work with a shotgun someday and kill everyone?"* kind of nervous, but more of a *"shit, I breathed near him and now he's going to decimate an entire continent because of my audacity,"* kind of nervous. The man was on the edge, and we all worried he was going to go to the dark side.

I wondered if finding his mate would somehow balance him out. Afterall, Cole had been a sarcastic daredevil before he met Mika. Yes, he was still a pain in the ass, and yes, he was still sarcastic as all fuck, but he seemed complete now—more balanced and whole.

Scuffling in the alleyway nearby drew my attention back to the here and now, and I peeked around the corner again. I was hunting a rogue band of Demons that were causing us a bit of trouble. Many might be surprised to know that not all Demons were under the control of me or my brothers. There were some who had branched off over the centuries and formed their own beliefs and groups. Every species had their oddballs, and these guys somehow got it in their head that they could do their own thing and get away with it. Sure, okay, maybe we had let it go on for a little too long, but who really had the time to chase them up? We had millions, no, *billions* of souls to deal with every day, and no one really wanted to go and hunt down a few stray Demons who were causing next to no drama.

Until they were.

We hadn't become aware of how extensive the problem was until Mika had found Cole. The number of Rogue's were larger than we originally thought, and more than that, some of the little fuckers were teaming up with our natural enemies—Angels. They were trying to de-throne a King of Hell in the hopes of taking it over and ruling it themselves. None of us were sure that was even possible, but it wasn't stopping them from trying.

So, now I spend a few days a month tracking down the strays and putting them out of their misery. Occasionally, I brought one back to Hell and held a demonstration for the others so they saw what happened to deserters and betrayers. It may seem cruel to those who did not know our ways, but it was not easy to keep control of so many Demons, and they respond to pain and fear more than time outs and quiet reprimands.

I watched now as a group of six Rogue Demons strode confidently in my direction and I ducked into a small alcove. I had come too late tonight for the unfortunate human they had butchered. Some of them had learned if they properly sacrificed a pure human and ate their heart, it would enhance their powers, albeit, temporarily, but it was still a power boost. Unfortunately, a lot of humans were paying for our oversight. We would have put a stop to it anyway, but Tomika was being very vocal about how mad she was on this subject, so each of my brothers and myself were topside a lot more than usual, putting Rogue Demons down wherever we could.

I waited as the group passed me before I stepped into pace behind them. None of them noticed me there to start with, and it wasn't until we got to the end of the alley that took us to a backdoor to a club, that the nearest one realized I was there. His steps faltered, causing him to stumble and I grinned.

"Hey there," I greeted cheerfully before I shot my hand forward. I smashed through his chest, crushing bone, muscle, and sinew. He gaped at me as I wrapped my hand around his still-beating heart and wrenched it from his body with a wet, sucking sound. The other five turned to look at me in shock as I dropped the ruined organ to the ground beside the twitching Demon. He wouldn't die right away, it took a lot to kill a Demon, but he would stay down for a little while.

"Good evening," I welcomed, smiling congenially at the group. "Get him!" one of them shouted. I rolled my eyes as the group rushed me, and drew inwards, finding them in my minds eye, linking each of their life forces to me before I clenched my fist, grasping the invisible ropes I'd connected to them. Each of them came to a jarring halt, their eyes wide and mouths gaping, but no sound escaped.

"We told you all to stay quiet," I reminded through gritted teeth, letting them feel the full force of my anger. These fuckers were some of the few who meant Mika harm, who meant my brothers harm. None of them could be permitted to leave.

One of them made a gurgling, wheezing sound, and I noticed it was the same one who had spoken before. The leader, I was going to assume. I lessened my hold on him and he gasped.

"We apologize, my King. We will leave now," he rasped.

I frowned. "Oh, there's no way you're leaving here tonight," I answered with contempt. His eyes flicked behind me, and I caught the merest glimmer of triumph there and spun quickly to get a fist in the face. Still gripping the Demons tightly, I struck back, my fist slamming into the face of the Angel who had snuck up behind me.

Fucking fuckers. If there was something we hated more than the Rogue Demons, it was these self-righteous dicks.

I tightened my hold on one of the Demons, draining him of his life and taking his energy into myself, boosting my power as I flung hellfire at a second Angel. He screamed in agony even as a third threw a small blade at me. It scraped my chest as I moved to avoid it, and the unmistakable burn of an Angel-Blade made me grimace.

"What do you winged dick-bags want?" I snarled as the Demon I'd drained fell to the ground, a lifeless husk. All my brothers and I had this ability, but we rarely used it as it was hardly a fair fight. Demons we may be, but we appreciated the art of a fair war, and so this was a last resort... or to get across a point. Not to mention, dividing our attention between a fight and holding the life force of several others to us could prove deadly if we were not careful.

"To rid the world of you, Devil spawn," one of them hissed. I rolled my eyes. Okay, Angels were typically lethal fuckers, but they all walked around in these black outfits with delicate model-like features, too pretty and perfect to actually be human but not good looking enough to be a Demon.

"Ouch. You'll hurt my feelings with words like that," I pouted, yanking the life force from a second Demon. I had no idea what the Angels were doing using Rogues, but they had an agenda, and whatever worked for them most certainly would not work for us.

The three Angels converged at once, and I had to move quickly to outmaneuver them. The space we were standing in was small and not conducive to a fight between celestials. We tended to break buildings, so we'd have to be careful here so as not to draw attention. Because as much as we didn't care if humans got caught in the crossfire, we were all at least able to agree that humans should not be given absolute proof of divinity. It was the one rule we all kept.

The fight was on, but it was nothing compared to what I was used to. I was playing with them, keeping them on their toes enough that they kept coming but didn't run scared. Every few moments I drained another Demon until only the leader was standing.

"Take that, you fluffy fairy!" I shouted, purposely throwing small balls of Hellfire at the Angel to keep him moving. Another rushed me from behind and I threw a series of flames after him.

"Go back to Hell, Demon filth," an Angel retorted, hurling a blade at me that narrowly missed my head.

"I am rubber, you are glue," I chanted in a sing-song voice and grinned, dancing around the Angel, playing with them. This group were not well trained. They most certainly should not be picking fights with a Demon, much less a King of Hell. I'd never let one of my Demons leave the Pit if they were anywhere near as weak as this lot.

"Your kind are not fit to walk the surface," the third one snarled,

lashing out with a well-timed kick. I dodged and skipped away.
I laughed. "Whatever you say, Halo-hugger."
The Angel pulled out his blade, and I paused feigning a gasp.
"An Angel Blade... Are you flirting with me?"
Ice-hot pain lanced through my ribs, and I bit back my shout of
pain—barely. I glanced down to see the handle of an Angel Blade
sticking out from between my ribs and cursed. Looking up, my
gaze clashed with the eyes of a fourth Angel who was smirking at
me.
"Mother fucker," I hissed, letting my anger bleed through.
"At least I'm not the dead mother fucker," he returned, smug
satisfaction clear on his face.
"Not yet," I replied, raising an eyebrow. I clenched my fist,
dragging the life force from the last Demon, using it to fuel my
power and mask my pain. Drawing deep inside, I unleashed a
wall of hellfire at the four Angels, done dancing with them. I
needed to get my wound looked at before it took me down.
Screams of agony shattered the night air, and I slipped my own
dagger from its sheath and got to work, coming in low and
slashing at the Angels, making sure to decapitate or rip their
hearts from their chests as I went. I stabbed each of them, tearing
them apart so that by the end of it, I was drenched in blood and
innards, and they were a mass of broken, bloody meat suits piled
together.
When the last one was added to the pile, I dragged in a deep
breath and grimaced as pain burned through me.
Fuck.
I had been cocky, dancing around and not keeping my senses
alert. I'd allowed an amateur Angel to get the drop on me, and I
could never let that happen again. Looking at the mass of
twitching bodies before me, I concentrated a stream of hellfire on

them, making sure to burn the bodies to ash before I let the flames die down. Not a single one would survive that.

I slid my dagger back into its sheath and leaned heavily against the brick wall beside me, taking a moment to get a handle on the pain. Shoving it down, I forced myself not to show it. Kings of Hell did not feel pain, at least, that was what we told everyone, and we had managed to keep the truth hidden for eons. I wasn't about to let on that we were vulnerable to it.

Closing my eyes, I imagined myself clean and was relieved when all the grime and blood was removed from my body. The sounds of humans became clearer, and I wrapped myself in shadow and sent myself away. I staggered to a stop several blocks away and hissed. I needed to go home; Mika could heal me.

I'd had this injury once before at a time when Witches were gone, and I'd managed to get my hands on the fucker who'd injured me and took some of his blood to heal it.

I groaned. Pain wasn't exactly a new thing to me, and pretending I wasn't injured was an art form me and my brothers had perfected over the centuries.

"You need a Healer."

I turned quickly to catch sight of an old man a small distance away, waving a hand towards my bloody midsection where my hands clutched my ribs. I mentally kicked myself. I *really* had to remember to scan my surroundings at all times. I was slipping; too used to passing through the years without an issue.

"Did ya hear me, son? You need a Healer," the old man repeated.

"No shit," I mumbled. The old man's eyes brightened briefly, and he seemed to be weighing his next words carefully.

"How did you get hurt, anyway?" he asked.

"I told a pretty boy he was a wuss. He didn't take too kindly to it."

The old man's lips twitched, and I sighed. I might as well go home; no one but Mika could do anything for me. Cole would be mad because my need would pull her away from him, and she'd have to put her hands on me.

I bit back a grin; it was always fun to get Cole riled. We all knew he and Mika were happy together, and none of us would dream of trying to take a woman from a brother, but it was fun to make Cole get all snarly and snappish. Besides, Mika and Cole were destined mates. There was no pulling them away from each other, even if one of us were so inclined. Sure, she was hot, and her sass was hilarious when she threw it around, but none of us were interested in going there, not really.

"So, you gonna go get that sorted?" the man asked.

I shrugged. "A doctor can't heal me," I answered, pushing off from the wall, and it took far too much effort to refrain from groaning.

"I didn't say you needed a doctor," he added with a squinty look, as if he were weighing my worth. "I got eyes, boy. You ain't normal. No, you need a Healer."

I raised my eyebrows at being called *boy*. He had no idea how old I was. He was practically a sperm, at least to me. But my attention snagged on his insistence of a Healer. Some humans called other humans Healers, but usually they were Faith Healers, and they were a load of shit.

"You know where I can find a Healer?" I asked, curious now.

"I might," he hedged, his sharp eyes considering me.

"But you won't tell me." I made it a statement.

He shrugged. "Like I said, you ain't normal. You need a Healer, but I don't think I want you near her."

My interest increased. I knew I could pluck the information from the old man's head in an instant, but I did him the courtesy of waiting. What could I say? I liked the crotchety guy's attitude and humor.

Could it be? Was he talking about a Witch? I had been hunting for one since Cole and Mika had gotten past their near-death experience over two years ago. I'd been looking for a Witch at the hospitals and shelters knowing that a Witch could not ignore her need to heal, not entirely. They could suppress it, but it was impossible to always ignore. There had been no flares of energy to suggest a Witch nearby, but if she knew what she was and was smart enough to hide herself, then there wouldn't be any trace.

"No, I'm not normal," I finally answered, deciding to be frank with the man. "And this is no normal wound. Without a proper Healer, one I suspect you know… it will never heal," I answered. It was the truth; I just didn't let on that I already knew where I could find one and be healed within an hour.

"Are you a danger to her?" he asked.

"Only if she's dangerous to me."

He watched me with shrewd eyes, his narrow frame trembling slightly. I knew it wasn't from cold or fear, but likely age and illness.

"Come with me," he finally answered and turned his back.

I waited a few beats, wondering if this really would be my lucky break. If she was a Witch, then she'd be able to see me even if I cloaked myself. Witches could see auras, so she'd know I wasn't technically a good guy. Would she even agree to help me? Did it even matter?

I frowned as I followed the old man, wondering what I was going to do. If this Healer was a Witch, would it be smarter to run away with her like Cole had done to Mika? Or would it be more prudent to allow her some freedoms while following her? I didn't want to have all the same issues Cole had with Mika. I didn't want to have to kidnap her. Besides, Mika was a different story. Not only was she Cole's mate, but she was also an untrained Witch. I had the feeling I was going to be dealing with one who knew very well what she was and how to use her magic. Restraining her probably wasn't the best way to go about getting her on my side.

Had she already met the Angels? Had they had a chance to brainwash her to their side and make her one of theirs? No... no that wasn't likely. The Angels were hungry for a Witch now that word had spread about their existence. They wouldn't let a Witch roam around on Earth, they'd keep her locked away in their realm to have as a personal Healer. I mean... I wasn't really any better. It would be great to have a Healer on hand all the time—one I didn't have to fight my brother for—but I wasn't up for the constant fighting kidnapping her would cause.

What if she's yours?

The thought came to me unbidden, and I squashed the small spark of hope and interest. No. It was so unlikely it was laughable. Besides, just because the prophecy stated each brother had a soul mate, didn't mean she'd be a Witch. It was just as likely she'd be a human without any magic.

"What are you, anyway?" the old man asked suddenly.

"My name is Adrik."

"I didn't ask ya name, boy. I asked *what* you are. Cause you ain't human, that's for sure."

"And what would you know of non-humans?" I asked, raising a brow. Just because he said he knew; didn't mean he really did. A lot of homeless people were a little nutty.

"I've been around a while, seen my fair share of things. I know there are things out there that people don't wanna think about, and I can see you're one of 'em. So... what are you?" he continued, never once stopping his walk.

I considered his question and how best to answer it. No humans, besides Witches, were supposed to know of the existence of Demons and Angels. They couldn't have absolute proof of the divine or things tended to get messy.

"I'm different," I replied with a shrug.

He made a scoffing sound and shook his head. "A blind man can see that. Alright, don't tell me. A man has the right to his secrets, I suppose."

I followed him in silence for a while, cursing the burning and stinging on my side. It wasn't unbearable, but I was exhausted, and I just wanted to go home. The pain would only increase as time wore on, but I guess one of the perks of growing up in Hell with eight brothers was that one learned how to never show pain. Pain was weakness, and I couldn't afford to be weak and rule over a circle of Hell. I was hoping it would be worth the extra wait to get this healed. I pressed my hand harder against my side, ignoring the blood that seeped between my fingers.

Up ahead, beneath the highway underpass, there were a group of tents set out, tables, and a couple of vans. The lights were dim in the growing darkness. As we got closer, I could see some of the tables had food set out, and people behind them serving others. Ah, they were do-gooders, probably spreading the word of God and infecting unsuspecting homeless people.

I rolled my eyes, already disgusted.

Fuck, I hated the church goers. They were always so goddamn righteous—pun intended. Most of them were giant hypocrites too, which always made it fun when they ended up downstairs with me and my brothers.

"Your Healer is here?"

"Do I look like I got time to waste draggin' you somewhere else?"

the old man returned rudely.

I grinned at his snark and followed his slower lead, looking everyone over carefully. No other Demons, no Angels... all humans. I couldn't sense a Witch anywhere, but if she were smart, then she'd have hidden herself well.

"Have you been healed before?" I decided to ask.

"Maybe," he murmured cryptically. I got the impression he was done telling me anything else until he knew if he could trust me or not.

"What's your name?" I asked the old man as we approached.

"You can call me Sol," he answered without looking back.

"Alright, Sol. Why are you bringing me to your Healer if you don't think you can trust me?"

"I don't trust anyone, boy. But you got an injury only a Healer can heal, and I gotta believe that I was late for the bus today so that I could find your sorry ass and bring you to her. Otherwise, I walked twelve blocks for nothin'," he snapped grumpily.

I grinned again. I liked Sol and his sullen attitude.

"A believer in fate?" I wondered aloud. He made a small sound of derision and shook his head. I kept my senses peeled the closer we got, but there was still nothing beyond the humans.

"You can call it whatever you want to call it, boy. But like I said, I've been around long enough to know a thing or two, and stuff happens for a reason, even the shitty stuff," he muttered.

"Like getting sliced with a blade?"

"Like me having to walk twelve blocks with my shot knees and having to listen to you talk like you just discovered the ability. Now, shut your pie-hole and go get healed," Sol huffed impatiently, pointing towards the larger tent. I chuckled as the old man muttered under his breath and headed for the table piled with food.

I stopped to take another look around, aware of the multitude of traps someone could have set for me or my brothers if they were smart. But those kinds of things usually left a trace, and all I was getting here was hopelessness, bad hygiene, and humans.

"Here goes nothing," I muttered under my breath before I wrapped myself in shadow and entered the tent. It was lit from within by several battery-operated torches and lights. There were several seats already filled with people and they were all facing a closed curtain. I was surprised; I figured this would be a show like the Faith Healers put on. I was expecting a stage and a chorus of singing religious zealots and lots of overacting as the "spirit of Christ" moved through them. Several people took up space, the smell pungent but not overwhelming. It was obvious everyone here was human, and I wondered if they'd ever been healed by this person before.

Sighing, I crossed my arms over my stomach, keeping pressure on the blade wound and waited.

CHAPTER TWO
CALI

I knew something was wrong.

The overpowering feeling of darkness swamped me, spread around the tent, and infiltrated my previously serene atmosphere like a slow stain. It wasn't evil, exactly, but it was certainly dark. I didn't let any of this show on my face however, or to influence my healing in any way, shape, or form. I needed to finish healing this little girl before I could handle what was out there. I didn't want to stop her session now, not when we'd finally started making some progress with her illness. She was suffering every day, and unfortunately, her condition was advanced and leading her to a short and somewhat painful life.

Sky, the twelve-year-old girl on my table, remained still and practiced the deep breathing I'd taught her. She was as calm as ever, never once feeling stressed or panicked as I worked. Her mother, Sara, was less so. I could understand the woman's unease and inability to remain still. She had seen every type of medical professional known to man, and I was her last resort. I didn't take offense to that. More often than not, I was the desperate last hope for many people, and I helped as many of them as I could.

Sara came to me four months ago, a total wreck, desperate, and hurting. Her daughter was in pain and had all but given up on a chance to live. I knew healing her would drain me; it would take a lot of time and effort. I'd desperately wanted to heal the young girl who had not even had a chance to live yet, but it had taken a lot of convincing with her mother to make sure she kept up with her visits to me. I could heal cuts and bruises, even broken bones and torn muscles and tissue... but a disease like this took a lot of power and finesse. It couldn't be done in one session, and I wasn't totally sure it could be done to completion. I had never tried to do it before. My Aunt Penny had healed a disease this extreme before, but she was a seasoned Witch and very capable. I'd been learning since I was a child, but never dared to take on a case like this before.

I'd been pleasantly surprised when Sara came back the next week after her first session with a little more hope on her face. After three weeks of my sessions, she came barreling in one day and almost tackled me in a hug. She'd taken Sky for another exam and the doctors were baffled by how her condition seemed to have improved since her last checkup. And every month since, Sky was showing signs of healing. I warned Sara that if I was able to heal her completely, that she and her daughter may have to move away. Doctors from all over would be wanting to run tests on Sky to see how this was possible, and I didn't want Sky to trade a short life with her disease for a long life being poked and prodded by doctors.

The feeling of darkness grew as time went on, and I focused harder on healing Sky.

Finally, I drew back, sucking in a breath and took a moment to steady myself.

"Are you okay, Cali?" Sky asked. I smiled softly and drew in a deep breath.

"I always am. I just need a minute after your sessions is all," I assured, squeezing her hands. Sara stepped up beside us, her bright eyes smiling at her daughter.

"I made another donation last week, Cali. I hope you're able to get those beds you were talking about."

"Thank you so much, Sara. You know I don't require any form of payment for my work though," I reminded, hating the idea of her feeling like she was obligated to give so much.

"It's the least I can do, hon. You're saving my daughter. If I could, I'd give you everything I have," she answered honestly. I smiled and patted her hand.

"We appreciate your donations."

I helped Sky stand up and be steady on her feet. "Okay. You're all ready to go. I'll see you again next week, okay?"

Sky gave me a quick hug which I hurriedly returned and walked them to the tent flap that led to the waiting room. Just as Sara was opening the flap, I pulled her back gently and caught sight of the man responsible for all the darkness.

Only he wasn't a man.

He was a Demon, but not like any Demon I'd ever seen before. I mean, not only was he hot beyond belief, but the sheer power that radiated from him had me drawing in a sharp breath. He wasn't someone I wanted to mess with, and since Demons and Angels seemed to be on the hunt for my kind again, seeing him out there meant I had been found. He was also in a *lot* of pain. The sheer amount of it was excruciating, but it wasn't showing even a little on his face. The only sign that he was injured was in the way he held a hand to his side, blood seeping through his fingers.

"Are you okay, Cali?" Sara asked softly.

"Yes," I said quickly, and then realized I had her hand. "Sorry, can you please announce that Mr. Jefferies is next?"

Sara nodded slowly and stepped out. As soon as she was gone, I hurried to my bag, threw in my candles, crystals, and talismans, and zipped my bag shut. I was out the side door before Sara made the announcement.

Mr. Jefferies didn't exist. It was a code phrase I used among my regulars to alert them to clear out and that something was wrong. They would make sure everyone who was new got out quickly and safely.

I looked over my shoulder as a steady stream of people exited the tents, a few stopping to pack up the food platters and dismantle the tables. Unfortunately, I'd had to put in procedures such as these many times in the past. I couldn't risk Angels or Demons finding me, and I sometimes ended up with humans after me, the kind looking for a news story or a medical marvel they could run tests on. I wasn't interested in being a part of either.

I made sure my concealment charm was strong as I merged into the crowds on main street. I could disappear here, and that was what I needed to do.

I rounded a corner and turned to look over my shoulder, making sure no one was following me when I ran into something hard. I gasped, and a hand shot out to catch my wrist, the grip tight and warm. I glanced up, already knowing it was the Demon I'd seen. I opened my mouth to curse him, and he tugged me upright, pressing a hand over my mouth.

"Please, help me," he whispered roughly. I sucked in a sharp breath, freezing for a moment at the intensity of his pain, my eyes glued to his bluer than blue eyes. He took his hand from my mouth, and I backed up, tugging my wrist away from him.

"Why should I?"

"I am going to die. I was stabbed with an Angel Blade."

"Your kind would abduct me and hide me away, why should I help a Demon?"

He shook his head. "I am a King of Hell."

I raised an eyebrow and took another slow step back. "That

makes me want to help you even less."

A cold finger of fear traced up my spine and I mentally prepared a spell, drawing my magic from within me to protect myself.

"What if I told you I can protect you?" he asked.

~

ADRIK

I watched her magnificent eyes swirl with distrust and heat, the combination somehow alluring. This was her... it had to be. The sudden flare of desire and need I felt was unlike anything I had ever experienced before. She was my mate; I was sure of it... and yet... the prophecy. It stated I'd have to follow her blood trail to find her. She was standing in front of me, uninjured. Instead, I was the one who was hurt and bleeding. She was mine, I knew it with a certainty I'd never had before, like she was a missing part of me I'd finally found. She was beautiful, with a curly mane of strawberry blonde hair and pale green eyes. Her creamy skin looked soft; her cheeks flushed slightly. She was taller than Mika and slightly curvier, her body meant to be gripped and held, to lose yourself in.

"I wouldn't believe you even if you promised such a ridiculous thing," she returned hotly, shaking me out of my thoughts. Distrust and unease were clear across her face, and I let my agony wash over me, causing me to stagger. I lifted a hand to hold myself upright against the underpass and caught the flicker of concern on her face.

"Please. I am in a lot of pain," I pushed, knowing she could feel my injuries because I was projecting it.

"That's not really my problem," she murmured, but there was no heat to her words.

"You are a Witch… this is what you are meant to do," I groaned, looking down at my hand now coated with thick, red blood.

The Witch pressed her lips together and looked around us, her need to heal clashed with her instinctual reaction to run and hide.

I allowed my pain to wash over me again, pushed it out so she gasped and clutched her chest, her eyes swinging back to me.

I knew she had made up her mind to heal me before the next words passed her lips.

"Fine. But we need to get away from here. Follow me." There was a bite in her tone, but I nodded and staggered after her, not needing to put on much of an act with how much my injuries ached. My legs wanted to crumble beneath me, the fire and ice that ran through my veins was almost enough to make me shout and curse.

I followed the Witch as she led me off the crowded streets and back beneath the bridge to a different section of the underpass. Most people had cleared out now, leaving us alone. She gestured to a broken crate among a pile of discarded wood, and I took it to mean she wanted me to sit down.

"Let me look." She sighed, and I could tell she was determined to get this over with as quickly as possible. I couldn't allow that to happen, I needed to spend time with her, convince her she was in danger and that she needed me.

"Shirt off or on?" I asked. She shrugged, choosing not to answer. I carefully tugged off my jacket and placed it beside me on the crate and started to lift my shirt but groaned and hissed, pain ricocheting all through my body.

"Here, let me," she ordered, her voice strained with concern. I hid my smile and nodded. I could have waved the clothes from my body, but this was so much better, even with the pain.

The Witch helped me remove the bloody and torn material, and I watched as she paused briefly, her breath catching and her gaze heating as she looked at me. I purposely tensed, allowing the definition of each muscle beneath the tapestry of tattoos to be visible to her. She lowered her gaze, her cheeks turning pink, and I wanted to shout in victory. I quickly buried the emotion. She was a Witch; she would sense my every emotion.

"I want you to know, Demon King, that if you make a move to take me or cause me harm, I have the ability and the will to hurt you. I will make sure your attempt to hurt me is the last thing you ever do. Is that understood?" she asked softly, but there was a will of iron in her voice that was impossible to ignore.

"Are you single, Witch?" I asked as if she hadn't just threatened me. Honestly, the thought of her fighting me made the front of my jeans incredibly tight. She blinked quickly and dropped my shirt, her gaze jumping back to mine.

"Excuse me?"

"Are you single?" I repeated, keeping my tone light even though the thought of another male with his hands on her made me recall every form of torture I could use on him.

"What does that matter to you?" she asked, stepping closer to look at my wounds.

"I want to know what my chances are of winning you over," I said with a shrug, wincing and hissing loudly when the wound tugged and burned painfully.

"You have no chance with me. You're a King of Hell," she pointed out. "I can almost guarantee you there's nothing that would tempt me to cross that line."

"*Almost* guarantee isn't a total guarantee. I like my chances." I watched her lips tug slightly in a repressed smile, but she ducked her head again before I could coax it out.

"You're awfully sure of yourself," she murmured, stepping to the side to look at my back.

"As old as I am… I should be. And you, dear Witch, are quite the catch."

"Of course I am. I'm a Witch and you want to have me as a secret weapon," she returned a little sharply.

"I'd prefer to have you in my bed than as a weapon."

She paused again, her eyes wide and cheeks staining pink. I liked that I could shock her with my words.

She shook her head. "You are incredibly forward."

"I'm decisive and determined," I corrected.

Rolling her eyes, I watched as she drew in a deep breath and centered herself. I could feel her humor, the way she didn't want to think I was funny, the way she detested that she was physically attracted to me, but she was determined to remain distant.

Hmm… I'd have to see what I could do about that.

"Do you believe in destiny or fate?" I asked.

"Of course," she whispered and brought her hands to my torso, directly over the Angel Blade wound. I hissed and bit back a curse.

"I think it was fate we met tonight," I forced out in a pained breath.

"Oh?"

"Yes. I got stabbed by an Angel Blade, met an old man who recognized me as something not human and knew I needed a Healer and not a doctor. He led me to the camp which led me to you… a Witch, a species of human we thought were extinct."

She didn't reply to that, and I gave her some time, closing my eyes on the blinding heat she was pushing toward my wound. I had left getting healed a little late, the lethal components from the blade had almost had enough time to work its way throughout my whole body. If she hadn't healed me when I asked, I wasn't sure I'd have had enough energy to call for Cole and Mika to save me.

One of the Witch's hands slid across my bicep, and I felt the heat intensely. I allowed my desire for her to wrap around us, let her feel that I wanted her. Her lips pressed together again, a small frown on her face and I ducked my head to hide my grin.

"We should get to know each other," I announced.

"Why?"

"Because we're going to be seeing a lot of each other. I assume you'd want to know me, and I certainly want to know about you," I answered.

"I am disappearing after this healing and you'll never see me again," she explained.

"Nope. Fate has other ideas. We'll see each other again. My name is Adrik," I introduced. She didn't respond, but I could feel her exasperation was tinged with humor. I was getting to her.

"I have eight brothers; we each rule a circle of hell. I hold dominion over the second circle," I continued happily as if she were interested. She was a little, but not enough to engage. Ignoring this, I continued anyway.

"My parents are happily betrothed and enjoying their time together away from their children."

This statement made her pause and her eyes opened. She frowned, and I could see confusion clear as day across her face.

"Your parents?" she asked. I nodded and waited. "As in…" She trailed off, looking uncertain.

"Lucifer and Lilith," I finished for her.

"And you say they're… happy?"

"That surprises you?"

35

"Well… yes," she answered, blinking quickly. I shrugged. "Despite what you had to have heard, they're not what everyone thinks they are. My father was like any son abandoned and disowned by his father for simply breaking a few rules. He was angry and resentful, ready to tear the world apart. That was until he met my mother, and she calmed him in a way he hadn't known was possible and showed him how to make the best of a situation. She became everything to my father, and he made sure she knew how much he treasured her. She knew all too well what it was to be cast aside as well, and together they bonded and became, in my opinion, a greater love story than Adam and Eve," I explained, still able to see the way my father and mother looked at each other. It had been a long time since we'd seen them, and none of us expected to see them again.

"Wow," the Witch whispered, stunned. I grinned and let the moment draw out before she shook herself and went back to healing.

"Anyway," I continued when it was obvious she wasn't going to say anything more, "I love the color blue, I hate vegetables, and I believe that whoever invented the harp needs to be strangled with one."

She shook her head in confusion, but that humor was back in her mind, even though she refused to show it.

"I have a thing for strawberry blondes, especially those with a sassy mouth and a backbone," I added. She rolled her eyes and moved back to healing me, her hands warm and moving slowly. Another tug from deep inside me, an urging to claim her was building in strength, only cementing my belief that this woman was mine.

"Cut it out," she hissed, a small frown creasing her forehead.

"Cut what out?" I asked, even though I was fairly sure I knew what she was referring to.

"Stop projecting your pain. I can feel it without you helping it along, I could feel it before you even entered my tent," she ground out. I grinned, uncaring if she could sense my amusement or not.

"Maybe I just wanted you to put your hands on me?" I suggested. Her nails dug into my skin briefly in retaliation, and I groaned, my cock jumping in my pants. She opened her pretty eyes, her face far too close to mine. She swallowed hard, and I could see she realized the reaction she'd caused in me and had been unprepared for it. I wanted to reach into her mind, to influence her, to make her want me, but this woman wasn't like Tomika. She was practiced in her art; she knew how to cloak herself and she knew how to shield her mind. If I tried, she'd think I was trying to be underhanded and sneaky, and she'd never trust me. I mean, by swaying her mind I was doing exactly that, but I was feeling close to desperate.

That wave swept over me again, that urging, that yearning, gaping hole in my chest screaming at me to claim her, to take her.

Fuck.

Her lids went heavy, her lips parted, and her eyes turned heated, as if she were feeling everything I was.

If this was what Cole went through with Mika, then no wonder he couldn't resist putting his mark on her. He was totally blindsided, unprepared. At least I knew there would be something coming. I never would have predicted it was this powerful though. Never in all my existence had I felt something like this.

"What is that?" she whispered breathily, her hand trembling as it moved across my chest to heal the smaller cuts.

"Power," I replied softly, forcing myself not to lean forward and sink my fingers into her thick, strawberry blonde hair and drag her mouth to mine. I don't think there was ever a time I'd wanted a woman so badly.

"It's more than that," she countered, blinking as if to clear her thoughts. I didn't bother to respond. I didn't want to outright lie to her, but I wasn't going to tell her more than she could handle. Finding out she was destined to be my mate was not something she'd take easily. Unlike what my brother assumed when he met Mika, I knew this feeling was more than chemistry. I knew what was happening and what we were meant to be. I wasn't going to force this woman to be with me, or to accept this. She needed to do it on her own. Besides, she was a seasoned Witch… I had every confidence she knew how to harness her power to put up a hell of a struggle.

The thought made my cock twitch again.

Her gaze narrowed and she raised an eyebrow. I grinned, happy to let all my steamy desires show on my face. The Witch flicked her gaze away, and I caught the small flush up her cheeks. Fuck! She was more than tempting when she went all innocent on me like that. My mind instantly flashed to what it would be like to pull her hair away from her neck and kiss it, nip at it. I'd strip her of all her clothes and have her screaming my name with a few strokes of my fingers and tongue—

"Stop!" she hissed again.

"What?"

"You know what." She glared, her cheeks flushed darkly, her breathing a little heavier. "You know I'm a Witch, then you know I'm an empath, and I can feel everything you're feeling. Stop. It," she gritted out. I grinned again, and she went back to healing me. I desperately wanted to slip into her mind right now, hear her thoughts, see if she was having trouble concentrating as her hands slid over my bare torso and arms.

"You know I can't let you leave here unprotected," I said softly. Her hands paused for a moment before they resumed, and she shook her head.

"I don't need your protection."

"Whether you think you do or not is not the point. I know of you now, and obviously you know you're being hunted. I can't just let you vanish without seeing to your safety."

She raised an eyebrow in disbelief, a small, amused smile tugging at her lips.

"And you're going to be the one to protect me? You honestly expect me to believe you have no ulterior motive to wanting to know where I live and where I am at all times?"

"Oh, I definitely have ulterior motives," I admitted, and she paused to consider me carefully. "For example, I'd like nothing more than to lay you out on my bed and fuck you until you're so wrapped up in pleasure you can barely breathe," I admitted in a low voice, letting my desire for her flare out around us.

She inhaled sharply and paused, her fingers digging into my bicep and her eyes burning with heat. I bit back the growl that tried to escape at the scent of her arousal. It took more effort than I like to admit not to sweep her away and have my way with her.

Normally, I wouldn't have come out of the gate so early with my physical desire for her, but she was right, she was an empath and had likely picked up on my desire for her already. Besides, it made her feel safer to think that I wanted her for her body and not her power, so I was going to lean into it. She didn't need to know that I wanted her because she was my mate and fate had declared her to be mine.

"But since you are obviously immune to all my charms, I have a vested interest in keeping you safe," I went on, forcing a casual tone. She swallowed hard and I watched as she struggled to get her mind away from the image of us in bed together. I needed to give her something more, a reason to see me again, to not disappear on me. And I had exactly the right bait.

"And what interest is that?"

"I know another Witch," I shrugged. The look she shot me was full of disbelief and I shrugged. "You can believe me or not, that's up to you. She is married to my brother, but she wasn't brought up in the life and is self-taught. We can give her all the books we have and train her the way we see fit, but we're no replacement for another Witch with experience in her craft."

I was tempting her. I knew she had a soft heart, and the thought of a Witch alone and unable to properly use her gifts was not going to sit well with her.

"If you had another Witch, why did you not go to her to heal your wound?"

"My brother is rather possessive of her. He would allow it because it would hurt her not to heal me, but he doesn't like her putting her hands on another man," I explained with a grin.

"Why should I believe you?"

"You don't have to. Her name is Tomika, she's still young. She was healing celestials when they were unconscious because she knew enough to keep a low profile. She found my brother when he'd been stabbed with an Angel Blade and was dying. Mika healed him, and my brother has protected her ever since," I explained, skipping over all the kidnapping and fights. She didn't need to know *all* the details right away.

I watched her as she went back to healing me, but I could read her face as if it were words on a page. She knew there was more I wasn't telling her, but she was also afraid to ask.

"You're healed," she murmured. She moved to step back, but I was faster, drawing her hands back to me to hold her close. She was stiff, but she didn't yank herself out of my grasp.

"I want to protect you," I told her honestly, wanting her to read it. At the end of the day, she was a Witch and was valuable. But more than that, she was *mine*. My mate. My woman. No one was going to take her from me now that I had found her.

No one.

"I don't need you to protect me. I've been doing it well enough for years," she answered softly.

"And yet I found you."

She blinked slowly, as if just realizing this.

"You did," she agreed slowly.

"I would like you to come with me so I can keep you safe, but I know you'll never do that. So, I will watch over you from a distance. Of course, I'd rather be much closer in order to protect your magnificent body, but if it makes you feel better to have me somewhere else, then we'll start there," I explained.

She frowned. "Start?"

"Well, of course. You're going to be tempted by my body, my humor, and my charm. You'll find yourself swooning over me in no time, tempted to act out your darkest and most sinful fantasies on my naked form," I continued with such confidence that she blinked in surprise and then laughed.

I barely refrained from dragging her against me and claiming her there and then. That laugh… shit… I had a new respect for Cole and what he went through with his mate.

"You sound so certain." She grinned, and I wanted to cheer when I could feel her reservations about being in my presence melting away.

"I am," I nodded, widening my eyes at her. "You'll think I'm funny and cute, you'll start watching me when you think I'm not looking. Then you'll have dreams about me, the steamy kind that wake you up in a sweat with your body aching and throbbing, crying out for mine," I continued, dropping my voice an octave. She inhaled sharply and I smiled slowly, gently reaching up to touch her face. My fingers tingled at the contact, and I resisted frowning. How did touching her feel so electrifying?

"Then you'll start blushing every time you see me. You'll look for reasons to be close to me, to talk to me... to touch me. And we'll get close. We'll have inside jokes and secret looks. We'll spend more time together until one day... you just can't stay away anymore. Then we'll make our way to the bedroom, and you'll wonder why you ever tried to keep your distance," I continued, painting a picture for her. Her pale green eyes were darker, slightly serious, almost glazed over in thought.

"You've thought a lot about this," she murmured.

I shrugged. "I know what I want, and I go for it. And I haven't wanted anything more than you, little red," I answered. She was no longer stiff, her body was softening, leaning unconsciously towards mine. She was standing between my knees, both of her hands in mine as I gently stroked the tops of them with my thumbs, her skin so damn smooth I couldn't have stopped had I tried.

"Cali," she corrected breathily. I tipped my head to the side in question, and she smiled gently. "My name is Calixta, but people call me Cali."

I smiled, and her gaze dropped to my mouth. Fuck, I wanted her to kiss me, to *want* to kiss me. But before she even looked away, I knew it wasn't going to happen.

"Well," she said and cleared her throat, stepping out of my space. "You're all healed now, and I need to be going."

"Alright, I'll walk you home," I agreed, standing.

Her eyebrows rose and she shook her head. "No."

"Okay."

She glared suspiciously. "You're going to follow me, aren't you?"

"Absolutely."

Cali sighed and shook her head. Her pale eyes locked with mine for a moment and she smiled gently, her expression taking on an almost angelically sweet expression. I had a second of unease before she threw her arms out, sending me flying back into a cement pillar. I grunted as my back took the brunt of the hit and before I could react further, she was moving her fingers in complicated patterns, locking me in place with a spell. I blinked in surprise at her speed and strength. With a sweet smile, she winked and ran away from me, her figure getting smaller and smaller. I was stuck, helpless, totally unable to move. I could feel the strength of her spell lessening with every ounce of power I poured into it, disintegrating it, but she was already so far ahead. Grinning, I shook my head and laughed, amusement and lust warring with each other as my beautiful Witch disappeared from my view. She was sugar and spice, with an innocent face and the fiery determination of her kind.

She wasn't going to come to me easily. In fact, I anticipated a lot of work on my part to break through her walls and have her rely on me, want me, seek me out.

I was going to have a lot of fun doing it.

CHAPTER THREE
CALI

"Make sure you reinforce your protections around your home and yourself. Go over the concealment charm again, make sure there are no chinks in your armor," Aunt Penny reminded, and even through the phone her voice was laden with worry and tension.

"AP, I'm fine, okay?" I assured, using the nickname I'd always given her since I was a kid.

"You're fine *for now*. Honey, you healed a King of Hell. This isn't just any celestial, it's the Demon equivalent to an Archangel. He knows you exist now; he knows your face, he probably got in your head and knows more about you than you think."

I sighed heavily and let myself fall backwards onto my bed, my eyes on the ceiling as she continued to warn me about all the danger I was in.

"Have you considered my offer?" she finally asked.

"You mean to come with you to the Amazon and heal people in remote tribes?"

"You would be safe here, Calixta. They don't look for us in remote places, and these villagers could use all the help they can get."

"I know," I answered softly. Penny raised me when my parents had died in an accident when I was six. She was basically the only mother I had ever known, and she had instilled in me a deep respect for my abilities and the responsibilities that came with them. No matter what I did in life, my first responsibility always had to be to my gift and the serving of others, it was why I was here, why I was born into a family of Witches.

"I can't leave here, Penny," I sighed, rubbing my tired eyes.

"I know," she mumbled, but I could hear no reprimand. She knew what I did here was important. "Just… be extra careful. I don't like the sound of this Adrik Demon, and I certainly don't like the way he made you feel."

I could picture her deep frown as she paced.

"It was… unexpected," I agreed, not daring to tell her that a part of me craved to feel that way again.

Adrik was powerful, he wore it like a second skin. I had a feeling he could take out a room full of demons with little more than a flick of his wrist, he could see into me in a way no one else ever had, and my reaction to him had been more than surprising. I'd never reacted that way to anyone in my life.

We knew nothing about one another, and yet… the way he looked at me was like I was to be revered, protected, saved. In between the sinful looks so heated I was sure it was against all the laws of nature to possess, there had been something else flickering in his eyes, some other emotion. He obviously knew what I was and how rare my kind were now, but he hadn't looked at me with greed and triumph. More like… awe.

I shook my head and sucked in a deep breath.

"Just… be careful, Cali. I can't lose you, and if you need me, you know how to reach me. I can lend you power from here, so don't hesitate if ever you are desperate for help. Please," she reminded.

"I know, AP," I sighed. "Thank you for being here for me. And you stay safe too. Just because you're in a remote place does not mean you are safe."

"Love you."

"I love you too."

We hung up and I blew a strand of hair away from my face as I continued to stare at my blank ceiling. Before getting home tonight, I'd redoubled my concealment charm and had already checked the protection of my home. I didn't need Penny to remind me how to look after myself, but I knew she did it because she worried. I turned thirty last week and I had been practicing my craft since before I could speak in full sentences. Witches had power from the get-go, and it was imperative we learned to handle it.

I frowned, something Adrik had said coming back to me. Did he really have another Witch? Had he been lying? The idea of a lone Witch surrounded by Kings of Hell didn't sit right with me, especially one who had never had a proper teacher to show her the true extent of her powers. I was sure being involved with a powerful Demon King gave her many chances to grow her powers, but they didn't fully comprehend how it felt to wield magic like ours, and my skin felt itchy at the thought of her relying only on Demons for guidance.

And was she truly married to Adrik's brother? Or had his brother taken her as his bride against her will? The thought had my hands burning with the need to hurt him. If she had grown up alone, then it was likely she didn't know how to defend herself without feeling the pain she'd landed on her opponent, which meant she had little to no chance to defend herself against a Demon King. But... I gnawed on my lower lip, thinking back to Adrik. I didn't sense any of that when he spoke about the Witch. There was a fondness there for her, an almost brotherly love. I couldn't imagine him allowing someone he cared for to be mistreated... so, maybe this Witch was happy?

I groaned and shook my head at myself, putting my phone on charge by my bed before I crawled under the covers. Maybe, if she truly was not a prisoner, Adrik could organize for me to meet her somewhere I felt safe. I needed to put my mind at ease, I needed to know she was okay and had a handle on her powers. There were so few of us Witches left, we needed to stick together where possible.

I closed my eyes, and it was like I was back in that underpass with Adrik's fingers stroking my cheek. I could still feel the powerful pull towards him, the yearning, the desire to kiss him, to let him lay claim to me in some way I didn't understand. I had just met the man, but something within me recognized him on a level that seemed impossible. Being a Witch, I had learned to listen to that part of me, deep down, but what it was telling me was so far outside the realm of normal that I was hesitant to listen. How had a simple touch made me want him so much? And why hadn't he taken advantage of my moment of weakness? He was a King of Hell, and it was obvious he wanted me in more ways than one. Why had he not played on my moment of lapsed judgment and kissed me? I knew I would have been helpless to resist. He may be a Demon King, but he was hot and smoldering, and we had the kind of chemistry people wrote about but rarely experienced. It was like a drug: dark and lulling and so hard to resist.

I felt myself sink deeper into sleep and didn't fight it. My house and myself were protected and shielded, AP knew of the possible danger, and I needed to get some rest to continue my healing tomorrow night.

During the day I worked at an animal shelter. I could sometimes heal their minor ailments, and at the very least, soothe them and bring them a sense of calm and peace instead of fear and aggression. And no, I did not allow a single animal to be put down. While we didn't have a 'no kill' policy—yet—I always made sure to get every animal a home, and if I couldn't do that before their time was up, I fostered them until I could find them suitable homes. I could not miss a day of work, or I risked losing an animal, and that guilt did not sit well with me.

Sleep finally pulled me under, and I let it take me, feeling my body relax and my mind rest...

"Interesting," a voice mused behind me.

I spun around to find Adrik there, dressed as he had been before, his hands in his front pockets as he looked around. I did so too, startled to find him here with me. Where was *here*, exactly?

I was surrounded by moonlit mountains, a stream cut through the earthy structures and ran with a gentle current before me. The mountainside was clear with thick, lush lemongrass, and white flowers bloomed, turned upwards towards the bright silver moonlight. The air was warm, and there was a gentle breeze. All around me the scenery was beautiful, but there was a lagging sensation in my mind, almost like it was taking me a second or two longer to remember what I was going to say. I recognized the signs of where I was...

"What am I doing here, little red?" Adrik asked. I turned to look at him again and shrugged, my eyes wide as I looked around.

"Where is here?" he asked instead.

"Uh... Hekate's Mountain... it's a place of magic and healing. I've only been here once," I answered in awe. I'd been sixteen and officially given permission by my Elder—my aunt—to use my magic as my own and when I saw fit. I'd trained and proven myself responsible and careful.

"Interesting," he muttered, glancing around.

"How did I get here? And *why* are *you* here?" I asked.

"This is your realm, your dream. You just pulled me into it," he replied distractedly with a shrug. I tasted no lie in his words, and my mind snagged on the word *realm*.

"We're in a psychic realm," I mused quietly, part in wonder. I hadn't ever done this before. I knew it was possible, but the need had never been there and honestly, I'd never really investigated how to do it.

"Yes," Adrik answered unnecessarily. "I told you that you'd start dreaming of me."

I turned back to look at him and pressed my lips together at the slow, appraising look he was giving me. Oh no… Psychic realms were very tricky, but anything that happened here would be as if it happened in real life. And with the way Adrik was looking at me, I knew exactly what he wanted to happen.

"Stop that," I gritted out.

Glittering, dark blue eyes met mine, that sinful smile creeping onto his face, the heat in his expression enough to have me shifting uncomfortably.

"But why? This is your dream, and you pulled me into it, which means that your subconscious mind is trying to fulfill some desire you are refusing yourself in the real world," he pointed out, moving closer, his every movement a glide of rippling muscle.

"Just because I might want something, does not mean I should have it. There are some things I want that are bad for me, and you are likely to be the worst of them all," I pointed out, refusing to back up even as he continued to stalk forward, slowly, almost like a jungle cat ready to pounce.

"Sometimes it feels good to be bad," he returned, the cadence to his voice sending goosebumps up my arms.

"Adrik," I warned, but my voice wasn't as strong as I wanted, not as commanding.

"You don't trust me." He made it a statement.

"Can you blame me?"

"Not at all."

"Why do you *want* me to trust you?" I asked, my voice quiet. A cool wind picked up around us, and I was in awe that I could feel it, despite not *actually* being here.

"Because I'm not going to let you go now that I know you exist, and it would be easier to be around you, to get you to listen to me when I know danger is near if you trusted me," he answered. There it was again… he was telling the truth, but there were elements of concealment in his voice, something he was holding back. I studied him carefully, wondering how I would get that information from him. Yes, he wanted to protect me and keep me from harm, I recognized the truth in his words, but he also had an ulterior motive, and it wasn't as simple as sleeping with me, even though I was sure that was part of it.

"You're not telling me everything," I told him softly, deciding to test him. His blue eyes glittered back at me, and he shook his head.

"No, I'm not."

"Why?"

"Would you believe me if I told you that you weren't ready to hear it?"

I frowned and scrutinized him further, wondering how I could force the truth past him.

"You want me to trust you, but you won't be totally honest with me?"

"Sometimes the whole truth is not what is good for you. I want to tell you, but only when I know you're ready to hear it," he answered slowly.

"You mean, only when you're sure I won't go running in the opposite direction," I corrected.

His lips tilted up in a small smile and he edged closer so that I had to tip my head back to look at him. Neither of us spoke for a time, and I wondered what it was he was thinking so hard about.

"I want you to trust me," he murmured, a small frown creasing his forehead as if he weren't sure how to go about that.

"Trust is earned."

"How do you suppose I earn it, then?" he asked, his blue eyes searching, reading me in a way I wasn't familiar with.

"Who says I want to trust you?"

His face cleared, and I watched a small, knowing smile curve his lips, drawing my attention to the scruff on his face and his defined jawline.

"It isn't wise to lie to yourself. Be honest, look within yourself. There is something inside of you that *wants* to trust me, that is reaching for me, urging you to be around me and let me close. I know it scares you, and every other part of you has been conditioned to hide from and mistrust me and my kind, and it is not without reason," he began, his voice a low rumble, his eyes locked with mine and shining with honesty.

I pressed my lips together, wanting to refute what he'd said, but he was right. Since I'd laid eyes on him, fear had mixed with excitement and an odd sense of relief. There was something about him that called to me, causing parts of me that had lain dormant to writhe and cry out with yearning. Something inside me recognized him… as if he were a part of me or was supposed to be.

I could feel the power here, even in my dream. Hekate's Mountain was a place of deep magic and safety, it was a place that called to the very essence of my power and allowed me to regain my strength and feel my magic to its deepest roots. Here, I was safe.

"What do you propose?" I asked, swallowing hard and allowing myself to recognize the need inside me. I didn't understand it, and it scared me, but I couldn't go on ignoring it. Adrik took a long look at me, almost as if he were reading me, trying to find a way to build a bridge where the ground was rocky and unstable. Because he was right... I had every right to fear him, to want to run and hide and protect myself. His kind and the Angels were the reason Witches were almost extinct, and why we had to go to such measures to protect ourselves and stay hidden.

"I want you to open your mind to me, and trust me not to go looking through it, not to go wandering and searching for more than you are willing to give me," he answered. The immediate refusal was there in my mind, on my tongue, but something about the look in his eyes froze them there. He was asking me to be completely vulnerable to him, so vulnerable that I was almost more willing to have sex with him than I was to do this.

I allowed myself to sink into my magic, to allow the energy and guidance of Hekate and her mountain to guide me, to let me feel what was right. Confidence, power, and assurance poured into me. My Goddess was here, providing me with safety and power. He would not dare try to take control of my mind in a place as formidable as this, even in a psychic realm. Was that true trust then? If he were afraid of repercussions, would this really be an act of trust?

"Does Hekate scare you?" I whispered.

"Not as much as she should."

"Why not?"

"Because while she may decide to take me if I betrayed your trust in this place of power, I have eight brothers who would hunt for whoever took me, and they would destroy them—Witch, Goddess, or anything else. Hekate cannot afford such a war, and so I know she will not do something to start one," he answered easily, as if the idea of destroying a Goddess was not a horrific idea.

"And that is supposed to make me trust you?" I frowned.

"No. It is supposed to help you see the reason I will not betray your trust is not because I am frightened of a Goddess. I will not betray your trust because I want to earn it, because the idea of betraying you hurts me in a way I do not understand," he continued, frowning slightly as if the idea of my pain confused him.

Honesty, clear and pure, rang from the depths of him, and hearing it, feeling it, settled something deep inside me. I was nervous, I was scared, but for whatever reason, I knew I could trust him to do this.

"You won't wander?"

"No."

"You won't go looking through my memories or plant an idea or a dream? You won't try to manipulate my emotions or desires?" I pushed.

"As tempting as it is... no. I want you to trust me."

"And do *you* trust *me*? Will you grant me the same access to your mind that you are asking of me?"

He paused for a moment, and I waited. The fact that he was considering it without blindly agreeing only made me feel safer in allowing him to enter my mind. I was powerful, and it seemed he knew just how strong I was. If he hurt me, I could hurt him too.

"I have access to my brothers' minds. It would not just be access to myself I'd be potentially granting you," he said slowly. I stilled and drew in a deep breath. I hadn't considered who else he would have access to.

"And you would have access to my aunt, the only person I have left to me," I admitted, my heart thumping hard now. That news seemed to ease something in him, and I realized he was as cautious of me as I was of him.

"I give you my word, Calixta. I will not do more than be there with you," he assured.

"And I promise the same," I agreed on a shaky whisper. I could feel his anticipation rise, his need to prove himself, his determination to be rigid and stick only to the particulars we'd agreed upon.

After a moment of silence, I closed my eyes and focused on the warding in my mind and the mental barriers I'd worked on since I was a young girl.

My breath caught when I felt his hands slide over mine, and I turned my hands over slowly so that we both stood, palm to palm. The heat of his body wrapped around me, and I wanted to sink into it, melt against him. He was a King of Hell, and yet somehow, he felt like safety to me, like warmth and protection. When I felt a gentle brush against my mind, I stiffened, but did not throw up my barriers to protect myself. I allowed him to brush against me again, melt into my consciousness so that he was in my mind. It was a slightly uncomfortable experience, but it also felt good… a moment to treasure. I felt his hands on my face as if he were stroking my cheeks, his lips brushing my forehead even though he hadn't moved his physical body, and neither had I.

I slowly reached out to him, felt the masculine frame of his mind, the darkness that embodied him. He was dark, yes… but there was not the taint of evil I had expected. Intrigued, I reached further, stepping into his mind to wrap myself in him. I imagined raising my hands to slide up his chest, to feel the hard edges of his body. Hearing his sharp intake of breath had me biting back my smile, proud that he was as affected by this as I was.

Something between us shifted. I had no idea what it was but there was something here, something powerful and old, something that merged us together in a way I couldn't accurately explain. It was as if pieces of us were intertwining so deeply that they would never untangle. What was more... was that feeling it happen didn't cause me to run in the other direction. It felt like I was piecing together parts of me I hadn't known were missing.

My heart pounded harder at acknowledging it, and my blood rushed loud in my ears. Adrik's hands moved from my cheeks to slide in my hair, and I tipped my head back, skimming my hands over his chest and shoulders to link at the back of his neck. We held each other, and I felt his forehead press against mine.

I knew neither of us had moved our physical bodies, that we were both standing inches apart with the palms of his hands hovering over mine, and yet his strong fingers were tangled in my hair, his skin against my hands, his breath in my lungs.

We were tied together somehow, tethered in a way I didn't know was possible. Still, I wasn't scared. I was in awe of it, of the purity I could see in those invisible bonds that glowed brightly between us.

"You're not exploring," I pointed out. I *felt* his small smile rather than saw it.

"Why would I want to go further when simply being here is like coming home?"

Home.

That really was what it felt like to be here, to have him in my mind and me in his. How that was possible, I was unsure, but right in this moment, I was positive I wasn't supposed to be anywhere else but here.

Neither of us moved, we simply stood in this moment, soaking in it, marveling at the raw beauty of it.

Trust.

It was probably not smart to trust a King of Hell, and in the waking world I would be screaming it from the rooftop. But somehow right now, I knew that trusting him was the single most important thing I could have ever done. Like I was accepting a part of my destiny that had not yet been revealed to me.

Hours or days could have passed, but neither of us moved, too content to be here and feel each other. Every emotion that passed through him went through me and vice versa. I could feel his awe, his trust, his joy and how completely he cherished this moment. It was feeling his emotions that helped quell any kind of anxiety that had remained.

"I don't want to leave," Adrik whispered.

"Do we have to?"

"Hours have passed, and it will be daylight soon," he murmured. Sighing, I nodded. His lips brushed my forehead again, ethereal and intangible, but the feeling was there all the same. I slowly released my hold on him and slipped from his mind and back to my own. Adrik did the same, and when I blinked to open my eyes, it was to clash with his incredible midnight blue ones.

"Thank you for trusting me," he whispered.

"Thank you for being trustworthy."

Adrik slowly raised his hand to my cheek as he had done in our minds, and I felt the spark on my skin as he stroked it.

"How is this happening?" I whispered. He looked pained for a moment, and I let him work it out.

"I know something… but I do not think you are ready to hear it."

"And you get to make that choice, why?"

He shook his head and watched his fingers against my face as if he were transfixed.

"Can you trust me to know this? I will tell you in time, but for now, this way is best," he assured. I opened my mouth to protest, but I could still taste his honesty and feel it radiate from him, stronger than ever. Something had changed between us, something had linked us together, bound us more acutely than ever.

"I might surprise you," I said instead. Adrik's smile was slow and devastating.

"Your existence surprises me... everything else about you is just a bonus."

"Adrik?"

"Yes, Cali?"

"I want you to kiss me," I whispered quickly. His stroking fingers paused, and his dark eyes snapped back to mine. I felt his heart slam hard against his chest, felt his breath still in his lungs and hope spark in his ocean blue eyes.

"Then you shall get what you want. I cannot have my Witch unsatisfied," he agreed, that familiar heat back in his eyes.

"*Your* Witch?" I questioned with a raised eyebrow. His hands slid suddenly to my waist, and he hauled me against him. My lips parted in surprise, and I clenched his leather jacket in my hands. "Yes... *my* Witch."

"Do I get to claim ownership over you too?" I joked.

"Please do," he answered without pause. "I *am* yours, Cali. You don't realize how seriously I mean that right now, but I do." My stomach fluttered at his words, at his honesty and resolve. He really meant it.

"Kiss me," I demanded shakily. For reasons I could not explain, I needed to feel his lips against mine more than anything else.

Adrik smiled and leaned down to capture my mouth with his. His lips were soft and warm, and his tongue flicked out, enticing my mouth to open. I did as he silently requested and sank into him as he controlled the kiss, deepening it. I sighed into his mouth and slid my hands up to his hair and fisted it, pressing into him. There was a low, rumbling growl from deep inside him and he devoured my lips, one of his hands sliding up to bunch in my hair and tilt my head more to the side, the small bite of pain sending a spark of arousal though me and a gasp to escape me.

I'd never been kissed with such passion and heat in my entire life. Sensation and emotion flowed between us so that I didn't know what was his and what was mine. Possession, need, desire, and lust swam together. Awe and triumph swirled amongst the already cluttered emotions, but the feel of Adrik's mouth on mine, his hand in my hair and on my waist were distracting. The scent and taste of him were intoxicating and addictive, and I found myself desperate to be closer to him. Clothes were a barrier that needed to disappear.

I gasped when Adrik pulled back, both of us panting, my eyes wide with astonishment.

"We need to say goodnight," he decided with a shaky breath.

"Why?"

"Because I can feel what you want, and if I take you up on your offer right now, you'll be mad at me later and feel as though I took advantage of you," he explained, and I could feel a small wince in his mind.

"What is it?"

"I never thought I'd be the one turning down sex," he grumbled. I laughed, the sound surprising me and he grinned, his eyes bright as if me laughing were some kind of prize. Shaking my head, I brushed my thumb over the scruff on his jaw and sighed.

"Goodnight, Adrik."

"I'll be seeing you soon, little red," he assured. I leaned in to kiss him again and he didn't leave me waiting, his kiss hard and insistent. With a forceful tug, I stepped away from him, and seeing one last grin on his face, I forced myself awake.

I came to, staring at my ceiling, my heart pounding, my body aching for more, and a smile on my face. I knew AP would kick my ass for doing what I had just done, but I couldn't find it within myself to regret it. Biting my lip, I took my time warding my mind once again to protect me while I slept. When I was sure the wards around my home were secure, I sighed and sank back into my mattress. I closed my eyes, and could have sworn just before I fell asleep, that I could feel Adrik's arms wrapped around me, keeping me secure and safe as I slept.

CHAPTER FOUR
ADRIK

"What has you in such a good mood?" Malik asked as I looked over the number of new souls headed for my circle of Hell in the next month. Yes, we Kings had actual book work to do. Souls were a currency, stock, and only a fool would let things get so out of hand that he had no idea of his numbers.

"What?" I asked distractedly, looking up from the new projection sheet.

"You. You were smiling," Malik pointed out, looking at me as if there was something wrong with me. I wanted to smile again, I could feel it there beneath the surface, and considered what to say. I had found my mate; I knew who she was and where she was. And last night? Our shared night in a psychic realm had been next level for me. Nothing and no one had ever made me feel like that, which was saying something when one took into consideration how old I was. From what I knew about Cole and Mika and how their unions went, there were four levels of which I had to lock Cali to me. Our minds would be locked together from our first psychic dream—check. With our first physical joining we'd lock our bodies. When I could finally put my Mark on her, our souls would be forever joined. And then there were our hearts.

I wasn't as jaded as my brother; I didn't consider loving someone to be the end of the world. But I did have doubts as to how a Witch—the very essence of light and healing—could fall in love with a King of Hell. Although Mika had fallen for Cole, and it was obvious how crazy they were about one another. Maybe it would be possible for Cali to love me the same. Could I love her? I'd never truly loved a woman before. I loved my brothers, but that was a different kind of love.

"Ouch!" I snapped, regaining my balance after a book hit me in the head. I turned to glare at Malik, and he rolled his eyes.

"For fuck's sake… you found her, didn't you? Your mate?"

"How do you know?"

Malik scoffed and dropped into a cushioned seat nearby, his long legs stretched out in front of him and his fingers steepled together on his chest.

"You have that same stupid, sappy look on your face that Cole does whenever he's thinking about Tomika… which is almost always. Fuck, you guys look so pussy whipped. I thought maybe Cole was being dramatic, but now seeing that look on your face…" Malik trailed off, shaking his head so that his dark hair fell disheveled around his shoulders.

"Your time will come, brother," I muttered, bending to pick up the book.

"So, what's she like? What's her name?" Malik asked, looking quite at ease. I considered what to say to my brother. I knew I could trust them, always. It was unthinkable that one of my brothers would betray me or try to hurt my mate. But she was a Witch, and they were so rare…

"Her name is Calixta," I finally muttered, sighing heavily before I leaned back into my chair and rubbed my thumb and forefinger together.

"She hot?"

I glared at my brother, red-hot anger ripping through me at the thought of him looking at her as one of his women, as a warm body to fuck and discard.

Malik grinned and shook his head. "Fuck man, if this is how we're all going to turn out, then I am more than happy to wait my turn," he said with a small chuckle.

"Well, it's your turn next, fuckface. From the first to the last— You are the ruler of the third circle," I reminded.

That wiped the smirk from his face.

"What else do you know about her? How did you meet?" Malik pressed.

I can trust my brothers, I reminded myself.

"I got stabbed with an Angel Blade last night," I finally answered, sitting up straighter. Malik raised an eyebrow and looked me over, not seeing any evidence of a lingering wound. After another moment, his eyes widened, and he leaned forward in interest.

"You mean, she's a Witch?"

I nodded and sighed. "Yup. She's not like Mika, though. She is powerful and knows her craft well. She's been soothing her need to heal celestials by healing the humans who are homeless and broke. They all keep her secret in return for help," I explained.

"Fucking hell," Malik muttered in an astonished whisper.

"Yep."

"So, do you think… Are all our mates Witches?" he asked.

"I think there's a good chance. I guess we'll get a better idea when you find yours," I answered.

"What if I find her too late? I mean, what if she's mortal?" Malik asked. I thought about it for a moment and shook my head.

"I get a feeling there is a lot at play here we don't understand. We won't find our mates until we're supposed to. It's been two years since Cole met Mika and I'm only now finding Cali. It could be ten years until you find your mate, I guess it all just depends on what destiny has in store for us," I answered.

We both sat in silence for a little longer before Malik spoke again.

"So, if you know where your Witch is and who she is... why aren't you with her?" Malik asked. I shifted uncomfortably for a moment and a small smile crept over his face, growing into a shit-eating grin.

"She fucked you up, didn't she?"

"No," I snapped.

"She did!"

"Okay, it was one little spell I wasn't prepared for. She's powerful. Like I said, she's not like Mika, she knows what the fuck she's doing, and she doesn't hesitate. We haven't dealt with Witches for over two-hundred years. I was not prepared," I defended. Malik laughed and shook his head, pushing himself to his feet.

"So, are you going to sulk here or go after her?" he asked.

"I'm not sulking," I defended. "It was kind of hot how powerful she is."

"Gross."

"I'm letting her think she's warned me off. I know where she'll be tonight, and I'll see her then," I added.

"Alright... well, let me know if you need any backup," Malik offered, bumping my shoulder with his fist as he strode past me.

"Will do," I called, but I knew I wouldn't... this was something I needed to handle myself. I thought back to our night and grinned. She had no idea what she was in for.

~

"You're back."

I turned around to see Sol, the old man from last night, behind me, his milky eyes staring at me shrewdly.

"I am."

"Why?"

"I don't see how that's any of your business," I replied, raising an eyebrow.

"If you're here for our Cali, then it is my business. That girl is a miracle, and she don't need no trouble from someone like you," he refuted, stepping closer. My admiration for the old man grew another couple of notches when usually my disdain for being argued with would have overruled. I wasn't a hard ass, but my life as a King of Hell had afforded me a certain regard, and no one argued with me except my brothers. Yet, here was this mortal giving me the evil eye and warning me off from a woman I wanted. He knew he didn't stand a chance against me if I wanted to take him out, he knew I wasn't human, that I was something else. Yet he was willing to put himself between me and Calixta to try and protect her.

"I don't mean her any harm, Sol. She needs protecting, and I'm here to do just that," I assured, turning when I felt her presence. She was a breath of fresh air, of life itself. Her strawberry blonde hair was tied back in a high ponytail and her enchanting eyes were bright with happiness and warmth. She was a goddamn beacon of light and purity, it almost hurt to look at her. That ever-present pull in my chest was urging me forward, an alluring voice in the back of my head whispering to me to Mark her, to make her mine forever. Deep down, I knew that voice and the urge to claim her would never leave me until it was done, but I could hold off... for now.

"Are you gonna protect her from yourself?" Sol asked, coming to stand beside me as we looked at her.

"I'll never let harm come to her if I can help it, and I'll never hurt her," I promised.

"That wasn't what I asked."

"I know," I answered with a one-shouldered shrug. "But that's all I can give you."

Sol made a small sound of discontent but didn't say anything further for a moment. I watched Cali take in the sight of all the extra tables set out with items like bags, sleeping bags, clothes, canned goods, and toiletries. There were racks of jackets and blankets and shoes. Other tables held several platters of food and drinks.

Cali cared about these people, and so I had to care. She wanted to look after them, so I'd brought a range of items that could help, especially as the weather grew colder and the nights longer. I wasn't evil like mortals thought I was, I was a King of Hell, which meant it was *my* job to punish the assholes of the world. However, I *had* grown rather numb to the suffering of mortals on Earth and hadn't made much of an effort to care for them in quite some time. Cali's eyes were wide, and her lips parted in disbelief as she took in all the new items I'd provided. Several of the transients stopped to talk to her, their amazement and gratitude obvious. I could practically see that light inside her burn hotter and brighter.

That tug inside me got stronger, so strong I almost stumbled towards her to Mark her and lock her soul to mine for all time, but I resisted. She needed time, and I was going to do better than my brother, I was going to give Cali time and as much of a choice as I could.

Cali's head swung in my direction and her gaze clashed with mine. I watched her pause for a moment, her bright eyes widening and then burning with something more. It seemed as though the events of the previous night played out between us, bringing with it that intense feeling we'd shared and had been reluctant to let go of. I could still feel her mouth on mine, the way her breath felt in my lungs, the feel of her soft, pliant body pressing into mine, and I could tell by the look in her eyes that she remembered too.

"Alright, well, I don't need to stand around and see this," Sol muttered, shaking his head, obviously picking up on the undercurrents between my mate and myself. I grinned and Cali's face flushed, but she started towards me anyway. "You look after her, boy," Sol reminded.

"Always."

Cali reached us, her gaze still locked with mine, and I watched as she slowly dragged her attention to her friend.

"Hello, Sol. It's good to see you again. Will you let me look at your leg tonight?" she asked the old man, her obvious affection for him clear on her face. It was like a wave of warmth, acceptance, and healing came from her to wash over us.

"I'm just fine, sweetheart. This leg has been carting me around for decades in this condition, I can do it a while longer while there are others here who need your help more," he assured.

Cali frowned. "Please come and see me tonight, just for a few minutes. I won't be able to repair all the damage in that small amount of time, but I can ease the pain you're in. Please?"

I watched Sol's face soften and his pride war with his need to give Cali what she wanted. It was hard to resist her, especially when she asked to help like that.

"Alright, love, but only for a few minutes. I don't want you wasting your energy on me," he assured, but his tone was stern.

Cali's smile was radiant, and I watched the old man soften some more as he looked at her. I could feel their bond, strong and tangible, something like father and daughter. There were many years of shared troubles and laughs between them.

Sol turned to look at me and gave a small jerk of his head. "Boy."

"Goodnight, Sol," I replied, grinning. This guy was great, full of fire and ire, and I found it hilarious that he continued to call me *boy* even though his entire life barely equaled an afternoon in my lifespan.

I watched him hobble away before I turned back to Cali. I didn't bother to restrain myself from stepping in closer to her, tasting her sweet scent in the air and drawing a lungful of her into my body. I was addicted to the smell of her now, there's something unique that was all her.

"I don't feel any injuries on you," she pointed out softly.

"That's because there are none."

"So, you thought you'd show up and do what? Try and distract me?" she asked, raising a thin eyebrow, her lips tilting up slightly in a small smile.

"And provide help," I added, nodding to the extra tables.

"You?" she gaped; her eyes wide as she turned to look at everything. She swung back to me, frowning. "Why?"

"Why not?"

"I hope you're not helping just to get something from me," she said suspiciously, her brows furrowed.

"I'll do anything I can do to get what I want from you," I answered honestly. "But no. I did this because these people are important to you, and so are important to me."

"Why?"

"Why?" I repeated with confusion.

"Why are my wants and needs important to you? What do you get out of it?"

I paused as I considered what to tell her. I was not, of course, going to tell her that there was an ancient prophecy which stated she was my mate and therefore the single most important being to me, but I had to tell her something.

"You are a Witch," I answered with a shrug. "You are determined to be out here alone, healing, when there are thousands of celestials on the hunt for one such as you. These people are important to you, and you refuse to leave them. So that leaves me no choice but to be here and help in any way I can."

"You're not telling me everything."

"No, I am not," I agreed softly. She studied me a moment longer, her gaze searching and scrutinizing. With a small shake of her head, she sighed and stepped back.

"Last night didn't mean anything," she finally said, her chin lifted defiantly.

I grinned. "Last night meant everything."

She glared and turned on her heel to march towards the tent that had been set up for her to heal her people in. Last night had meant the first bond sealed between us. I was confused at first; Cole had said when he and Mika completed the mind bond, that they'd had sex. I was expecting to need to do the same with Cali, but we had not done so, and yet I'd felt the bond complete, felt the link in our minds forge and a new pathway between our minds to appear that had not been there before.

The moment she'd shown trust, the moment she'd allowed me to take control in a way that left her vulnerable, had been the moment it happened. So, perhaps it was not about physical intimacy in our psychic realm, but about trust. I frowned as the line in the prophecy meant for me flitted across my mind again. *The second shall follow her blood trail.*

I was supposed to find my mate by following her blood trail. So how was it that I'd found Cali without her blood? There was no doubt in my mind that she was my mate, there was no way she could be anything else, but the prophecy…

I shook my head. Maybe I'd speak to my brothers about this and get their opinions. For now, I needed to be here to protect my mate and do whatever I could to convince her that she belonged with me.

CHAPTER FIVE
ADRIK

I watched as Cali finished healing Sol's leg, going further than what the old man was happy with, but I helped to keep him distracted while Cali healed him, determined to do everything she could for him before he pushed her away. She was majestic when she healed, utter purity and light. I was drawn to her in a way I'd never been to another living being, and I found myself craving a way to carve myself a place in her life, so deep she'd never be able to dig me out.

When Cali finished healing Sol, I helped the old man off the table with only a few mumbled curses and snarky comments about how he was more than capable of doing it himself.

I watched Cali as she got to work emptying her herb dish. According to her, she needed different herbs for each patient, as they each required something different. Her back was to me as she hummed under her breath, and I gently reached out to see what she was feeling. She was content... happy. Her mind was clear as she worked, and I knew she was in her element helping those who genuinely needed her.

Slowly, I stepped towards her, making sure to keep my footsteps light and soundless. My gaze was drawn to her waist and spectacularly curved ass. The woman had curves for days and my fingers itched to sink into her flesh and grip her tightly while I did pleasurable and dirty things to her body. My gaze traveled up her waist to the curve of her breasts and further up to the graceful column of her neck. Who knew a neck could be sexy? I sure didn't, but Cali had a neck I could picture kissing, nibbling, and sucking on.

She turned suddenly and gasped, stumbling back when she found me only a few inches behind her. I shot out a hand quickly, pressing it to the small of her back to keep her steady and to bring her flush against me.

"What are you doing?" she whispered, surprised.

"You look far too tempting standing over here. I needed to be closer," I answered honestly. She swallowed hard and her gaze skittered around the room as if looking for someone to save her. I smiled slowly and watched the heat pour into her cheeks and the way her breathing kicked up ever so slightly.

"Scared, little red?" I asked. Her pale green eyes flashed, and she straightened, tilting her chin up stubbornly.

"Of you?" she scoffed. I smiled wider, pulling her tighter to me. "Do you want me to be scared of you?"

I shook my head. "Only if you're into that. I hear playing hunter and prey can be quite... invigorating."

She laughed nervously and shook her head. I didn't speak and simply raised my eyebrow. Her laughter died away and she drew in a shaky breath, her pupils almost eclipsing the color of her eyes.

"It has been too long since I kissed you," I murmured, dragging her closer.

"Technically, you haven't kissed me at all, we were in a dream," she whispered, her voice breathy.

"Hmm... let's correct that, shall we?"

Cali didn't pull away, her gaze dropped to my lips, and I bit back a groan. I didn't wait to give her time to think, I swooped down and captured her lips with mine, coaxing her mouth open within seconds. She felt and tasted exactly as she had in our psychic dream. She made a sound in the back of her throat, and I wrapped both of my arms around her, hauling her closer to me. Triumph grew as her hands slid slowly up my arms to link behind my neck and her body moved against mine. She was intoxicating, the taste of her was something I would forever crave and never get enough of.

"Cali?" someone outside called, shattering our heated moment. I groaned against her mouth and then she pulled away, almost panting. I gazed down at her dazed expression and couldn't help the smug smile that curved my lips.

She glared. "Don't look so pleased with yourself. You're so old I bet you had a pet dinosaur. If you didn't know how to kiss a woman at least that well, it would be sad."

I threw my head back and laughed, completely shocked at my own reaction. But this woman—my mate—had a way about her that made me so fucking happy.

Cali smiled, surprised, but pleased.

"Cali?" the person called again.

She sighed. "I'm needed."

"You're needed here too, red," I reminded, grinding my hips against hers. Her face warmed and she ducked her head. With an exaggerated sigh, I released her, and she smiled at me

"I'm going to go help pack up, I'll leave you to it," I said as I stepped back. Cali didn't respond, but the heat in her cheeks and eyes made me feel somewhat better about having to end our moment.

I left Cali to pack up her things within the tent and gave the volunteers a hand to break down the tables and chairs and load them into the van. I could have waved my hand and had all this finished, but they were human and that wasn't how things were done.

I kept myself fully entrenched in Cali's mind while I worked, determined never to let her far from me and to protect her, even when she insisted on doing it herself. I was happy to find her in a state of happiness and contentment.

This mate-bond stuff was crazy.

I wondered if she knew the bond was there; if she could feel it or had simply overlooked it. I hadn't bothered to speak to her using it yet, wanting to see her face and gauge her reaction first, and I wanted to have an answer ready for her as to how and why we now had a direct link to one another.

Almost an hour passed when the last van was loaded up and the driver waved us off. I stood beside Cali in the darkened area and looked down at her.

"I should get home." She sighed, looking tired.

"Let's go."

"You're not walking me home, Adrik. We have talked about this."

"No. You said you didn't want me to know where you lived, and I admitted that I'd follow you anyway and then you sucker punched me with some magic to prevent it," I reminded, choosing not to mention I could have followed her had I wanted to, but it had seemed important to her that she win this one little show of independence and power.

"Right, so what's to stop me from doing it again?" she asked, her lips curving into a small smile.

"Other than the fact that you really want me to walk you home and spend as much time with me as you can?"

Cali shook her head and bit back a smile but didn't deny it.

"You know if I wanted to find out where you live, I could, right?" I reminded her.

She sighed and swung her arms. "I know," she muttered.

"Don't sound so pleased."

"I'm not," she admitted. I let the silence drag between us as we slowly began walking and thought about me walking her home and therefore knowing where she lived.

"What is it that truly bothers you?"

Cali didn't reply right away, and I refrained from delving into her mind to feel her emotions for her. Tomika had hated Cole when he invaded her mind like that, and I was attempting to learn from my brother's mistakes.

"You are a King of Hell," she finally said.

"And?"

"And? Isn't that reason enough to refuse to give in to this attraction between us?" she asked, looking out at the velvet night sky rather than at me. "You specialize in torture and pain, and I crave healing and peace. We are as different as oil and water, and yet you insist on trying to blend us together."

"I think you underestimate how fun blending with me could be," I joked, waggling my eyebrows. A grin tugged at her lips and her eyes sparkled with humor, but she ducked her head and shook it without replying. Heaving an internal sigh, I considered her words more seriously before answering.

"If we were not meant to blend together on some level, then why do we feel this pull toward one another? I have been alive longer than I care to think about, and never in all my time have I ever felt such a pull toward another being. Never. That may sound like a line, but I know you can sense my honesty," I explained. There it flared again, that desperate, almost painful urge inside of me to Mark her as mine. The intensity of that craving grew every moment I was in her presence, and I was beginning to wonder how long I would be able to refrain from giving in to that urgent demand, because I knew as long as I left her without my Mark, the urge to claim her would never go away. I took a moment to pull it back, gritting my teeth as my palm tingled and that voice in my head whispered how much easier all of this would be if she were already tied to me.

"Attraction isn't reason enough for me to tear up the foundations of who I am and rebuild myself, ignoring and allowing the things you do on a daily basis so we can enjoy each other's company," Calixta began, turning to face me. I stopped walking and watched her tip her head up to study me, her beautiful eyes serious.

"Attraction is not the right word," I countered.

"Oh?"

"No, attraction is too weak a word, it's something felt between animals and humans," I answered and stepped in close to her. Cali's eyes widened slightly but she did not retreat or show signs of fear. Lowering my guard slightly, I flooded her with what I felt.

"When you touch me, it is as if a trail of fire follows in the wake of every stroke of your fingers. When I touch you, I learn a new level of craving beyond anything I have ever known," I began to explain, feeling her heart flutter and her breathing increase.

"The scent of you is imprinted in my mind forever, and I crave it like a drug I never want to give up. I am a master of all things pain and torture, you are right. But not being able to touch you when I want, *how* I want, is a new kind of pain I've never felt before. Watching the light in your eyes shine when you do good, when you help people, has me hypnotized. Seeing your smiles, each of them meaning something different, has become a new favorite hobby of mine, as is trying to discern precisely what each one means. I can *feel* you when you're close, and every cell of my body reacts to your presence and comes alive," I continued in a low voice, knowing she was getting overwhelmed, but I needed her to see, to feel, to properly understand the torture I was putting myself through in order to give her the time she needed to adjust.

"Adrik—"

"And when we kissed last night, refusing to go further with you was hands down one of the hardest things I have ever had to do," I cut in. Cali blinked slowly, her gaze becoming slightly unfocused. I inched closer, and my hands had a mind of their own as they slid to her hips and pulled her gently against me. I could feel her desire as it swamped me, and I concentrated hard not to get swept away in it.

"You're evil," she whispered breathily, her gaze on my mouth.

"Am I?" I stroked her cheek softly. "Or am I simply the darkness you've been taught to fear?"

Cali's mind was a haze of desire and lust, her usually clear thoughts overrun with ideas of kissing me and running her hands over me.

The need to kiss her, to devour her, to make her so breathless with desire that she would almost pass out from lack of oxygen was almost unbearable. I wanted her skin to feel alive, her heart to drum harder and for her to be lost in *feeling*. I let the moment build as I inched closer to her, my own heart pounding and my cock growing heavy and hard at the feel of her pressed against me. As I leaned in closer, I paused, something out there pricking on my radar.

Someone unwelcome was nearby.

The air suddenly felt thick and electric with power. Clouds were darkening overhead, and the threat of rain seemed inevitable. Yet, there was more. Cali froze, blinked, a small crease appearing on her forehead as she slowly looked around us.

Shit.

"Do not speak, Cali," I warned. She stilled, her eyes flying back to my face, her mouth parted in surprise. She opened her mouth to comment, and I shook my head.

"Not a word, red. We need to get out of here," I added. She frowned and shook her head at me.

"While I really want to know how the hell you're able to speak into my mind, I can feel the power increasing in the air. What is it?"

"I'm not sure, but—"

I didn't get to finish my sentence because there was a blinding flash and the sound of thunder directly in front of us. The almighty boom was enough to make Cali lose her balance and she began to fall. I grabbed her hand and yanked her behind me as the ground shook and the power in the air caused the hair on my arms to stand on end. The flash of light accompanying the sound was blinding, and I closed my eyes and spun, pressing Cali's face into my chest to protect her eyes from it. When I was sure it was gone, I turned and looked over my shoulder as a shout of pain shattered the air and another rumble of power shook around us. Two Archangels battled against a lone figure, their white wings almost luminescent. As much as I hated the bastards, there was a certain appeal to seeing them in action. We called them fluffy fuckers, but the Archangels were deadly, and to see them in the midst of a fight was indescribable.

The figure they fought also had wings, ash-black and huge in comparison to the Angels. Where the Angels were lithe and flexible, regal, and too perfect to be human, the dark winged one was battle-scarred and rough around the edges, but there was a cloak of power to him I'd only ever seen a handful of times in my life.

"What is he?" Cali whispered beside me, her voice filled with fear and awe.

"*A Nephilim,*" I replied, watching the fight before me with a little reverence myself.

"*Wait... Nephilim are real?*"

"*Rare, but very real,*" I answered, scanning around us to see if anything else was amiss.

"*Are they... evil?*" she asked, and I knew her compassion was getting the best of her. As an Angel scored a deep gouge on the Nephilim, I scanned Cali, worried she was feeling their pain. But she knew enough to keep her guards up and was only getting the barest echo of their wounds. I wasn't happy about it, but it was better than her feeling the full brunt of it.

"*We should go,*" I suggested, tightening my hold on her hand.

"*But it's two against one,*" she reminded, a tinge of outrage in her voice.

"*Trust me, it will take more than these two to kill him. Nephilim's are incredibly powerful, and this one seems... oddly more so,*" I answered, frowning as I watched the lightning speed with which the Nephilim moved. Archangels were the mightiest warriors Heaven had to offer, and he was dancing around the two of them like they were nothing. Come to think of it, the other Nephilim I had seen over the years did not have wings like his. Theirs tended to be a gray-white kind of color, not the ash-black I was seeing. What was different about this one?

"*Is the Nephilim evil?*" Cali repeated, and I recognized the stubbornness in her voice. Gritting my teeth, I shrugged.

"*Not exactly. They are part human, part Angel,*" I explained, watching as the Nephilim took another slash of a blade.

"*Help him?*"

It was a plea, one that tore at me. She was using that voice, the one that made completely sane people do irrational things just because she'd been the one to ask it.

"This being does not need my help, red. He is more powerful than you know," I tried to explain. While none of my brothers had ever gone head-to-head with a Nephilim, I was not confident that any of us would walk away from a real fight with one, at least not in one piece. We tended to leave them be; we had no issue with them. Angels saw them as filth, as abominations. They were the one thing Angels hated more than Demons. It was ironic since Nephilim only existed when an Angel and a rare type of human did the naked tango, and a child was a result. There were some humans out there with a special gene, very rare, but it was only those humans who could produce a part Angel baby.

"Adrik, please. He does not deserve to be hunted because of what he is," Cali pleaded.

"Does that go for me too, red? Will you continue to put limitations on us and what we feel because of what I am?"

Cali's expressive eyes showed so much emotion, so many insecurities, questions, and fears. I waited, the battle raging on.

"I don't fear what you are... I fear who you are," she explained softly. I frowned, her words sinking in slowly. Was a King of Hell the only thing that made me who I was? Was my entire identity wrapped up in torture, pain, and ruling a circle of Hell? Or was there more to me, something I had that I could offer my mate that would make being tied to me for an eternity worth it? My gaze flicked to the battle that was increasing in violence and blood and sighed.

"I don't want you here," I explained.

"I am not leaving, but I will protect myself and remain hidden and out of the way if that's what it takes for you to help him," she agreed with relief. My immediate reaction was to say hell no and take her by shadow back to my realm where she'd be safe. But one look at those pleading green eyes, feeling her need and steely resolve

gave me pause.

Fuck!

Gritting my teeth, I forced myself to have more confidence and trust in my mate. I knew she was powerful and could protect herself for a time, but the thought of her being caught off guard and whisked away while I was helping a fucking Nephilim made me want to destroy the dark creature as well just so there would be no more chances of her asking me to do something so needlessly stupid. I wasn't kidding when I said the Nephilim was powerful. Nodding slowly, I agreed to Cali's terms, fully prepared to leave the Nephilim to whatever fate awaited him if she so much as moved an inch toward us in order to help.

"Your word, Calixta… that you won't try to help. I will leave the Nephilim to perish if you try to intervene."

Her eyes narrowed for a moment, her pride pricking at being told what to do, but I knew she could feel how determined I was to keep her safe and how ready I was to pull her away from here if she could not truthfully vow to remain safe.

"I promise."

I watched her a moment longer, needing to be sure. She was my mate, my other half, and nothing mattered as much as her safety. Her happiness would always be second to her wellbeing. Sighing heavily, I leaned down and kissed her hard and set her aside. I watched as she properly warded herself and coated herself with a spell that made her less noticeable. Swearing under my breath, I turned away from her and stalked toward the battle, hoping the Nephilim didn't try to attack me as well.

Knowing how it felt to try and balance my mate's happiness with her safety, I had a new appreciation for the constant struggle Cole went through. We all thought him dramatic for some of his actions regarding Mika, but the others didn't know the gut-wrenching fear of losing their mate. Cali and I were not even bound, only by mind, and the thought of losing that connection, of losing *her,* was a new level of fear I'd never experienced myself.

I turned my attention back to the fight and watched the Nephilim strike out with a long black bladed sword, his dark eyes narrowed on his opponents. As distracted as the Angels were with the Nephilim, I knew I had a good shot at helping here. Without pausing, I wrapped myself in shadow and sent myself a few feet behind one of the Archangels. Her long hair was braided down her back, as perfect as the rest of her. Usually, I would partake in some banter and dance around for a while, but I was incredibly aware of my mate not far away, and I worried someone would find her and take her.

Without giving a warning, I drew on my power and sent a jet of hellfire at the Angel. She shrieked and spun around, her blue eyes finding me, her face contorting into an expression of rage and pain as the flames consumed her.

"T'Nari!" the other Angel roared.

The Angel I now knew as T'Nari continued to scream in agony as she tried to put out the flames. Hellfire wasn't like regular fire, and so was not so easily put out.

The Nephilim noted my presence but did not stop his fight with the other Archangel. I considered intervening, offering a hand, but I could tell by the lazy way he fought that the Nephilim had been bored and eager for a fight tonight. I wasn't going to take away his plaything.

"Aren't you going to help?"

I almost startled at the sound of Cali's voice in my head, and something deep down soothed at hearing her reach out to me first and speak in such an intimate fashion.

"The Nephilim is bored tonight. I have seen them in action before, and he is simply playing with the Angels. I do not wish to ruin his fun."

"Are you sure?"

"Absolutely. And this Nephilim seems different than the others I have encountered. He is more powerful," I assured, a little apprehensive at the thought. The other Nephilim I had encountered over time had been staggeringly strong, their reflexes and abilities were something my brothers and I were weary of. But the winged warrior before me wore power like a second skin.

I kept an eye on the Angel fighting his dark-winged companion as I finally strode towards the female Angel who was only now able to lessen the flames. Whether I was helping this creature or not, I wouldn't turn down an opportunity to rid the world of an Angel, especially one so high up on the food chain. Where my brothers and I were at the top of the Demon food chain, there were only nine of us. There were approximately one-hundred-and-twenty Archangels still in existence—they could stand to lose a few.

T'Nari was panting and still crying out in pain, but she was distracted. I knew it would be honorable to wait for her to heal a little, but I didn't feel any guilt in being less than honorable where one of her kind were concerned. Besides, I had already waited until she'd put out the flames. She spun back towards me, her skin bubbling and sloughing off her body and her hair gone. Drawing my sword from thin air, I watched her eyes widen briefly as she raised her own blade, but too late. I swung hard and fast, the blade smooth and sharp as it went through her neck like a hot knife in butter. Clean and quick, it was a death she more than likely hadn't given any Demon. I watched her head roll for a moment and realized this kill was the fastest I had ever delivered a death blow to an Archangel. Usually, I loved to play around, dance, draw it out and make a game of it. When you'd been alive for eons, you found fun in things others never would.

"T'Nari! No!"

With his eyes on the now lifeless body of his companion, the last Angel became distracted, and the Nephilim took his shot, striking out with a powerful hit to the chest, his fist breaking through bone, muscle, and sinew to tear the beating heart from his opponent. The Arch froze, his face a mask of pain and disbelief as his legs gave out. I stepped back and watched him crumble. He wouldn't die yet, but he'd be in terrible pain. Only too aware that Cali could feel the echoes of his pain, I flexed my fingers on my sword and stepped towards the dying being.

"What are you doing?"

I froze as the Nephilim acknowledged me, his black eyes glittering and narrowed.

"Helping."

"Why?"

"Why not?"

"Do not play games with me, Demon King. I want to know why you would provide me with what I can only assume you meant to be assistance, when in the past our two kinds have avoided one another," the Nephilim inquired, stepping closer to the twitching body.

I reached for Cali in my mind, and I could feel her discomfort, but there was no pain.

"I do not answer to you." I shrugged and lowered my sword but did not put it away.

"No, you do not. Nor I, you. So, I would appreciate you answering my question."

I considered the Nephilim and shrugged.

"Would you believe me if I said someone asked me to help you?"

"If you are referring to the Witch hiding in the shadows, then yes," he answered.

I refused to react or show any emotion at all. I had no idea if Nephilim needed or wanted Witches. Being so rare, and because we had done our best to keep our distance from them in the past, there was very little we actually knew about his kind. From what I understood, however, Nephilim's could heal one another. They had no need of a Witch in the way Demons and Angels did.

"You can come out now, Witch. I mean you no harm, but I do question your sanity to remain in the presence of a Demon King," the Nephilim continued before he finished off the Angel at his feet with a lazy slice of his blade. I studied the black blade with admiration; it was beautiful. While we considered Angel Blades to be the only weapons capable of killing a King of Hell, that wasn't exactly true. Nephilim Blades were just as deadly and had the added bonus of killing Angels as well.

The Nephilim wiped the blood from his blade before looking over my shoulder.

I felt Cali's approach and ground my teeth together. Without taking my eyes from him, I backed up slightly until I stood before Cali, blocking her from reaching him or making herself any more vulnerable than she already was. The Nephilim's black eyes watched me curiously, his face emotionless before they slid back to Cali.

"Witch, why are you in the company of a being who would hunt you and keep you prisoner?"

"He is persistent, and will not take no for an answer," Cali answered with a shrug.

"Has he harmed you?"

I stiffened and drew myself up, preparing to pull Cali away the second he showed signs of wanting to attack.

"No, and I do not believe he is capable of it. Not where I am concerned," she answered kindly. The Nephilim looked between us with scrutiny, as if he did not believe her words, but finding no untruth in them.

"You are aware that his kind are hunting yours again?"

"Yes."

"And still you remain in his presence. Why?"

Cali sighed and I startled slightly when I felt one of her hands drop to mine, twining our fingers together.

"What are you doing, red?"

"Showing him he has no cause for concern."

"Adrik is protecting me. I trust him," she answered aloud. Again, the Nephilim looked between us and slowly shook his head.

"You are injured... Can I heal you?" Cali asked when silence persisted. I bit back my immediate refusal to let her anywhere near the creature, knowing that forbidding it would only spur on her desire to go to him simply to prove a point. Cali's laughter echoed in my head, and I felt a brush of her fingers across my lips as she caught my wayward thought.

"Thank you, but I do not require your assistance," the Nephilim answered.

"Are you sure? I can feel your injuries," Cali pointed out, frowning. The Nephilim tipped his head slightly in acknowledgement, and I frowned at the small, crooked curve of his lips. Was he trying to smile?

"Stop it," Cali reprimanded in a hiss, but I could feel her humor.

"What? It looks painful."

Cali gave me a mental kick in the shins, and I tried not to laugh.

"There is something between the two of you I am not seeing," the Nephilim announced. I didn't respond, and thankfully neither did Cali, although I wasn't entirely sure she knew what was going on between us. When neither of us elaborated, the Nephilim shrugged.

"I can see that you are close... which could present a problem. There will not be an Angel on Earth who will not try to take you from him, many Demons too."

"I have been cloaking myself my entire life, I will continue to do so," Cali shrugged.

Silence fell and she stepped forward. I was quick to pull her back and she sighed, turning more fully to look at me. Her green eyes softened slightly, and she raised a hand to brush my cheek gently. *"Trust me,"* she whispered. I could feel an urging in her, an instinct to extend her hand, to exchange pleasantries, to show this creature kindness. I did not understand her need, but I could feel it. Taking her hand from my face, I held it tightly and prepared to whip us away in shadow in an instant. I stepped forward with Cali, and she held out her other hand and smiled.

"I am Calixta, but you can call me Cali," she introduced. The Nephilim, for the first time, looked surprised. He glanced from me, to Cali, and then at her hand before he slowly took hers. Her hand was so tiny, engulfed entirely by his, only reinforcing to me the knowledge that she was intensely vulnerable right now.

"Amazarak," the Nephilim introduced, his voice gruff as if he didn't use it often.

"May I call you Zarak for short?" Cali asked with a radiant smile. The Nephilim frowned slightly, a small flicker of wonder crossed his face, but nodded.

"You may. I have never had a shortened name before," he replied slowly, seemingly unsure.

"My friends call me Cali, and I'll call you Zarak," she beamed.

"Friends." The Nephilim seemed stumped, considering this word as if it were unknown to him.

"You don't have any?" I asked.

He shook his head slowly and shrugged. "Only other Nephilim."

"That must be lonely," Cali whispered sympathetically.

"We are not here to be his therapist, woman."

"He needs friends," she argued, and I could feel the compassion rolling off her in waves.

"He is not an animal at your shelter in need of a home. He is a powerful immortal."

Cali gave the mental impression of the middle finger and I sighed, part of me wanting to smile at her fire.

"I am going to assume you have been stalking me, because I never told you where I work," she pointed out.

"I warned you that you need protecting at all times. You call it stalking, I call it being a bodyguard."

I could feel her mental eyeroll and bit back a smirk, knowing I'd won that round.

"We need to go, Cali. You need to go home," I said out loud. She glared at me, and I raised an eyebrow. She was in danger out in the open and had now gone and made friends with a being who was used to being a loner and answering to no one. I was not pleased with this development.

"Thank you for your kindness, friend Cali," Zarak said, bowing slightly. I rolled my eyes.

"You're more than welcome," Cali returned, beaming. With a nod at me, Zarak stepped backwards, and with one powerful beat of his wings, he took off into the night sky.

CHAPTER SIX
CALI

"You can leave me alone while I'm shopping," I told Adrik as I finished putting a handful of apples in a bag. I'd originally come in for milk, but decided to get my weekly shop over with while I was here.

"I could, but then I'd be thinking about you alone and unprotected," Adrik returned, his voice warm and smiling. I bit back my own smile and looked around surreptitiously. Adrik wasn't *with* me, he was working, but he hadn't left my mind for more than half an hour, and he refused to leave me while I was out in public. This wasn't the first time I'd spoken to someone in my head before, but I'd never done it with such ease. Speaking to others this way was a drain on my energy to maintain the connection. With Adrik, it felt as natural and as easy as breathing.

"I don't think it's likely I'll be accosted by Angels in a supermarket." The thought of bumping into one of Heaven's warriors in the snack aisle was enough to make me snicker. An older woman frowned at me, and I smiled and hurried on.

"You never know, little red, they can show up anywhere," he warned, but I could tell he was enjoying being with me even when he couldn't. I tried hard not to think about the fact that he was a King of Hell and that his job required him taking in human souls to torture and rip apart until they were so damaged that they became Demons. I tried not to picture him taking pleasure in someone's pain. The Adrik I knew versus the one in my head were so different, I just couldn't believe it was true half the time.

If it weren't for that perpetual flow of darkness and power I felt on him, that clung to him, I'd think I was crazy.

Then there was the other thing I was trying not to think about. What was this connection I felt with Adrik? Why was I so drawn to everything about him, and why was he insisting on keeping me close? It was almost like he'd decided I was his, and I had no say in the matter. I knew he was hiding something from me, he'd told me as much, and promised to tell me when he thought I was ready to hear it. Knowing he was hiding something important from me should have made me more than happy to cut him out of my life and run in the other direction. Yet... I sighed. The thought of cutting him out made me want to cry, and the thought of leaving him behind made me feel sick. Both of those reactions in themselves should be massive red flags—they were—but I couldn't do anything more than let this thing between us play out. It was likely going to be horrible, and I was probably going to kick myself good and hard when whatever he was keeping secret came to light. For now, though, I just couldn't bring myself to care enough to leave him.

"Will you be out much longer? I do not like the fact that you are out there unprotected for so long," Adrik continued.

"Almost done," I assured, grabbing a salad bag. Usually, I made my own from scratch, but since moving to my new place, my garden was still in the works and not quite ready yet. AP thought it was crazy that as a Witch, I hadn't made the garden my first priority. I loved nature, all Witches did, but I had been so focused on the animals at the shelter that I had overlooked the flora side of things for a while. I did admit though, I felt more at peace with all the greenery I'd brought into my gardens and my home.

As I walked down the aisle, I felt Adrik's hands on my hips, sliding up my waist to my breasts. It was almost as if he were standing right behind me, his front pressed to my back. I sucked in a sharp breath and paused for a moment.

"Adrik!"

"Keep shopping, red. I'm just playing," he murmured, and I swear I could feel his hot breath on my ear. Over the last few days, we'd teased the line of this kind of behavior, but we'd always put a stop to it, as if we were too worried neither of us shared the restraint to stop from going further.

I pushed on, trying hard not to concentrate on the feeling of his hands cupping me, his fingers teasing my nipples. A hot flush of heat struck hard, and I drew in a deep breath, keeping my gaze averted from the other shoppers. There was no way they could know, but I still felt like they would somehow clue in if they saw my face. I knew no one else could see him, no one else knew what was going on, but it was so hard not to react.

"I can't concentrate."

"Then perhaps you should leave," he suggested, his teeth gently grazing my neck. I bit my lip and tried to concentrate on my mental list. I still needed bread, I had to go get bread.

"You make me so hard, little red, I'm aching for you," he murmured with a soft groan. My heart began to pound harder at the need in his voice, and I tried to steady my breathing.

Shaking my head at myself, I strode on, trying my hardest not to act as though anything was wrong. Adrik's fingers continued to pluck and roll, his teeth raking back and forth over the pulse point in my neck. I could feel the heat of his body pressing up against my back, his hard cock drawing my attention. I looked around me quickly, almost certain I'd find him there, but he wasn't. I felt him rock hard against me and between my legs started to throb and tingle.

What did I need again? Right, bread. I hurried along and took two loaves off the shelf and dumped them into my cart as Adrik's fingers tortured me some more. Screw it, I could shop again another day, I needed to go.

Adrik's low chuckle against my ear sent a shiver down my spine as I pushed quickly to the check outs and sent out a quiet thank you to the universe that there was one free. As I started unloading my cart, I felt Adrik's hand slide beneath the waistband of my jeans.

"What are you doing?!"

"Giving you incentive to move your sweet ass to the car, and get home where I know you are safe," he murmured, his voice deep and rasping, as if this was affecting him as much as it was me. I stiffened and kept my head bowed away from the cashier as I struggled to keep my expression neutral.

"If you're so worried about my safety, you can just shadow your way here and stay with me until I'm home," I suggested desperately.

"Ah, but then I would not be able to put my hands on you like this," he reminded, chuckling low, his voice like fingers stroking my skin.

"I'm out in public, Adrik. Could this wait?" I pleaded as he stroked me gently between my legs. I felt as though my underwear was still there, so he hadn't gone beneath it... yet.

"You're taking too long, red. I'm not stopping until you come... twice. Whether that is at home or in public is up to you," he warned. I wanted to ask him to stop, to wait, but another part of me refused to let the words out. My body had been on fire for him since we'd first met. The nights we spent together in my head, kissing deeply and only lightly touching had left me desperate for more. I knew he wanted me, and I could feel how hard it was for him to restrain himself from pushing the issue to go further. I'd been secretly wishing he'd throw caution to the wind and just take me already, but he hadn't, and now here we both were,

horny, desperate people who had reached a breaking point.

"You make my cock so hard, red. Can you feel it? Do you feel how much I want to fuck you?" Adrik moaned.

"Hi there, how is your day going?" the young man behind the counter asked. He had to be barely twenty-one.

"I'm well, thank you," I answered unsteadily as I finished loading my groceries.

"Any plans for the rest of the day?" he asked cheerily, and I didn't miss the way his eyes raked over me, lingering for a moment on my breasts. And great, he was chatty. Adrik stroked me again, slow, and languid and I clenched my thighs together and forced a smile.

"Not a lot, just going home to do some housework," I lied. And probably spend some time with a battery-operated toy because this was torture.

"I need you, Calixta. I want to feel your pussy wrapped around my cock, I want to taste you, touch you, leave my mark on you," Adrik continued, his words having just as much effect on me as his touch.

"That doesn't sound too bad. I'm here until seven tonight, and then my friend Tommy…" the boy continued, but I blocked him out. Adrik's low laughter rumbled in my ear and his fingers continued their slow torture.

"I think this boy likes you."

"So?"

"So, how do you think he would react if I made you come, right here and now? What do you think he'd say if he knew you could feel my fingers between your legs and my mouth on your breasts?"

"Your mouth on my——"

I gasped aloud when I felt as if a hot mouth sealed around my nipple, suckling strongly, fingers still stroking my clit.

"Are you okay?" the boy asked, pausing for a moment, his wide eyes searching my face.

"Answer him, red, or I go further," Adrik warned when I didn't speak right away.

"Fine. Sorry, I'm just not feeling well and need to get home. Do you think we could hurry this along?" I asked, forcing a smile as Adrik sucked harder, his tongue flicking out wildly. I ducked my head and pretended to be looking in my handbag and closed my eyes as the sensations rocked through my body.

"I could make you come while he watches, red. Do you want that?" he threatened, his voice low and raspy, sending a tremor to my very core.

"No, don't," I replied, my voice breathy even to my own ears.

"You look a little flushed, can I help you to your car?" the boy asked, handing over the last bag.

"No!" I cried and then cleared my throat when he stared at me, wide-eyed. "I mean, no thank you. You have been such a great help," I assured and handed him my money. "Keep the change."

He mumbled a confused goodbye as I directed my cart out the large doors. Adrik's chuckle made my stomach flutter, and he continued his torturously slow assault.

"There, I'm out of the supermarket and on my way home. You can stop now," I explained somewhat desperately, loading my groceries into the car.

"I said you'll come twice before I stop," he reminded me as I pushed my trolley into the trolley bay.

"Adrik," I warned, almost stumbling as I felt his fingers slide beneath my panties. I gasped and planted my palms flat on the side of my car when I reached it and closed my eyes as he slid a finger inside me. Goddamn, how was this even possible? How did it feel so real?

"Get in the car, red," Adrik instructed, stroking me deep. I bit back

a moan and unlocked my car before sliding in, locking it behind me and panting aloud.

"You need to stop," I pleaded with a moan, unsure how I was supposed to concentrate enough to drive home.

"I can't stop. I'm stroking my cock right now, little red, thinking about how you'd feel, thinking about the scent of you. I need to come, and so do you," he answered, groaning low and deep, the sound sending a spiral of pleasure through me.

"Start the car, baby. Get moving."

Gritting my teeth, I did as he ordered and managed to get out of the parking lot without causing an accident. I only lived five blocks away, I could get there safely. I could picture Adrik on his chair or lying on his bed, his shaft in his hand as he stroked his hard length, slow and tight, his moans echoing in the room. Just then, Adrik slid two fingers inside me, and I cried out, momentarily closing my eyes but I forced them back open, gasping, trying to concentrate.

"Adrik!"

"I wish I were beside you right now, watching you, touching you," he groaned, and I could hear how much he wanted me, his voice was laden with desire and lust. I was so close... so close...

I gasped as I reached a red light and closed my eyes.

"More," I hissed, rocking my hips. It felt so real, I could swear with my eyes closed that he was there. Adrik stroked me hard and fast, curling his fingers just so, his thumb circling my clit and dragging me ever closer.

"Come, baby. I want to hear you moan," Adrik whispered in my ear before his mouth was back on my breast. Oh shit... so close, so close.

"Yes! Adrik, don't stop!" I cried, clutching the steering wheel tighter. Almost there...

"Yes!" I cried out, my hands slamming into the roof of the car, my back arched and hips rocking against a hand that wasn't actually there, but *oh yes* did it feel real. I gasped and panted, slowly sliding back down in my seat. My heart was thundering hard, and I could still feel his fingers inside me, his mouth kissing my breasts and flicking at sensitive nipples.

A horn beeped and I jumped, having forgotten for a moment where I was. My gaze caught on something beside me, and I turned to see a guy in the car next to me, his eyes wide and mouth open in shock.

Shit.

It had to be obvious that I was having an orgasm.

I gasped and froze, unable to think of what to do or say. The car behind me honked again and I jumped into action. My face flooded with heat, and I quickly drove off, a laugh working its way up my throat.

"I hope he enjoyed the show," Adrik chuckled.

"I can't believe that just happened!" I shrieked. If I hadn't been driving at that moment, I'd have buried my head in my hands and wished for a hole to open and swallow me whole.

"I am not done yet, little red. I promised you two," Adrik reminded.

"This has to wait until I'm inside," I replied with a groan, feeling him beginning to stroke me again. I didn't even bother to fight it this time, too high on the first orgasm he'd given me to care much anymore. I forced myself to concentrate on the road as he began touching me all over, sometimes biting gently, pinching and stroking. I was in a haze of stimulation when I managed to pull into my driveway.

"You are not safe until you're inside," he reminded before he began flicking my nipple with his tongue again. With a groan, I stumbled out of my car and opened the trunk. I took all four bags

at once and staggered to my front door, moaning out loud. My body was on fire, it was throbbing and aching, and I just needed him to stop... or keep going. I staggered into the house and slammed the door shut behind me, dropping the bags on the floor.

"Lock it, red," he ordered. I did as he said and stumbled down the hall to my room where I barely made it to my bed before he began thrusting his fingers deep again.

"Adrik."

"Take off your clothes, red. I want to see you," he ordered, his voice husky and deep. I didn't even care anymore; my body was screaming for more and I wasn't going to deny it. I mean... this wasn't *really* sex. I wasn't actually giving myself over... right? This didn't count!

I stripped off my clothes in record time and was back on my bed as I felt him nip and lick his way down my chest to my stomach, his fingers tracing my inner thighs. I closed my eyes and just let myself feel, imagining him here, imagining him stroking himself.

"Are you hard, Adrik?"

"I'm always hard for you, Cali, but yes. I have my cock in my hand, stroking it, so ready to come. I want you to touch yourself," he answered, his voice strained.

"Why?" He was doing a good enough job on his own.

"Because I want to watch you stroking your pussy while I make you come." Biting my lower lip, I did as he asked, sliding my hand between my legs. At the same time, I felt his hot breath on me, and I gasped when I felt him stroke me with his tongue. I dropped my head back and groaned at the sensation of him feasting on me, his tongue and teeth dragging me towards the edge.

"Are you stroking your pussy baby? Let me see," he ordered, his voice ragged. I opened my eyes and looked down at myself and I heard

him groan as he looked through my eyes.

"That's it, red. Keep playing with yourself. Come for me, I'm so close."

"Let me see," I whispered in a ragged gasp.

After a moment, I found myself looking through Adrik's eyes. He was in a high-backed leather chair, and his hand was wrapped around his thick, hard cock, moving up and down the long shaft. I moaned at the sight, transfixed. I could feel his mounting pleasure, the way he was holding off until I got there too.

"Adrik, I need…" I trailed off, not knowing what it was I needed.

"Come for me, Cali. Good girl, I know you're almost there," Adrik coaxed, a small moan accompanying his words. I gasped and rolled my hips when I felt his mouth on me again, his fingers sliding deep inside me, stroking, teasing, bringing me ever closer to the pleasure he promised.

"Faster," I whispered, my back arching as my fingers continued to flick and swirl against my clit, his fingers stroked me inside while his tongue lapped at me. He did as I begged and I was panting, gasping, my muscles locking tight and my pleasure mounting.

"I feel you, red. Come for me."

A light blew behind my eyes and sounds were momentarily muted as I screamed. My orgasm didn't wash over me, it hit me like a goddamn freight train, carrying me away so fast and hard that for a moment—or maybe several—I couldn't breathe.

I heard Adrik shout my name, felt his pleasure overwhelm him as he came, his back arched and heart pounding, breathing ragged and uneven.

I don't know how long it took for sound to return or for my breathing to start up again. My head pounded in time with my heart, and I felt sweaty.

"Adrik?"

"Hmm?"

"I forgot to get milk."

There was a moment of silence before he laughed, and I smiled at the sexy, sated sound of it.

"Next time…we're doing it in person, red," he replied, groaning exhaustedly. I grinned and lay flat out on my bed, my body throbbing and rippling with pleasure, my mind gloriously blank.

CHAPTER SEVEN
ADRIK

Two full weeks passed since the day at the grocery store, and we still hadn't had sex. At least not physically, but I made sure to visit Cali every night and I didn't leave until she was crying out my name. I wanted her so badly I was worried I'd do something stupid soon and Mark her. Thankfully, I had enough self-control to keep distance between us whenever that urge was getting too strong to resist. My aching cock wasn't happy with me. Yes, I got off every time I touched her from a distance, but it wasn't going to keep me going for long. I could feel how it was only taking the edge off for her now too, which made me happy because it meant that sooner rather than later, she'd want the real deal, and I would be ready when that happened.

We did not see the Nephilim, Amazarak, again, and I knew that concerned Calixta even though she tried to conceal it from me. I made an effort to conceal my jealousy that she was concerned about another male more than me. I knew her feelings about him, and they were not as intense as her feelings for me, but the very fact that she had another male on her mind was enough to have me grinding my teeth at an unusual rate.

Besides that, nothing new happened. I kept tabs on her every day when she went to the animal shelter, I brushed her mind and coerced her with my words, tempted her and slid vivid fantasies into her head. She sometimes reciprocated and I'd fallen off my chair more than once at feeling her hand on my cock at random moments in the day.

I closed my eyes as I lay in bed and sent myself to her, feeling her laying in her bed, slowly drifting off to sleep. I imagined wrapping my body around her, pulling her close to me. Almost immediately, her body relaxed, and a small smile curved her lips. She could feel me, and her body knew it was safe in my arms. We hadn't yet completed a single other bond, and I was slowly going crazy. My body was on fire all the time, hard and demanding release, but no matter how many times I jacked off to her little fantasies or to the memory of her, it was never enough. My palm was basically itching all the time, urging me to Mark her, and something deep inside which I could only assume was my soul, screamed at me whenever she was near to bind her to me, to make us complete.

I could feel her discomfort, but she had no idea why she felt that way. I wanted to tell her, but something in the back of my head kept telling me to wait, that this wasn't the time. Cali was fighting her attraction to me, fighting her need to reach out to me throughout the day, to not feel me with her at night. But every night, she dragged me into another psychic realm. I was a goddamn fucking saint for not taking her body yet, for not urging her on until she couldn't think straight. The times I entered her mind and made her feel my touch were only going to keep us sated for the time being. I could taste her desire on the air whenever we were near, feel it burning beneath her skin, hear it in the whisper of her voice and taste it in her kiss. But she was strong, and she was fighting with decades of thinking that I was the definition of evil. I tried to prove her wrong. I was with her every time she set up the tents to heal, I continued to bring food and clothes. I spent time with the homeless and sick, doing what I could to help. I protected her every night despite her insistence that she didn't need me.

Sol was slowly warming up to me, but every night he warned me not to hurt her, to protect her.

Malik was the only one who knew I'd found my mate yet, and he was giving me shit for not having completed the bond yet, but he didn't know the struggle and what it would be like to be the cause of his mate's pain or misery. Cole had explained once that he'd messed up with Mika, refused her request to join him on the surface to close a case she'd been working, and when he'd come back, feeling her numbness and a disconnect between them turned him into a raging idiot, angry and anxious and out of sorts. I could only imagine.

Everyday Cali and I spent together, I felt myself fall a little more in love with her. I knew it was happening, and I wasn't going to do a goddamn thing to stop it. This woman was mine; she was universe approved and I knew that being in love with each other, trusting each other with that knowledge, was another bond that needed to be forged. As far as I was concerned, it couldn't happen soon enough. I knew Cali was falling too, but she fought it so hard, refusing to look at what it was she felt towards me for too long. It scared her.

Without warning, I blinked and found myself in my study, but I wasn't *truly* in my study. Another dream.

"So... this is where you work?"

I spun around to see Cali sitting in my desk chair, her legs crossed and propped up on my desk, her smile knowing and teasing.

"When I'm not with you, yes."

"I gotta say... it's not what I expected Hell to look like," she mused.

"That's because it's not... not really. This is simply my realm, my home. Sure, Hell is right next door, but this is just my space," I answered, stepping close to her. Her eyes brightened with interest, and she took another look around, slowly getting to her feet.

"So, you chose this desk, this chair… you read these books?" she asked, rounding the desk to look around more carefully.

"Yes."

She smiled and kept looking and I sat down instead, just watching her in my space. I liked her here; it was where she was meant to be. I wanted her to want to know me, to see my home and my things. Stretching my legs out in front of me, I laced my fingers over my abdomen as she looked around. She was wearing a simple yellow and green sundress that complimented her eyes and skin tone perfectly. Her breasts were emphasized, and my palms ached to hold them. I raked my gaze slowly downwards, drawn to the dip in her waist and the curve of her hips, all the way down her long, tanned legs. Steamy thoughts of them wrapped around my hips as I sank into her tight, wet heat had me hardening uncomfortably. The idea of fucking her for hours made me shift slightly to give my growing erection some space.

"Adrik," she whispered, her cheeks flushed and her body responding to the need of mine. I could feel every ounce of desire and restraint in that one whispered word. Groaning, I dropped my head back to look at the ceiling, counting backwards from twenty in an attempt to remain in my seat so I wouldn't push her against the bookcase and fuck her senseless.

"I can feel your craving," she continued, and from the sound of her voice I knew she'd come closer.

"You have to keep your distance for a moment, Cali. I am practicing self-restraint, and it's not something I've had to do before. I'm not very good at it," I warned, refusing to look at her.

"It hurts me to feel you so in need."

"Cali, stay back. Please," I insisted, feeling my grip on my restraint slipping.

"What if I could help you a little?" she asked. Images of her on her knees, my cock in her mouth, her hands stroking me filled my head. My breath caught at the possibility, but I wasn't sure I was strong enough not to take her body completely, not to fulfill my every desire.

"No."

"It might help?"

"Cali," I gritted out and slowly raised my gaze to hers. "If you touch me, I will snap. I am trying hard not to push you down onto my desk, lift your dress and bury myself inside your body so deeply you'll feel me there forever," I admitted, my voice rough, my heart thumping hard. "My need to fuck you so hard, that you go hoarse screaming my name is almost too much. I want to bury my face between your thighs and *feast* on you until you can't take it anymore. My body is screaming for yours so loudly, it's hard to hear anything else. So please. Stay. Away." I ground out, my breathing heavy.

~

CALI

Adrik's desire was beating at me relentlessly, building with every second, his yearning for more causing my own fantasies to grow. A pulse beat relentlessly between my legs at his words, and I felt myself reacting to him, my panties damp and my heart pounding hard. The imagery in my head was vivid and powerful, and I knew he'd unintentionally done it, his need so great he was having a hard time controlling it.

The hardest part for me, however, was admitting just how badly I wanted him to fulfill every one of his fantasies. My every waking hour was filled with thoughts of him. If I went for longer than twenty minutes without touching my mind to his, I felt uncomfortable, achy, and alone. And when he finally touched my mind, it was a soothing balm on a deep and ever-present burn. My dreams were always filled with these psychic visits. My daydreams were flooded with the idea of being in his bed, in his arms, feeling him fill me and take me, bringing me to heights I *knew* he could take me to. He was nothing like I imagined. Adrik wasn't the evil being I'd grown up thinking he was, and if he were hiding it or pretending, then he was world-class. I trusted my intuition, and it was never wrong. Everything inside me screamed that Adrik was important to me, *the most* important thing to me. We were meant to be together; we were meant to complete each other in a way I didn't quite understand. Something told me he knew, though. He knew what this intangible connection was between us. He'd asked me to trust him, that he knew something I did not, but that I was not ready to hear it. It was driving me wild not knowing, but I also felt I could trust him. I was desperate to talk to someone about all of this, maybe my AP, but I already knew what she would say. She'd tell me to run far and fast, and to never look back. She wanted me to keep my distance from Adrik and leave him behind. But the simple thought of never seeing him again, touching him, hearing his voice… it left a deep pit of despair in my gut I didn't understand.

No, staying away from Adrik wasn't an option.

So then, where did that leave us? Because I was causing him a good deal of pain by making him keep a leash on his desires. I knew he wanted me from the very first moment we met, and if I were honest, I'd wanted him too. I'd never met someone so sinfully sexy in all my life, someone who wore sex and sin like a second skin, who exuded power and dominance. So, if I already knew it was impossible to say goodbye to him, what was I meant to do? Because keeping us on this permanent standby was not realistic but the thought of pursuing some kind of relationship with a King of Hell had me terrified for my soul.

Then there was that feeling in my gut that told me this was right.

"Adrik, I want to help you," I began, edging towards him. The closer I got, the tighter he wound in on himself, as if my nearness was causing him physical pain. I felt his determination to keep his hands to himself, to not touch me or allow even a small moment of weakness. He honestly thought if he gave in a little, he'd never be able to stop himself.

But I didn't want him to stop. What was the point in giving in only a little, in dragging things out when it would inevitably go the way we both knew it would? Keeping my hands to myself had been torture these last few weeks. Indulging in vivid, steamy daydreams and fantasies meant to tease him just weren't enough. I wanted the real thing, and I wanted it now.

"Adrik," I whispered again, my body aching.

His dark blue eyes snapped open, the burning fire in them enough to steal my breath. His gaze heated exponentially when he finally caught onto my feelings, felt my decision.

"You need to be sure, Cali. Because I cannot stop this time, it's too powerful," he warned, his voice deep and low, sending a shiver of desire down my spine. I watched his knuckles whiten as he gripped the arms of his chair, as if he were physically holding himself in place.

"I want this, Adrik. I *need* this," I admitted, uncaring now that voicing it left me vulnerable.

Adrik shot up out of his chair so fast I stumbled backwards. He was there in front of me, his hand pressed to my lower back, his other hand tipping my head back to look at him. The pounding of desire beating at him was so strong my legs almost gave out.

"Not here, baby. You need to lower your wards to your home and let me in," he rasped.

"Adrik——" I shook my head.

"I am not properly fucking you for the first time in a psychic realm. I want to be with *you*," he insisted. I was almost a puddle at his feet and sucked in a breath, nodding. I trusted him. I knew he wasn't going to hurt me. Having him in my home was not going to make a difference.

His slow smile was full of sin and heat. Quickly, he pressed a hard, devouring kiss to my lips and then—

I shot up off the bed, my heart pounding and body pulsing with need. My breath was coming faster, and my entire body felt like it was vibrating with my want of him.

"Let me in, little red, or I'll huff and puff and blow your house down." The words were playful, but the dark desire in them had my anticipation kicking up several notches. My breath caught when the full realization of what I was doing sank in, and I had a moment of hesitation.

"Adrik…"

"I need you, Calixta. Can you feel how much I crave you? My desire? How tight and aching my body is, waiting for yours? I know you feel the same. Knowing you need me as much as I need you but not giving you what you need has been a pain unlike any other."

Of all the things he could have said…

"Come inside, Adrik," I invited while pulling down my wards. I stood from my bed on shaky legs as I heard my front door open. As soon as it closed, I pulled my wards back up and sucked in a breath. I scanned around my room, taking in the laundry in the

hamper and my crumpled bed sheets. God, what was I thinking? I ran my shaky fingers through my hair as I heard him approach, I could feel him getting closer.

I jumped when my door slammed open, and I gasped at the sight of Adrik in my doorway, his dark eyes glittering with heat and sinful intent. Hunger rolled off him in waves, swamping me, overwhelming me. He took three slow steps forward, every movement a glide of rippling muscle, his eyes locked onto me. I was suddenly feeling like he was very much the Big Bad Wolf. My heart was pounding, trapped in my ribcage, my lungs unable to take a big enough breath as he came forward, the air around us crackling and snapping with electricity, chemistry, and pheromones swirled until it was too hard to think, too hard to breathe.

Adrik stood before me, a mere inch away, his heat reaching me. My skin was sensitive, itchy, like the clothes I wore were too confining, too uncomfortable.

I tipped my head back to look at him better, his dark eyes almost black with need.

"One last chance, little red," he forced out, and I could feel his restraint weakening. Everything he wanted was within reach and he was still giving me another chance to say no.

"Ye—" The word was lost as he brought his mouth crashing down on mine, his fingers sliding into my hair to bunch there. I moaned into his mouth and sank into him, gripping his shirt tightly in my hands and bringing myself flush against him.

Desire. Lust. Desperation. Hunger. Greed. All of it was mixed together so tightly it was hard to distinguish one emotion from the other. But I no longer cared to think or analyze, I was acting on nothing but instinct. I gripped the hem of his black T-Shirt and began yanking it up. Adrik broke away long enough to pull it swiftly over his head before he was back to kissing me, his hands working at the waistband of my shorts. He tugged and I whimpered. With a growl, he snapped his fingers, and I drew in a sharp breath, suddenly naked. I gaped at him, taking in his entire nude form with awe. I knew the man was sexy, but seeing all of him, naked, tanned, tattooed, muscled, and… ahem… *hung*… I was beginning to wonder how I had even postponed sleeping with him this long.

"Fucking perfect," Adrik groaned huskily, echoing my thoughts, and I dragged my gaze back to his face, noting the hungry way he looked at my nude body. Done wasting time, I lunged at him, and Adrik caught me, his wide hands gripping my backside as I wrapped my legs around his waist. He groaned low and deep, the sound setting off little fireworks in my body. Adrik stumbled backwards until the backs of his legs hit the edge of my bed and he sat down with me astride him. I rocked my hips, already slick and ready, so desperate for him I was almost sobbing.

"Now," I pleaded, grinding against his hard length again, needy and on edge.

"So greedy," he said with a moan against my lips, a smile tugging at his mouth. "So hot."

He slid a hand between us to test my readiness, two thick fingers slipping inside my heat. I moaned and closed my eyes, so close to the edge already but not willing to go over yet.

"Adrik," I whimpered.

"Do you want my cock, little red?"

"Now. Give it to me now," I demanded, trying to angle my hips so his fingers would go deeper.

"I haven't even tasted you yet," he reminded, sliding his fingers from inside me. My eyes fluttered open, and I watched as he sucked one finger into his mouth. The groan that rumbled through his chest had me trying to squeeze my thighs together in reaction. His dark eyes glittered lustily back at me, and I kept rocking against him, the feel of his shaft sliding against my clit so damn good.

"You taste so fucking edible," he whispered harshly. Slowly, he brought those fingers to my mouth and wiped them across my lips. I hesitated and he grinned and leaned forward, devouring my mouth, tasting me there so thoroughly it was like he would die if he didn't.

Dizzy, panting, it took me several seconds to realize Adrik was lifting me. It wasn't until the head of his cock was at my entrance that I gasped. With one, hard stroke, Adrik impaled me on his shaft. I tore my lips from his mouth and cried out as he filled me. *Yes!* This was what I needed.

I circled my hips as I rocked, taking him deeper and deeper, my body struggling to take his length.

"Fuck yes. Take all of me, red, don't stop," Adrik groaned, his fingers biting into my hips so hard I knew they'd leave bruises, but I didn't care. I healed fast, and I wanted his mark on me, I wanted to see evidence of our night together.

Deep inside, a part of me awoke I didn't know existed. It glowed bright and hot, and I felt an answering call in Adrik. Something between us had been created, something timeless and unbreakable. I felt closer to him in a way I had never experienced with another being, tied together with strands so fine, and yet, I somehow knew them to be unbreakable.

A sharp pain on the side of my neck yanked me out of that place and back to the present. I gasped and then moaned as Adrik's tongue toothed the bite he'd left on my neck where he sucked gently. I rocked my hips, taking him deep, grinding against him as I chased that familiar high.

"You feel so fucking good," Adrik bit out. I moaned as he thrust upwards and then gave a shout of surprise as he spun us quickly, so I was pressed into the mattress and he stood above me, sinking deeper. My back arched and he brought my feet up over his shoulders as he leaned into me and began thrusting hard and deep, claiming me, taking me for his own.

"Adrik!" His name tore from me in a surprised groan.

"Your pussy feels so good, Cali. I want to keep fucking you," he moaned. I was so wet, and he filled me so perfectly, I wasn't sure anyone had ever fit me so well. I bunched my bed cover in my fists so that I had something to hold onto as he angled my hips to thrust deeper and harder. My cries of pleasure mixed with his groans. My climax was so close, and yet I felt like he was keeping it at bay, drawing out this moment, taking from me every ounce of pleasure he could wring.

"I want you to come on my cock, Cali. Scream for me, baby," he demanded through gritted teeth. I watched the pleasure etched onto his face, the almost tortured expression as he held off his own pleasure to make sure mine was spectacular. I could feel it building from deep within, and Adrik was drawing it out, working my body in a way no one else ever had.

His hands gripped my ankles, but I could swear I felt them on my breasts, his mouth sucking on my nipples, every part of my body being stroked by him, overwhelming me with pleasure.

"Adrik."

"That's it, red, come for me," he ordered. Again and again, he thrust hard and deep, rocking his hips in a way that he ground against my clit, dragging me closer and closer to that edge. I raised my hands above my head and gripped the bedding there, my back arching and eyes closing as I got closer.

"Yes, yes, yes!" I chanted, pleasure exploding from deep within me,

washing over me.

Adrik roared his own release as he came inside me, his body locking tight, his eyes closed and face awash with pleasure and relief. He shook slightly and I moaned, smaller shocks rocking through me, over and over as I rode out the wave of release. My heart pounded almost painfully in my chest, my breath coming fast and uneven as my body continued to convulse around his length. Adrik groaned, small thrusts keeping my body spasming with smaller jolts of pleasure.

"We're doing that again tonight," I decreed in an uneven whisper.

Adrik's dark eyes found mine and he smiled with satisfaction before he slowly pulled out. I winced slightly and he leaned down to kiss me, slow and deep.

"I'm nowhere *near* through with you tonight," he replied. Grinning, I wrapped my arms and legs around him and pulled him closer, kissing him until we were forced to pull apart for air.

CHAPTER EIGHT
ADRIK

I am not going to let guilt get the better of me.

I repeated those words to myself over and over throughout the next two nights. Cali and I barely left her bedroom, and when we did, we ended up fucking on every surface in her house. For two days, we enjoyed each other in almost every possible position and every conceivable way we could think of. Cali was as hungry for me as I was for her, and we were both insatiable.

I smirked to myself when I remembered how she'd ordered Chinese food for us over the phone, and I made her keep talking with my head between her legs. Listening to her breathy words as she struggled to get us food while I brought her pleasure had been a highlight of the evening. She'd almost shouted the address at the other person and threw the phone as she came screaming. Seeing how red Cali's face was when she took our food from the delivery driver had been priceless. I'd read the guy's mind, and he'd definitely heard Cali come because she hadn't hung up the phone before throwing it. Not realizing Cali had been in my head as I read his mind, she'd discovered this too.

I'd spent a little extra time on my knees asking for her forgiveness for that. Yes, my face had been buried against her pussy at the time, but it had been an effective apology.

Every time we finished driving each other to the brink of insanity with pleasure, I'd hold her and feel that bond between us burning bright and hot, a reminder that she didn't know what it was or what it meant, and that I could possibly be making a huge mistake in keeping it from her much longer. I stood by my original assessment. If I had told her in the beginning that we were fated to be mates and that we needed to complete four parts of a ritual in order to be bonded together for all eternity, she would have run for the hills, and I'd have never seen her again.

But now...

I was more than halfway in love with this Witch, and despite her constant attempts to hide the truth from herself, I knew she was falling for me too. If she fell in love with me completely and told me she did, that would make three of the four parts of the bond complete, and the only thing left to do would be to Mark her and bind our souls.

Could I really do that without telling her?

No.

But if I did tell her, she would disappear. Considering we were already bonded in our minds, I felt reasonably comfortable in knowing I'd be able to find her. Neither of us could go very long without reaching for the other mentally. I didn't want her to come to me because she had no choice, I wanted her to *want* to be with me.

However, didn't choosing not to tell her about the bonds make her choice null and void anyway?

I bit back a sigh and watched as Cali finished tying her shoes. As much as we wanted to stay in bed together a little longer, Cali had a job she couldn't neglect, and I wanted to see my brothers. It was time to tell them I'd found my mate and fill them in on my predicament. Maybe they would have some solutions to offer.

"I'll pick you up when you finish work," I told Cali as I slid my shirt on.

"You don't need to do that."

"I know, but I don't like you walking alone, and nothing is more important to me than your safety," I explained, leaning in to kiss her upturned mouth. She rolled her eyes but smiled anyway, raking her fingers through her hair to put it up in a messy ponytail.

"Let me take you to work?" I asked.

She laughed. "Adrik, I can do this myself, honestly."

"I know." I shrugged. "But let me take you by my way of transport. Ever traveled by shadow?"

"No." She shook her head, eyes wide.

"Let me show you?"

Gnawing on her lower lip for a moment, Cali nodded and smiled. I waited as she gathered her bag and belongings before pulling her in close to me.

"It can be a little disorienting the first time, so it might be better if you close your eyes," I warned. Cali nodded and hid her face in my chest. My heart turned over at how small and vulnerable she was in my arms; at the trust she was showing me.

Taking in a deep breath, I wrapped her tightly in my arms and wrapped us in shadow, thinking of the shelter she worked at. Cali gripped my shirt, her gasp lost in the whirlwind of shadow and air before we came to a stop. I held her closely as she swayed slightly, the travel making her slightly dizzy.

"Woah," she whispered, slowly lifting her head to look around. "That was so fast!"

"My favorite form of travel," I nodded.

"And so much better for the environment," she mused. I laughed and shook my head. Of course she, as a Witch, would think of the benefits to the environment.

"Don't leave here without me, okay?" I urged her.

"I will wait, but if you're late, I'm heading to the underpass tonight to do another healing on Sky. She's made a lot of improvements and I want to make sure we don't have any setbacks," Cali told me. I bit back my demand that she do as I asked and stay put, but I knew that would go over as well as a cat in water.

"I'll be here," I finally answered. Cali grinned and leaned up onto her toes to kiss me. I didn't make her wait. Kissing Cali was one of my favorite things to do now. I could do it for hours and never get bored of the taste of her, the feel of her lips, the brush of her tongue or those small sighs of pleasure she made without even realizing it.

"Have a good day, little red," I whispered against her lips. Cali grinned and kissed me quickly once more before she entered the building. I waited outside a moment longer, keeping myself a shadow in her mind until I was sure everything was okay.

"Brothers... I need you. Meeting in the Arrival Room, now." I sent out the call to each of my brothers, preparing myself for advice I probably wasn't going to like, but no doubt needed to hear. I was too close to this, I needed other options on how to break this news to Cali.

~

"Two family meetings within the same decade... what's the occasion?" Harkyn asked as he swaggered into the room, his eyes on me, that perpetual smirk on his face.

I looked over the faces of each of my brothers as they took a seat at the strong table, their gazes ranging from knowing, to curious.

"Where's Nova?" I asked, not seeing my other brother and ruler of the sixth circle of Hell.

"Still hunting Mika's sister. She's wily and keeps giving him the slip," Cole answered as he strode forward.

Tomika had finally told Cole and Donovan about her twin sister a few years ago, and Donovan had set out at once to find her. Mika was concerned that her sister would be picked up by an Angel now that everyone knew Witches were still around. Nova had made a pact to Mika's ancestor, Tabitha, centuries ago that he'd look out for her kin. Having failed in that task two centuries ago, Donovan saw this as his chance to fix his mistake and keep Tabitha's descendants safe. I had an inkling that Nova was chasing more than just a chance to correct a mistake and keep a promise. It was more than likely that Mika's sister was his mate. I was fairly certain I wasn't the only one who had this idea, but none of us had enlightened Mika to that possibility in case she took it the wrong way. The woman may only be a little over five-foot tall, but she was prone to hurting people when they pissed her off.

"So, he's not coming?" I asked. The words had no sooner left my mouth than there was a great *whooshing* sound, and Donovan shadowed into the Arrival Room and strode towards the table.

"I'm here," he announced in a gruff voice. He looked like hell, and I bit back my initial observation. Donovan had gained the nickname Nova not because the word fit within his full name, but because in a fit of rage and anguish, he had decimated an entire field of Angels like a supernova when Tabitha and her family had been murdered in front of him. The guy had a temper if he wanted to unleash it.

"You look like shit, brother," Cole announced, and I ducked my head. Cole, however, had no qualms in pointing out that our brother looked less than his normal self.

"Go fuck yourself," Nova grumbled darkly.

"The hunt not going well then?" Malik asked, smirking. "Tell me, how does one tiny little Witch continue to elude you? We're practically as old as Earth itself, and you're chasing a woman who has barely hit thirty."

"Like I said... go fuck yourself," Nova snapped.

"Why are we here?" Devlin asked, pulling everyone back to the matter at hand.

"I found her," I blurted out without any preamble. "I found my mate."

Silence met my declaration for several long moments which was then followed by a feminine shout of joy. I turned around to see Mika standing in the doorway of her and Cole's realm, her eyes alight with happiness.

"Tomika," Cole ground out in a low growl.

"As if I wasn't going to eavesdrop anyway. Come on, guys. I know it's just been the nine of you since... forever, but there is a woman in your midst now, and apparently another one on the way," Mika answered, stepping closer to the table with a bright smile.

Cole was up in an instant, inserting himself between his mate and the rest of us. None of us took offense, we all knew it wasn't fear that we'd hurt her or take her... it was jealousy and possessiveness in its purest form. He just couldn't stand the thought of another man near her. I was beginning to understand that burning demand to keep Cali as far from any other males as well.

My chest tightened and I reached automatically for her in my mind. Her warmth spread through me instantly, soothing me, and I felt her internal sigh of relief at my touch. I took a moment to note that she was grooming one of the shelter dogs and imagined myself brushing a small kiss to her neck before I pulled away again.

"What's her name? Where does she live? Is she human?" Mika shot off, stepping around Cole to look at me animatedly.

"Just what we need, more women," Corvin grumbled.

"A woman is exactly what you need, Corvin. When was the last time you got laid?" Mika returned, crossing her arms over her chest to smirk at him. My eyes widened in shock, and I glanced at my other brothers, their expressions much the same. Cole, ever so slightly, inched back in front of his mate. I flicked my gaze to Corvin and was surprised to see the barest glimmer or humor in his eyes before it vanished.

"My sexual needs are not for you to worry about, little sister, however, I am sure it pains my brother greatly to know it is a concern of yours. So please, continue to think about it," he returned and if I didn't have better control of my expressions, my jaw would have hit the floor. Did Corvin just make a joke?

"Her name is Calixta, and she is a Witch," I announced when I could think of nothing else to say. I would consider that little conversation between Corvin and Mika another time. Since when did they talk enough for her to feel so comfortable speaking to him like that? Then again… Mika wasn't known for her shy nature. She probably decided enough was enough and threw the comment out there to see how he would respond. It certainly wasn't how any of us would have guessed.

Devlin let out a large breath at my announcement and sat back in his chair. "Do you think it is a coincidence, or that we're all destined for Witches?"

I shrugged. "It could be a coincidence. I guess we have to wait and see if Malik's mate is a Witch to draw a more conclusive answer."

"What's she like? When do we meet her?" Mika asked, frowning at Cole who tugged her back against him when she got too close to me for his liking.

"And why is she not with you now? She is a Witch and your mate. Why is she unprotected?" Corvin asked softly. I stiffened slightly, unease coiling in my gut. I wasn't scared of my brother or wounded by his question, but Corvin just had that effect on us. "She is a Witch well-trained in her practice, and she knows how to cloak herself. More than that, she's not shy about using her magic on me if I try to force my will upon her... which actually brings us to the reason I called you all here today," I continued, bracing my hands on the table. I waited as Cole tugged Mika back to his seat and pulled her onto his lap.

"Cali is a powerful Witch, but she has grown up her entire life knowing us to be evil incarnate. It has taken many weeks for her to see me as anything more. We have already completed two of the bonds without her knowledge, and I worry about completing any others without informing her of what it means," I admitted. Malik made a whipping noise, and I glared.

"I pity your mate, brother," I snapped.

"Hey, I just call 'em as I see 'em," he defended, holding up his hands in surrender. "But look at it this way, Adrik, no matter what, you two are destined to be together, there is no escaping it, no matter what you tell yourself or her. She could fight it, as could you, but you had no choice in binding your souls, Cole already explained that. Now, there is no leaving you. She will have to accept it," Malik concluded with a shrug.

"Actually," I cut in and sighed. "I have not Marked her."

More silence.

"How?" Cole asked, frowning. "When I met Mika, the feeling was overwhelming, impossible to resist."

"I know." I nodded. "And while I feel the need to Mark her, and yes, it's growing harder every day, I still have not."

"How?" Cole demanded.

"I don't know." I shook my head. "But that brings me to the other problem... the prophecy."

"What about it?" Harkyn asked, leaning forward interestedly.

"It's not exactly accurate." I frowned.

"How?" asked Mika.

I sank back into my seat. "The prophecy says I will find my Mate when I follow her blood trail… but that's not how I found Cali. *I* was hurt and I ran into a homeless man who said he knew a Healer. He didn't know specifics about Angels and Demons, but he claimed to have been around long enough to know there were beings like us out there who were not human and that we needed Healers, not doctors. He took me to a woman who maintained she was such a person. And there she was, in a tent, healing the homeless."

"That would have helped her need to heal celestials at least. She could keep a low profile but still do something to soothe the burning in her soul whenever one of you got hurt and she ignored it," Mika explained slowly.

"You're positive she's *your* Mate?" Cassius asked, raising an eyebrow. I glowered and straightened up at the implication. My brothers too, stiffened, the possible repercussions of what Cassius suggested seemed to echo around us. If she were not *my* Mate and we'd slept together and it turned out she was meant for one of my brothers, I wasn't sure if a relationship between me and that brother would survive.

But the thought of her being meant for one of my brothers brought out a rage in me I didn't know I was capable of.

"Be very careful of what you say, Cassius. I will not tolerate a single one of you going near her to try and stake your claim. That will start a fight you are not prepared for," I warned, my voice set low. My anger was boiling and building beneath my skin at the very thought of her being taken from me by one of them, the thought of her touching them, sharing her body, her mind, her smiles with them. The armrest of my chair shattered beneath my hands, and I looked down in surprise.

Instantly, Cali was there in my mind.

"Are you okay?" she whispered worriedly. Her presence was an immediate diffuser, and I sucked in a sharp breath.

"I am, little red, thank you."

Her fingers traced my face, and her lips brushed mine before she slid away from me again. The room still pulsed with volatile anger and an almost feral possessiveness, something I knew they could all feel coming from me.

"O-okay," Mika drew out slowly. "I think we can safely say she is your mate, Adrik," she added carefully. I could feel the waves of assurance and calm she was putting into the room, and I didn't fight it as it washed over me. Drawing in a deep breath, I allowed for Mika's soothing presence to tamper down my fury Cassius's words had brought out in me.

"Your mate soothes you, even from far away," Corvin pointed out, his steady eyes on my face.

"She felt my anger," I agreed.

"Anger is a soft word for whatever that was," Malik mumbled with wide eyes.

"How then, do you explain him finding his mate in a way the prophecy did not dictate?" Cassius asked, but there was no challenge in his voice, simply puzzlement.

I sucked in another breath before answering. "That is what I want to find out. I have no doubt she is mine. I do not believe the first two bonds would have been possible to complete if she were not. But it is bothering me that I can withstand the pull to Mark her and that the words of the prophecy did not match what happened. The two must be connected somehow."

Another moment of silence passed.

"Okay, we will circle back to that one. Why are you waiting to bind your souls?" Tamas asked.

"I'm falling for her, I feel it. I can see she feels the same toward me… and…" I trailed off, running a hand roughly over my head.

"You feel guilty for lying to her," Mika supplied. I met her gaze across the table and nodded.

"Just bind her to you, brother. No matter what, it will happen anyway. Why wait?" Harkyn suggested. Mika glared at him, and he widened his eyes at her as if looking for a reason.

"I want her to come to me because she wants to be with me." Malik made the whipping noise. I opened my mouth to tell him to fuck off, but Mika waved her hand at him, and his entire chair tipped over backwards. Harkyn, Tamas, and Cole burst into laughter, and I grinned and shook my head. Her green eyes were burning angrily at my brother as he stumbled back to his feet.

"What was that for?"

"A preview for what you're in for when you find your mate, dear Malik. Because if she doesn't knock you out of your chair on a regular basis to keep your ego and smart mouth in check, I'll be the one to do it," she warned. Cole grinned and leaned forward to nip at Mika's shoulder. Her eyes softened slightly as she twisted to look at her mate and I flicked my gaze away from them. I was grateful for Mika. She had made my brother happy, brought life to him I hadn't realized was gone. She made us all laugh and she gave us hope. I don't think any of us had ever truly considered having a life-long mate before, but now that the option was out there, I knew it was more than just me who wanted it.

"She is fiery," Cali whispered in my mind with amusement. I snapped to attention at once, closing that part of my mind. How much had she seen and heard? I had not even felt her there in my mind.

"Why did you kick me out?" Cali asked, and I could feel the small hurt in her voice.

"I did not know you were there. And this is... private. I cannot allow you access to my brothers or their mates... not yet," I answered softly, hoping she understood.

"Are you hiding something from me?" Cali asked, and I felt her stillness and she waited. I hesitated in answering, staring at my fingers while I formulated my thoughts.

"You already know I am. You will run if I tell you more, you will not give us a chance or see this through," I warned, already having told her some form of this in the past. She was silent a moment longer and I could feel her thinking things through, mulling over what she wanted with what was reasonable.

"If I ask... will you tell me what you're so afraid to tell me?"

Would I? Should I?

"We can talk about this more when I am done here. You have a job to get back to, and I need to finish up this meeting," I answered evasively.

"Nice non-answer," she replied with a little snark. I smiled and imagined my arms around her, holding her tight and pressed a kiss to her head.

"I will see you soon," I promised before I gently left her mind. I made sure to keep my guards up this time, not needing her to hear what we were discussing.

"And you, Adrik," Mika finally addressed, bringing me back to the conversation. "You are feeling guilty because you know Cali needs to know. Yes, she will be mad. I was mad and I *knew* what was going to happen. You've betrayed her, even though you were trying to spare her. But now you have to tell her before this goes any further. If you want to know for sure that she came to you of her own accord, if you want *her* to know that she chose you, then you need to tell her as soon as possible," Mika counseled.

My stomach actually knotted at the thought of telling her and I dropped my gaze to the table for a moment. I knew Mika was right… but I didn't want to do it. I was hoping my brothers would tell me I was doing the right thing in keeping this from her. But deep down, I knew it was wrong.

"You've already completed two of the bonds; you won't lose her forever," Mika comforted.

"What if she refuses the rest of the bond? She's strong, and she's powerful; she could find a way to resist."

"You cross that bridge if you come to it. For now… you need to tell her," Mika repeated.

"And the prophecy?" I asked, looking around at each of my brothers. They all looked as clueless as I felt, and I sighed. This was something we'd all have to think about for a while.

"Well, I'm out of ideas on this one. Nova, how is finding Mika's sister going?" I asked, determined to move on.

Nova sighed heavily and ran a hand over his short hair, his blue eyes tired.

"She knows she is being hunted, so getting close to her is nearly impossible. Unlike Mika, it seems she knows exactly what she is and has been learning somehow. She knows how to cloak herself and how to defend herself. Each time I catch up to her, she has already left. I can only trace her in the way of humans, and that is to follow a paper trail or digital footprint. She changes her identity every time she moves on," Nova explained.

"She's really that good?" I frowned.

"It looks as though she has been in hiding her whole life. She ran away from her foster home when she was fourteen and has been on her own ever since. I've been playing catch up on over twelve different identities since she first ran away, and it's only been a week or so since I learned of her most recent one. I have no idea who she is pretending to be right now," Nova continued.

"How do you know she is capable of defending herself if you are yet to catch up to her?" Mika asked.

"The only other way I've been able to track her movements is by the bodies she leaves behind," Nova grumbled.

"Bodies?" Mika whispered, looking worried.

"No humans, mostly Rogues and a few Angels. She is well versed in defensive and offensive magic," Nova continued, and I caught the small sliver of pride in his voice.

"What's your plan when you finally catch up with her?" Cole asked, and I knew he was worried because his brother was the one at risk, but Mika was this Witch's sister.

"I hope to restrain her long enough to explain who I am and that I know her sister. If she needs proof, then I'll reach out to the two of you to meet with us," Nova answered.

A small silence hung between us, and I watched the way Cole swept Mika's hair back to press a kiss to her neck. She sighed and relaxed back into him.

"In other news, I met a Nephilim the other night," I announced to fill the silence.

"Met one?" Corvin asked, his brow furrowing.

"Yes," I answered. "I would have preferred to keep my distance, but I was walking with Cali, and she saw he was outnumbered by two Archangels. She asked me to go to his aid."

"Did you explain to your mate that a Nephilim could handle two Archangels without a problem?" Tamas asked, quirking his eyebrow, his lips twitching in a smile.

I rolled my eyes. "Yes. But I couldn't refuse her," I admitted. Cole looked at me with understanding and I wiped a hand over my face and leaned forward. "Anyway, this one was different than the others. His wings were bigger and ash-black, he felt more powerful too. Have any of you seen a Nephilim like that?" They each shook their heads and looked surprised. "His name is Amazarak," I added.

"You exchanged names?" Cassius laughed.

"Again, not by choice. He could sense my Witch hidden in the shadows, and he wanted to know why I aided him when he didn't need it when we've all gone out of our way to avoid his kind in the past," I answered. "I told him she'd asked me to help, and I'd done so. Cali wanted to heal him, but he declined. I wasn't going to let her get that close anyway." I shrugged and then frowned at the idea of her putting her hands on him to heal him. Suddenly, I was feeling a lot more sympathetic towards Cole whenever he got mad because Mika wanted to heal his brothers.

"You said he could sense your mate in the shadows?" Corvin asked, flicking a small frown at Devlin.

"Yes."

"This is troubling. When have you ever known a Nephilim to sense one of us in the shadows before?"

I thought about this for a moment, my worry of the creature beginning to increase. Corvin was right; a Nephilim was an Angel-Human hybrid, neither of those two creatures could see into the shadows when we used them to conceal ourselves.

"You said there was something different about this one. Maybe we can look into it and find out what it is," Tamas suggested when no one else spoke.

"So how did you end up getting his name?" Cassius added. I sighed and shook my head.

"Cali introduced herself and asked him his name. He was surprised at being asked, and now they're... friends? I don't know. We haven't seen him again since, but hopefully he won't be a problem," I continued.

"Women," Cole sympathized. I smiled and then laughed when Mika elbowed him in the ribs.

"So then, Malik should be next to find his mate. Considering it took Adrik two years after Cole to find his, I think it's safe to say we don't have a real idea of when or where the rest of us will find ours," Devlin announced.

"And Goddess help the woman who is stuck with him," Mika muttered, shooting Malik a glare.

Malik grinned and leaned back in his chair, not a care in the world, his fingers linked behind his head.

"I tell you one thing... I won't be waiting around for her feelings to grow or any pansy-ass shit like that. If I find her and know she's mine, I'm Marking her and going to do everything in my power to get the body and mind bond completed as soon as possible," he stated emphatically.

I rolled my eyes and got to my feet.

"Thanks for listening. If any of you have any ideas about the prophecy and what went wrong, let me know."

CHAPTER NINE
ADRIK

"That's it, red, come for me," I encouraged as I continued to suck and lick at her pussy, my fingers sliding in and out of her, curling up and stroking her deep inside. She was splayed out on her kitchen table, her hands bound above her head and her legs over my shoulders. I just couldn't seem to get enough of the taste of her, the way she moaned, the way her breath hitched and her back arched. I was addicted to her, one hundred percent.

"Adrik!" she cried out as she came hard for a second time, but I wasn't done yet, I wanted more. I pulled my fingers away and stood up before I thrust my cock hard inside her. She screamed again, her back arching and her cheeks pink. We were both coated in a fine sheen of sweat, having gone at each other relentlessly from the second we arrived at her home. Cali had dropped to her knees the second we walked in the door and took me into her mouth and down her throat. She'd worked me as if I were her instrument and she, my master. Watching her on her knees, looking up at me, her pink lips wrapped around my thick, aching cock had almost sent me over the edge right then and there. I'd bunched her hair in my hands and fucked her mouth, watching the way she got pleasure from sending me over the edge. She refused to let me pull away, drinking down every drop of my cum like she was starving and it was her only source of sustenance.

Fuck, she was sexy.

I'd repaid the favor… twice. Now it was time for the main meal.

I wasn't gentle, but then again, Cali didn't need me to be. Drilling into her hard and fast, the table shuddered beneath us as I thrust inside her again and again. I watched her breasts bounce with every stroke and leaned forward to feast on them. I couldn't get enough of her. Since the first moment she had taken me into her body, I was hooked. Would it always be like this? Would we ever get tired of one another?

Cole and Mika had said it would only get more intoxicating as the years went on. I couldn't imagine anything better than this right now, but I was willing to wait and see.

"Adrik, faster," Cali pleaded, her fingers gripping the side of the table above her head where her hands were bound.

I grinned and did as she asked, kicking things up a notch. I could feel her velvet sheath tightening around my cock, strangling me, dragging me towards another world-rocking orgasm. Fuck, I'd never come so hard in my life more than I had with Calixta. I entered her mind, blended us so that my pleasure was hers and her pleasure was mine. Everything was heightened and so intertwined that it was impossible now to tell whose need was whose.

"I feel you, Cali. Come on my cock, you're almost there," I encouraged, my heart pounding, my breathing ragged. I could feel that all too familiar tingle starting in my toes and lower back, working its way to my core.

I stroked her inside her mind, touched her everywhere my hands and cock couldn't, flooding her with sensation and pleasure.

"Yes! Please... almost there," she whimpered.

"That's my girl," I praised, and then she screamed again, her eyes opening in surprise as her orgasm crashed over her. I gritted my teeth as my body tightened and I came hard, pouring my seed into her as her muscles rippled around me, dragging me in deeper, holding me as she milked me for every goddamn drop. I gasped and leaned over her, barely locking my legs so I didn't collapse. I pressed my forehead to her chest and brushed lazy kisses across her breasts as I struggled for air.

"I can't move," Cali groaned. I smiled against her soft skin and wished away her bonds. She sighed and lowered her hands to stroke my hair. Pleasure rippled through me at the curiously intimate action. I'd shared her body several different ways over the last few days, and yet something as simple as her stroking my hair felt that much more intimate.

"You're a fiend," I accused tiredly. I felt her laugh lightly and grinned, loving that I could do that.

"You're the one who spent the better part of the afternoon flooding my head with dirty fantasies."

"Hey, you're the one who jumped me the second we got in the door. I was helpless," I returned, slowly lifting my head to smile down at her. Cali beamed and stroked a finger down my cheek. Fuck, she was gorgeous.

"I need a shower." She sighed. I nodded and scooped her up, ignoring her feeble protest that she could walk. I knew she could, but I didn't want her to have to.

I sat her on the side of the tub and turned on the water. Cali grabbed a small bottle from the side of the bath and poured some of the liquid contents into the hot water. A flowery kind of smell wafted up and I smiled. This was what she smelled like all the time.

"Want to join me?" she offered. I had a momentary flash to what my brothers would say if I came back smelling like flowers, but then shrugged.

Fuck 'em.

"Try and stop me," I answered. Cali smiled and I helped her into the bath before settling in behind her. I groaned at the feel of having this drop-dead gorgeous woman naked and soapy in my arms.

"Comfortable?" she whispered lazily.

"Very," I murmured, brushing a kiss across her shoulder. Cali sighed and relaxed into me, and I closed my eyes on the feel of her and on this moment of perfection.

And then it was gone.

"Oh shit," Cali whispered.

"What?" I asked, snapping to attention.

"My aunt is reaching out to me... in my mind right now. She wants to know how my Demon King problem went."

"Demon King problem?" I repeated with a raised eyebrow.

"The last time I really talked to her was the first night we met... she was worried. I mean, I've spoken to her a little since then, but it's been quick recaps and to the point, I was able to avoid talking about you. Crap, how do I explain this to her?" she groaned.

"Just tell her the truth."

"And what's that? That I'm having hot, dirty sex with a King of Hell, but please don't be worried?" she joked.

"Sure, if you want. I was going to suggest you tell her that you're head over heels for a man who is just as crazy about you, and that he just so happens to be a King of Hell but that shouldn't matter because that's what he was born as, not *who* he is," I suggested.

Cali stilled in my arms and turned carefully to look at me.

"You're crazy about me?"

"You're a Witch, you can feel my emotions, you tell me," I suggested, lowering my guard so she could feel all of my emotions about her. Cali sucked in a sharp breath and her eyes went wide as she felt all of it.

"And you're lying to yourself if you try to tell me your feelings for me aren't the same. I feel them," I added.

"You can't know that," she whispered, but I could hear the doubt in her voice.

"I do, and I am ready to accept your feelings. But the question remains... will you continue to punish me by withholding them simply because of what I was born to be?" I asked, reaching out to stroke her cheek.

"Adrik..." She trailed off, uncertainty and guilt in her eyes.

"Just think about it. Go, talk to your aunt. I'm going to go, but I'll be back later tonight."

"Are you sure?"

"Yes. You need space to speak freely, and I have some things to take care of. I'll be back. Talk, and maybe think about what I said," I suggested, standing. I stepped out of the tub, and with a wave of my hand I was dry and dressed. I leaned down to kiss her soundly before I wrapped myself in shadow and left.

~

I woke to find myself in a plain brick room. There were no furnishings, windows, or doors.

Slowly, I turned in a circle, well-aware of the sensation that was dragging at me. I was in another psychic realm, but this did not feel familiar at all.

"Demon King," a strong, feminine voice addressed.

I turned the other way to see a woman standing before me, thick strawberry-blonde hair curling around her shoulders, slightly greying. She was older than Cali, in her mid-fifties, but I could see the family resemblance.

"You must be Aunt Penny," I greeted slowly.

"Why are you toying with my niece?" she demanded right away.

I drew in a deep breath and shook my head. "I am not playing with her."

She made a sound of disbelief and shook her head. "You are a Demon, and a King at that. You know no other way than to manipulate and toy with Witches and humans," she argued, her green eyes a shade or two darker than Cali's.

"Is that so?" I inquired, cocking an eyebrow.

"Do not play with me, Demon. I am not a young woman who can be seduced by your charm or good looks. I want you to leave my niece alone," she demanded, lifting her chin stubbornly. A part of me liked this woman. She was no-nonsense, strong, capable, and protective.

The other part of me itched to tell her where she could shove her orders and ideas about who I was and what I stood for. But she was Cali's aunt, and I had to tread lightly.

"What do you think I am doing with your niece?"

"Calixta is strong and capable. You want a Witch on your side, just like every other celestial out there. You'll do whatever you have to in order to get her, even go so low as to manipulate her emotions."

"What has Cali told you?" I asked, keeping my arms loose at my sides as I studied her.

The older woman shook her head. "She does not know what she's talking about."

"By your own words, you have said that Cali is strong and capable. Surely, such a woman could withstand my... what did you say? Charms? If your niece has finally confided in you her feelings for me, then you should have no reason to think they are anything less than authentic."

"I have no doubt about Cali's emotions. I have doubts about the truth and strength of yours," she countered.

"I believe you have wasted a trip to speak to me, Ms. Penny."

"Why?"

"Because you do not know me, nor would you believe any part of me I showed you because you would consider it a manipulation. Therefore, I have no way to prove to you the legitimacy of my feelings for your niece. This trip was pointless, because despite your disbelief that what Cali and I share is real, I will not stop seeing her just because you wish it. I have no qualms in admitting that I am falling hard and fast for your niece in a way I have never done for another being in my long life. And Cali is fast falling for me too, whether you like it or not," I explained.

"If you care for my niece at all, you will leave her life and never look back. You bring danger with you, Demon King. You are evil, you are the darkness, and you will snuff out her light. Being in her life has put a target on her back, and if anything happens to her, then you are at fault for not leaving."

"I will do everything in my considerable power to protect your niece and allow no harm to come to her," I assured.

"And yet it may not be enough," she snapped.

I didn't say anything to that because she had a point. Despite how powerful each of my brothers are, how powerful Cole is, Mika still died in his arms. Yes, she'd come back, but at the time we hadn't known that was possible.

"I can't let her go, Penny, it is as simple as that. I know you do not agree with it, and I know you disapprove. But I have been alive a very long time, and I know what I have with Calixta is powerful and rare. I won't let her go for anyone, not even you."

I could tell Penny was powerful, not the least of which was because of the power pulsing and crackling in the air around us. The very fact that she had managed to pull me into a psychic realm was my proof. Cali had been able to do it because we had a connection. Penny was able to do it because she was well-versed in the ways of magic and had considerable power, something I'd have to remember going forward.

"You're a selfish Demon. I should not have expected you to care about her more than you do your own feelings," she snapped.

"I *am* selfish, you are right. But there isn't a thing I wouldn't do to ensure Cali's safety and happiness. Now... if you don't mind, I would like to go back to the woman in my arms because I can feel her unease. She knows you are in my head, and she's not happy."

"You're not leaving here until I get through to you," Penny countered, looking superior in her ability to keep me here. I gave her a small, indulgent smile and shook my head.

"Goodnight, Penny. I truly hope you can come around on this and be happy for your niece," I added before I envisioned a door in the wall. Penny opened her mouth to speak, but I left before she could say another word.

"What did she say to you?" Cali demanded the moment I opened my eyes. I blinked up at her and smiled, wrapping my arms around her, and rolling until she was beneath me. Cali gasped in surprise and smiled, but her eyes were troubled.

I'd come back to Cali after she'd gotten off the phone with her AP just as I promised, and we'd spent another hour wrapped up in each other before drifting off to sleep. She had to have felt it when my mind was pulled from hers, even if she were asleep. I was guessing she knew it was her aunt simply because they had a bond much like me and my brothers.

"She was just warning me away and telling me she didn't like me. Nothing less than I'd expect," I answered, leaning down to kiss her.

"She didn't try to hurt you?"

I shrugged. "She might have tried, but I didn't stick around to find out."

"Wait, you were able to escape her realm? How?" She frowned. I chuckled and nipped at her neck and then pressed kisses all the way up to her lips.

"I have been alive a lot longer than she has, little red. I know how to leave a psychic realm when I want to," I assured. Cali relaxed beneath me, and I found her mouth again, chasing her tongue with mine, rocking my pelvis against her.

"Again?" she whispered with a gasp.

"I'll never get enough of you," I murmured and brought my mouth to hers as my hands got busy removing our clothing.

CHAPTER TEN
CALI

Sky was improving at an unprecedented speed.

I watched the little girl skip away with her mother, her smile wide and eyes bright as the illness that had been crippling her was beginning to recede. I felt drained and a lot more tired than usual, but it would be so worth it to give that girl another shot at life, or at least to keep her in the early stages of a disease that would otherwise have killed her.

Adrik brushed my mind gently, and I felt his concern. Biting back a smile, I sent him waves of assurance, hoping to put him at ease. Who knew a King of Hell could have such a tender side? I mean, no, he wasn't generally tender. When we were in bed together, there was a whole other side to him that I craved. He could be gentle if he wanted to be, if *I* wanted him to be, but there was something utterly and viciously beautiful at watching him lose control and take me with an almost animalistic desire.

Thinking of Adrik like that sent a rush of heat all the way through me to my core. I didn't understand how I could still be so desperate for him. I was positive that after spending a weekend in bed with him, he would be at least somewhat out of my system. But all sleeping with him had done was make my craving that much more intense. Not to sound cliché, but he was quickly becoming a drug I could not do without. I couldn't go longer than twenty minutes without touching his mind, feeling him in mine, or I became edgy and uncomfortable. Thankfully, he never left me longer than thirty minutes, but I wasn't sure what it would do to me if he stopped altogether. A small shiver worked its way down my spine at the thought, and I sighed in relief when he reached out to me again, warm and tender, protective, and safe.

I made my way to the tent flap and looked out. There were only a couple more, but I wanted to see Sol tonight. He had gone too long without another healing, and I knew the man walked practically everywhere. At his age, it wasn't a great idea.

"Sol?" I called out. I waited a few more minutes before calling again.

"Have you seen Sol?" I asked Adrik. There was a small silence, and I knew he was talking to someone.

"On his way," Adrik replied, and there was an amused edge to his voice. I looked up as Sol stumbled into the back room, glaring over his shoulder.

"I can walk myself, boy. You're lucky I don't have that cane people keep tellin' me I need, or I'd smack you round the head," Sol threatened.

"Calixta called for you, and you ignored her. That's rude," Adrik replied with a shrug.

"I keep tellin' ya, I don't need more healin'," the old man grumbled.

"Sol, it's been two weeks at least since I've done a healing on your legs and hips, and you know I want to give you a little relief at least that often," I reprimanded.

"You did a healing on me not long ago," he pointed out, glowering.

"Yes, but not on your hips and legs."

"You just healed that little girl out there from a disease that is slowly killin' her, sunshine. I can see how tired it makes you, and I don't want you wastin' ya magic on me."

My heart warmed at his concern and how much he cared for me. "I know." I nodded with a smile. "But you're important to me, and seeing you in pain hurts me. Just let me work on you a little, it won't take long, and you know it doesn't wear me out like some of the others do."

Sol glowered between me and Adrik. I could see he was calculating his odds of getting out of here without hurting my feelings, and there was no chance of it. Sol mattered to me, and I hated when he was hurting. He wouldn't let me get him into a shelter, he wouldn't take anything from these drives unless he was in dire need of it, and he was constantly looking out for me and the others out here. I just wanted to make walking less painful for him.

"You know I can't say no to you, sunshine. Just don't go puttin' in more effort than ya should," he finally relented. I smiled and nodded, waiting as he lifted himself onto my table. I glanced at Adrik who winked at me, and my cheeks warmed again.

I knew the man was dangerous, and he could flatten half the planet without much effort at all. Knowing it should make him repulsive to me, it should make me run in the other direction and never look back, but there was something intoxicating in knowing a man like him could look at me the way he did, and know he would do anything to keep me safe and see me happy.

"Get goin', boy. I don't need ya help," Sol grumbled, glaring at Adrik. With another grin at me, Adrik left us alone, but I knew he wasn't far. He was always a shadow in my mind and only a few seconds away at any point. At one time, I would have hated the idea of sharing my mind with someone so often, but considering I knew he needed to touch me as much as I needed him, it helped to even the playing field. Besides, he wasn't monitoring me and keeping track of what I was doing, he just needed the connection, the same as I did.

"That man—if that's even what he is—is dangerous, Cali," Sol warned as I got him comfortable on the bed.

"I'm aware," I answered without looking at him.

"He's the kind of man who would kill another just because he's bored. He's powerful in ways most people don't understand," he continued in an even, steady voice. I could feel his eyes on my face and kept mine averted as I fussed with the candles and herbs around me.

"What do you really want to say, Sol?"

"Don't let him go."

That did it. I dragged my gaze to his old, weathered face and frowned.

"But you just said he was dangerous."

"He is." Sol nodded and sighed. "But not to you. He's deadly to anyone else, but I don't think that man is capable of hurtin' a hair on your head."

A small burst of warmth spread within me, and I struggled not to grin.

"I got that impression too," I murmured, centering myself. Sol didn't continue our conversation, instead he laid back and let me heal him. I took another few moments to properly clear my head and got to work healing one of my favorite people.

Sol had been coming to see me for a little over five years now. Before I started healing regular people, my soul was on fire as I refused to go out looking for the Angels or Demons I could feel were in pain somewhere within the vicinity. To reveal myself was to sign up for a lifetime of misery and servitude, and my AP had taught me better than that. I'd needed to do something, and healing animals barely took the edge off. I knew healing humans would help more, but I didn't want to draw attention to myself from them, either. So, I went looking for the homeless who needed help, those who would be less likely to sell me out. It was an odd thing, that those who had barely anything would be more likely to keep their mouths shut about something that could potentially earn them a massive payday, than those who had every advantage.

It had taken a lot of time to earn their trust and to gather people who would come back regularly. Soon enough, most of them were waiting for me every week, setting up tables and booths to help one another out. Eventually, I found a few humans who helped the homeless and were more than happy to keep silent about me. True, they didn't entirely know what it was I did in here. I think they thought it was more of a spiritual healing and therapy that went on, but they still kept it all on the down low. Five years on, I'd done a lot of good for those who would otherwise have been left in the shadows. These were good people, and they just needed some help. Now that Adrik was here helping so much, we had been able to support a lot more people getting back on their feet. He had organized job interviews for several of them, rehab for others. Some of them just needed a small infusion of cash to be able to pay for a room so they could keep their jobs.

I frowned as I concentrated on Sol's hip. He'd left it so long in the beginning that the damage had been extensive, and it took a lot more effort to chip away at the problems that had stemmed from it.

"Do not overdo it, Cali," Adrik warned. I sent him an image of my middle finger, and his humor was instant. That's something else I loved about this man: he didn't take my attitude to heart. He tried to order me around and I fought back, then he laughed at my antics.

I was jolted momentarily from my trance and sucked in a sharp breath. Had I just used the *L word* in the same thought as Adrik? Was I falling for him? The thought had crossed my mind before, but I'd always been so quick to banish it that I barely remembered considering it. But now?

"Everything okay, sunshine?" Sol asked.

"Yes, just reorganizing my thoughts," I answered and quickly went back to work. I needed to set aside some time when I was alone to properly consider it, but if I were being honest with myself, with the pounding of my heart and the surging of my blood whenever he was near… I already had my answer.

I finished healing Sol far past the point that either he or Adrik appreciated, but I didn't care. I was tired, yes, and a little dizzy on my feet, but if it helped a man I dearly cared for, then I could suffer a night of weakness. I had Adrik with me, so I knew no one would hurt me, and I could sleep it off at home. Sol brushed a kiss over my cheek, snarked something to Adrik about looking after me, and then he disappeared with the others to where he slept of a night.

"The tables are packed up and the volunteers are leaving," Adrik informed me as he entered the tent.

"Good. I'm tired." I sighed.

"You pushed yourself too far tonight," Adrik reprimanded softly. I raised an eyebrow at him, but he stared me down. I could feel his concern more than his need to have his way, so I smiled and walked softly over to him.

"I have you here, so I'm not worried about getting home safely," I answered, leaning up to brush a kiss over his jaw. I stepped back, but his arms snaked out quickly and he pulled me back against him.

"Have I told you how much I love having you rely on me? How

happy it makes me that you trust me to protect you?" he
murmured, his amazing blue eyes warming.

"No, but I can feel it."

Adrik smiled slow and soft, and leaned down to kiss me. This kiss
was a little different. It was slow and intense, full of meaning and
purpose. The emotion rolling off him was strong and
overpowering, enough to make my knees weaken slightly and
butterflies to let loose in my belly.

Holy Hell, all that emotion… was this… did he…

I pulled back gently, dazed at the deep and overwhelming feelings
coming from him, and Adrik tucked my hair behind my ears.

"Let's go home, red."

I smiled almost drunkenly at him and nodded. I felt like a
schoolgirl with her first crush. The realization that he felt as
strongly for me as I did for him was a heady feeling, and I was
addicted to it. The words were there on my tongue, there in his
eyes, but neither of us said them. We stared at each other a
moment longer, the feeling heavy and tangible between us.
There was something there, burning hot and bright deep inside
me, reaching out for something inside Adrik that would tie us
together. I felt like all I needed to do was say the words and mean
them. The idea of being tied to him was scary and overwhelming.
No matter my feelings for him, he was still a King of Hell. I shied
away from that voice in my head that told me I'd need to think
about my feelings really soon and decide what to do about them.
I hated the thought because I knew once I laid all the facts out to
myself, I'd have no choice but to end this. He was a Demon
King, and I was a Witch. There wasn't a single reason on Earth
that we should be together.

His brother is wedded to a Witch.

I shut that little voice up. Yes, that was true… but I didn't know how that had happened. I didn't want to let Adrik go, but I was also at a loss on how this was supposed to work long-term. He was an immortal, after all, and I would die after a normal human lifespan. He would be my entire life, but I'd be a weekend in the span of his. There was so much to think about, and I slammed the door shut on it.

There was an intense pull to say those three little words, a seductive and dark lure that urged me to do it, but not knowing the meaning of that invisible tie I felt, kept the words safely in my mouth.

"Can we break down the tent, Cali?" a volunteer asked. I sucked in a sharp breath and jolted back from Adrik and smiled at the volunteer.

"Yes please, Eli," I answered. Adrik tangled our fingers together, and with another intense look we exited the tent and started walking in the cool night air.

Neither of us spoke as we walked, but my mind was racing a hundred miles an hour. Adrik often offered to shadow us back to my home, but I enjoyed walking at night and breathing in the cooler air, even if I wasn't feeling quite as strong as usual. A nice walk home would help me recharge.

We walked for a time in comfortable silence, and usually a stroll would help to clear my mind, but all the while my mind raced with the possibilities of my newfound feelings. I knew I cared for Adrik, and I knew he cared for me, but whenever the *L word* entered my mind in connection with the Demon King in any way, I banished the thought before it could fully form.

I closed my eyes and dragged in a deep breath, reaching out to get a better read of Adrik's emotions. He was… happy. Happier than happy, even. It was as if he were almost complete, a feeling he was unaccustomed to. I bit back a smile; at least we were even in this new development.

I wanted to tell him, I wanted to express my confusion and my doubt to him. I was trying to form the words in my mind when Adrik stiffened. I had less than a second to comprehend there was danger ahead when suddenly Adrik shoved me aside, concealing me in shadow and magic before he was thrown backwards, landing several yards away from me. I slapped a hand to my mouth to conceal my cry, reminding myself at the last second to remain silent.

Several Angels stood before us, forming a loose half-circle around Adrik as he rolled to his feet.

"And here I was hoping for a battle of wits rather than a physical confrontation. I guess it would be wrong of me to attack someone who was totally unarmed in that sense, though," Adrik quipped easily.

I watched him carefully, feeling the pounding pain in his back and head, but none of it showed on his face or in his movements. He was as graceful as ever, a cocky, half-smirk on his face as he surveyed his enemies.

"It's great to see you not let your education get in the way of your ignorance, Demon," the Angel smirked.

"Tell me how you really feel, Halo Hugger. I would do you the same courtesy, but I wasn't born with enough middle fingers," Adrik returned, looking as unconcerned as ever, but I could feel him coiled and ready to strike.

The Angel shook his head and sighed. "Look around, oxygen-thief, you're outnumbered. What you lack in intelligence, Demon, you more than make up for in stupidity."

Adrik grinned, and I noted the way he loved this banter back and forth. To him, it was the best part of a fight, but right now, he was more concerned with getting me out without them seeing me.

"And you are proof that God really *does* have a sense of humor," Adrik returned. "Now…" He sighed. "As much as I'd love to hang out here all night and trade insults, I have places to be. I was enjoying a nighttime stroll when you decided to put your hands on me. And don't tell me you weren't trying to feel me up."

"I was looking to disarm you," the Angel spat. "I'd much prefer to sever my own hands than to willingly touch you, spawn of Satan."

"And yet I felt your hands in places I'd never keep a blade. I do, however, own another weapon I *do* keep concealed in my pants, but that's just for the ladies." Adrik winked.

"Enough, Demon. You are in an area a Witch has reportedly been healing humans in, and I do not consider that a coincidence. I need to get to the bottom of your presence here quickly," the Angel responded, rolling his shoulders back.

"A Witch? Don't tell me so many of you actually believe they're back?" Adrik smirked, his voice dripping with derision as he shook his head.

"One of your brothers has one, Demon. Do not play games with us," the Angel snapped.

"He did have one," Adrik admitted. "Until you morons killed her. Your precious Alastair ran her through with an Angel Blade, remember?"

"She was healed."

"Was she?" Adrik tested. "Because I was there, and I saw her die. I watched one of my brothers carry her lifeless form out of there, and I watched as she was buried. The Witch is dead, and there are no others. What kind of bullshit excuse is this you're using to attack me?"

"We need no excuse to rid the world of you," another Angel spat.

Adrik heaved an exaggerated sigh. "You know what, shock me and say something intelligent and beneficial to the conversation, you winged dick-bag. Otherwise, I'm leaving."

"You know, a sharp tongue is no indication of a keen mind," the lead Angel pointed out, looking superior.

"And you're about as useful as a screen door on a submarine. What's your point?"

I glanced around at the five Angels as they traded insults with Adrik, reaching out with my other senses to get a better idea of who was feeling what. I had never trusted Demons, ever, and while I'd never looked at Angels as evil, they'd never managed to be allies either. But surely if a Demon King was capable of the goodness Adrik had shown me, it stood to reason that not every Angel was so blind too, right?

The leader and his second in command were manic, they believed to their very depths that Demons were the dregs of any being in existence. To them, Demons were beyond redemption in any sense and needed to be exterminated.

The third Angel was a follower, a soldier through and through. I looked to the fourth, hoping I'd find something different, but she was a carbon copy of the others, brainwashed and incapable of forming her own opinions, despite any evidence to the contrary of her beliefs.

When I turned my gaze to the fifth, it was with next to no hope, but I was shocked to discover a sliver of unease in this Angel. His expression didn't show it, but he didn't like that they constantly attacked Demons in greater numbers, overpowering them and for no other reason than because they were there. He didn't like what had happened to the other Witch. I frowned, digging deeper. He cared a lot about the fate of that Witch. Did he know her?

He frowned suddenly and turned in my direction. I froze, holding my breath. He seemed more sensitive than the others. He was looking right at me, but he couldn't see me—I knew he couldn't. I risked brushing his consciousness gently again, and drew back quickly, throwing up every mental barrier I had.

Had that been... It was impossible... Right?

I couldn't have felt the presence of a Witch in his mind... could I?

I turned my attention back to Adrik when he laughed at something the first Angel said, but I could feel him drawing energy from within himself, preparing to fight.

"No matter what, stay back."

His voice in my head was sharp and commanding, no room for nonsense. I sensed the underlying fear in him that they would take me away from him. It was the last thing I wanted as well, so I'd do as he ordered. But if he needed me...

"No, not even then, little red. Stay hidden, and do not reveal yourself."

I bit back my initial retort and instead stayed silent. I wouldn't make a promise I couldn't keep.

"What do you know of the Witch?" the lead Angel continued.

Adrik gave a dramatic sigh. "Are you always this much of a repetitive idiot, or just when I'm around?"

"Answer me, filth!" the fourth Angel shrieked, her hand tightening around her blade.

"Sweetheart, with brains the size of yours, it could explode and not even mess up your hair. I mean, I'm looking you right in the eyes, but I get the feeling someone else is driving. What part of *"Witches are extinct"* are you not getting?" Adrik returned, throwing his hands up in the air in exasperation.

"We don't believe you, bottom feeder," she snarled.

"Alright, honey, I'm going back to ignoring you so hard you'll doubt your own existence, okay?"

Adrik heaved another sigh, and with an air of forced patience I could only liken to a parent about to explain something very simple to his child for the hundredth time, Adrik looked at the others.

"Listen, fluffy fairies, I don't know what you all think you're getting at trying to throw around rumors that Witches are suddenly roaming the Earth again, but the joke is a flop," Adrik replied, rubbing a hand over his face in exhaustion, even though I could feel the way he was preparing to strike out.

"Witches are of the Earth, and so will never be truly gone from it. If one Witch existed, it stands to reason that others are—" the second Angel started.

"Cool story. In what chapter do you shut up?" Adrik interrupted, rolling his eyes. "I mean, are you lot always this stupid, or is tonight a special occasion? Witches. Are. Dead. I'm starting to get jealous of all the people who haven't met you lot. I know brains aren't everything, but with you fools, it's absolutely nothing," Adrik continued, shaking his head and staring at them as if they were the dumbest beings on the planet.

"Enough!" the leader shouted, and at that exact moment, Adrik shot forward with a Demon Blade in hand, swinging it upward to slice at the second Angel. He never saw it coming and fell to the ground, lifeless, blood splattering and spilling out around him. I hurriedly reinforced my mental walls to prevent myself from feeling their pain and stepped back slightly, hoping to give Adrik as much room to move as he needed. He was fluid in his motions; the second in command had barely hit the ground when he was onto the third Angel. Within five strikes of his dagger, Adrik had taken down another Angel. I bit my tongue to stop myself screaming out a warning as the female Angel slid up behind him,

her sword aimed low to run him through. I should have known
better. As she rushed forward to skewer him, Adrik rolled to the
side. Unable to stop her forward momentum, her sword ran
clean through the fourth Angel. She screamed her horror and
Adrik was up and moving again, his blade at her throat. With one
vicious and deep cut, he slit her throat, sending both Angels
toppling to the ground in a bloody heap.

I stared in horror, torn between disgust that the man I was falling
for was capable of such violence, and joy that he had not been the
one on the wrong end of a sword. Just as Adrik was moving
again, he was thrown backwards, his head slamming hard into the
pavement. I stifled a gasp when the fifth Angel turned to look at
the space I was hiding in again, his frown deep and eyes full of
concern.

Help him, I silently pleaded, wishing I knew whether I could trust
this Angel or not, desperate to do something. Adrik barely
missed a sword to the heart and rolled to his feet. I bit my
knuckles as I felt the white-hot slice of a blade across his
abdomen, the power of the Angel Blade working fast to take him
down. Adrik pulled from my mind completely, determined to
protect me from his pain. I felt his absence like the loss of one of
my own arms, but I knew it was for the best.

Only the first and fifth Angel remained standing, and only the
leader was fighting Adrik. The fifth Angel ran his hand over his
head in a helpless gesture, waves of indecision rolling off him.
What was going on with him?

Adrik sustained several more wounds, some deeper than others,
but he scored just as many on the leader. I began gathering power
at a faster rate, knowing I might only get one chance to help
Adrik, and that I needed to make it worth it. I'd had to fight
myself free of situations before, and while a Witch was meant to

heal, that didn't mean we had to simply take all the shit handed to us either.

The fifth Angel stopped his pacing and turned to face the dueling Angel and Demon, his mind made up. He took a single step towards them when Adrik was struck hard with the blade.

I watched him fall as if it were in slow motion. I caught the triumphant smirk on the face of the Angel as he raised his blade to thrust it into Adrik's chest. On instinct, I gathered my magic and threw it at the Angel.

"No!" Adrik's shout came too late, already knowing what I'd do but unable to stop me. Hellfire was gathered in his hands, but it was useless. At the same time as I threw my magic, I felt another kind of magic hit the Angel too, the combined forces sending him flying several feet away, his body singed and broken. His cry of agony would have usually sent me to my knees in guilt and pain, but Adrik was still down, blood still seeping from his body. The remaining Angel turned to look at me with wide eyes, the cloak of shadow now gone from my body.

I stared at him in disbelief. Why had he helped us? Why did he hurt one of his own?

I froze as I watched him, ready to defend Adrik if he took so much as a step towards him. Instead, he looked worried. He scanned his fallen brethren and turned to look at me again.

"My leader won't be down for long. Take the Demon and run. Cloak yourself, and for your own sake… stay hidden," he ordered, his words a low hiss. I frowned and he ran a hand harshly over his head.

"You're not going to try and take me?" I asked with a confused frown. He shook his head.

"No, sweetheart, I'm not. But you are not safe here, and neither is he," he said, nodding towards Adrik who staggered to his feet, hellfire swirling in his hand as he blocked me from the Angel's view. He was still bleeding, and I could feel his immense pain. "What do you want?" Adrik snarled. "What game are you playing?"

"You think your kind are the only ones with mates?" the Angel snapped, any gentleness in his eyes when he'd spoken to me was long gone. Mates? What was he talking about? Adrik didn't confirm or deny the Angel's accusation and he shook his head.

"We knew there was a Witch here, but now they know her face. My leader is not dead, and I cannot allow you to kill him. Take her, and don't let her come back," the Angel warned again, taking several steps back.

"Wait!" I cried, trying to get around Adrik, but he intercepted me. I peeked around his broad shoulders and looked at the Angel again.

"Will you tell me your name?"

"Red," Adrik warned with a growl.

"Hariel," the Angel answered quickly.

"Thank you, Hariel," I whispered meaningfully. He nodded, a small softness to his eyes and then he turned to his fallen Angel friends and gathered them together. All were dead except for his leader who groaned when Hariel moved him. We watched in silence as one moment they were there, and the next they were gone.

"Let me look—" I started but Adrik spun to face me so fast I gasped and stepped back.

"What did you think you were doing?" he shouted. I blinked quickly, shocked at the rage rolling off him.

"I was trying to help—"

"Help? You just exposed yourself, and you are in danger now more than ever. Your friends here that you help every night, they're all in danger now because you exposed yourself to the Angels!"

"You were injured. That Angel was going to kill you!" I shouted back, hurt.

"He was going to try, but at no point was I in any *real* danger, Calixta. I have been fighting these fuckers for eons; I knew what I was doing!"

"You were on the ground, no weapon in hand, and a sword aimed for your chest. How did you have that situation in hand?" I challenged.

"I don't expect you to understand because you're human, but I am a lot fucking faster and stronger than you realize, and there are times where I need for the enemy to think they have the upper hand before I destroy them," he snarled. I shook my head at him, biting back my arguments.

"You're throwing my humanity in my face?"

Adrik gritted his teeth and shook his head. Silence compounded between us, and my gaze fell once again on the blood seeping through his fingers.

"Can I heal you?" I asked, reaching for him. Adrik stepped away from me, and I knew he felt the immediate lash of hurt that hit me.

"What is your problem? I just want to heal you!"

"My problem is that you didn't listen to me, you didn't trust me when I told you I could handle this. I am in love with you, Cali, and I'd like to think that the woman I am in love with would show a little more respect for her own life."

"I love you too, asshole, and *I'd* like to think the man I'm in love with would take into consideration my happiness and my need to protect those I care about," I returned hotly.

"I am not like any of the men in your life before, Cali, remember that."

"And I will never be the kind of woman who lets others get hurt when she can do something to stop it," I reminded in a hiss, feeling hurt, angry, and strangely close to tears.

Something was happening.

I pressed my hand to my chest where I could feel that warm ball growing hot, the one that shone and burned whenever we made love or entered each other's dreams. There were those tiny links again, twining together, pulling Adrik and I closer and closer as if bound in some indefinable way. What was that?

"What's going on?" I asked, my voice shaky with emotion.

Adrik's dark eyes looked pained for a moment, and I caught the echo of frustration and a massive backlash of guilt.

"Adrik?"

I watched as his jaw clenched and he shook his head, swearing under his breath. He began to pace, his movements jerky and stiff, so unlike the usual glide of muscle I was used to. Guilt stabbed at him, as did the beginnings of panic.

I stepped towards him just as he lunged for me. Simultaneously, there was a flash of light and an odd rumble in the air, and when I looked behind Adrik, I found myself staring at Amazarak.

"Zarak," I greeted, surprised.

His coal-black eyes looked around us in a slow sweep before resting on us again, a small frown on his face.

"I tried to get here sooner, but I was detained. I could feel the energy of a fight, and the touch of a Witch, so I came to offer my aid," he explained evenly.

"Why?" Adrik asked, frowning.

"Calixta extended me the hand of friendship. I do not have any mortal friends, and so I came to help protect the only one I have," he answered as if it were so cut and dry.

"Thank you." I smiled softly, but my gaze darted back to Adrik. What wasn't he telling me?

"You're a little late," Adrik drawled dryly.

"It appears so," Zarak admitted with a small survey of the grounds again. His eyes settled back on me, and he frowned. "You need to get somewhere safe, Calixta. Those hunting you will not be gone for long."

"Please call me Cali."

"Enough with the pleasantries, we need to go," Adrik snapped. I glared at him and shook my head.

"I think it's time you start telling me what it is you've been keeping from me," I demanded. Adrik stiffened slightly and nodded curtly.

"Fine. But not here."

"I will try to get here faster if ever there is need of me in the future," Zarak offered with a small incline of his head.

I smiled. "Thank you, Zarak. I appreciate you coming to our aid." Adrik stepped back and pulled me in close to him. I felt his anger with me still simmering beneath the surface, and his fear. But there was also guilt, frustration, and a lot of anger at himself. With another small smile at Zarak, I closed my eyes as Adrik wrapped us in shadow.

CHAPTER ELEVEN
ADRIK

Rage was a watered-down word for what I was feeling. Anger at myself for not telling Cali about the bonds sooner was beating at me in a drum-like fashion. Fury at her for being so stupid as to expose herself out there was trying to override my anger at myself. More than any of it, was the cold, stark fear that tried to strangle me at the thought of those Angel's getting their hands on her. I never would have been able to get her back. I would have waged a war unlike any the world had ever seen to get her, all the while they could have been scaring her, hurting her. I'd have made deals with every Rogue Demon, every Nephilim, and every Demon under the control of Hell to get her back safely. She didn't know just how much I cared for her or what lengths I'd go to in order to keep her safe.

We arrived in the Arrival Room of Hell, and I let her go immediately, worried my anger would result in accidentally hurting her. I would never forgive myself if I harmed her—ever.

"Where are we?" Cali asked, her voice soft.

"Hell... almost," I answered and started towards my door. Pain from the Angel Blade was searing through me, tearing, and eating away at me, but I ignored it. After a few seconds, she hurried after me, and I looked back and saw her eyes wide with curiosity and apprehension.

"I want to go home," she whispered, her voice small in the echoing room of the Arrival Room.

"You can't. The Angels know who you are now, they will be

scouring the Earth for any hint of you out there. If they find you alone in your home, they will take you," I reminded, my fear burning hot again, almost smothering me.

"We need to make sure the people I heal every week don't go back there. I don't want to risk them getting hurt because of me," she insisted.

"Quite frankly, Cali, they are the least of my concerns."

"Of course they are. Why would it bother you that tens of innocent people could die? They're just humans. As a King of Hell, what are humans to you?" she argued, her eyes shining with unshed tears.

"They are *nothing*," I hissed, striding toward her until she was backed against the wall. Her pale green eyes were filled with tears and wide with apprehension. I could feel the guilt, worry, and fear coming from her, and it was making me crazy. "When it comes down to a choice between your safety and theirs, they mean *nothing* to me, Calixta. Everything—everyone—will always come second to you," I ground out, moving in close so that there was barely an inch of space between us.

"I don't want to be with a man who would make such a choice," she whispered breathily, a single tear rolling down her cheek.

"Too bad because you're stuck with me. You need to get this through your head, Cali, and you need to do it quickly. Your safety is of the utmost importance to me, second even to your happiness. If I must choose between what makes you happy and what makes you safe, I will always choose the latter. Now, you can help me make this possible, or you can fight me every inch of the way. In the end, if it comes down to it, I will burn the world alive to ensure no one can ever hurt you. Do you understand?"

Cali swallowed hard, her eyes wide and her expression one of pain and sadness. I knew this wasn't what she wanted to hear, and to know I put that look on her face was a dagger to my heart. But a flash of the earlier fight lit up inside my mind, the moment she'd revealed herself, the momentary surprise and triumph on the face of the Angel about to try and kill me. The instant she'd done it, fear had taken over me. It wasn't even anger at her ignoring my order, it was a bone-deep, soul-chilling, gut-wrenching fear I was unfamiliar with and did not care to feel again. Every possible pain the Angels could put her through to make her do their bidding flooded my mind in less than a millisecond, and I was overwhelmed with pure terror for her. Pain shot through me again, reminding me that I had an Angel Blade wound that needed healing. Cali sucked in a shaky breath and blinked, looking down at where the blood soaked my shirt.

"Let me heal you?" she asked, her voice breaking.

Gritting my teeth, I shoved away from her and strode angrily back to the door and pushed it open.

"Come inside; we need to talk," I ground out.

Cali needed to know; it was time. I wanted to tell her when the time was right, I wanted her to make the decision to bind our Souls and bring us together completely, but that was looking impossible now. I had wanted to do things different from Cole, to have my partner willing and consenting to our binding, but nothing was going the way it should, not even the fucking prophecy. I watched Cali and she struggled to pull her emotions back and wiped at her face before she lifted her chin and stepped slowly towards me, her apprehension and hurt beating at me, but that would change.

She would hate me soon.

~

CALI

Cautiously, I stepped toward Adrik as he stood in a doorway, his dark blue eyes serious and studying. Swallowing hard, I stepped past him and into the room, my eyes darting over every inch of it, trying to take in as much as possible. It wasn't what I was expecting.

The ceiling was high, dark wooden beams stretching from one side to the other, the walls were exposed brick, old, and so beautiful.

From my place in the doorway, I could see almost everything. There was an incredibly large fireplace that took up several feet of wall to my right, the ornate engravings in the stone visible even from where I stood. There was a stone staircase beside it that disappeared into shadow, and something told me I *really* didn't want to go down there. My gaze slid around the room, noting the beautiful architecture, the rugs, and lavish furniture. I took a couple of steps in, arching my neck to see a massive platform tucked around a small corner. That was supposed to be a bed, but it would have been better suited as a family share-bed. I couldn't help but appreciate the cherry wood four-poster frame it was on, however.

Judging from how close the other door had been to Adrik's in the hallway and how much room was in here, I was guessing there was some serious magic involved. The kind where these rooms were actually bigger on the inside than they appeared on the outside, an entirely new realm perhaps.

There was so much more to see, but at that point, I heard the door behind me close and my breath caught. Turning slowly, I watched Adrik as he leaned against the door, his arms crossed over his chest, his dark eyes watching me. I could feel his pain stabbing at him, sinking into his body. With the exception of the blood on his shirt, it was impossible to tell he was hurt. How did he do that?

"This is your home?" I asked, my voice a little more breathless than I'd like. Fear and dread were mixing, making me more antsy than normal.

"Yes," he answered.

"Are you going to tell me what it is you've been keeping from me?" I asked, not altogether sure I wanted to know. But the fact of the matter was I *needed* to know.

Adrik didn't reply, he just watched me a few moments longer. Even his mind was closed to mine, something that was uncomfortable and a little hurtful. After a long, tense moment, Adrik pushed off from the wall and moved over to a bookcase to his left. He slid a large book from the shelf and flicked through it until he came to a page at the end. Watching me, his eyes flickering with unease and caution, he handed it to me.

Frowning, I looked down and began reading the scrolling writing.

The Prophecy of The Nine

From the first to the last, the Brothers Nine will fall...

The first will face death and prevail,
The second shall follow her blood trail.

The third will endure his deal of time,
The fourth need only await his sign.

The fifth will betray his woman of binding,
The sixth will save she he must be finding.

The seventh will take her to keep her safe,
The eighth will have to rely on Faith.

The ninth alone is left to find,
She who was taken, now hidden by design.

From first to the last, the Brothers Nine must fall,
Or chaos reigns, and they will destroy it all.

"What... what does this mean?" I whispered, although with the way my heart was pounding, I already had an idea.

"I am the second brother of nine," he replied softly.

"This... is a prophecy about..." I trailed off, unable to continue.

"Our mates, and how we'll find them."

I slammed the book shut and put it on a nearby table, my mouth suddenly dry. "And you're showing me this because..." I trailed off again, unable to speak the words. Because no, there was no way it was even possible.

"Because you're my mate," he answered evenly. The words hit hard, but they were exactly as I thought. My soul knew it, felt it, and had been experiencing a bond unlike any other for the past several weeks. I'd known he was different, meant for me somehow, and yet...

My eyes flew open and landed on the book, and I frowned. Slowly, I shook my head and turned back to look at him, both relieved and saddened.

"But I am not your mate."

"You are."

"No, I'm not." I shook my head. "The prophecy states you'll find your mate by following her blood. That wasn't how we met," I reminded. Adrik shook his head and scratched at the side of his neck

"We're working on what happened. Cole found Tomika exactly as stated, but something is different for us. Cole also couldn't prevent himself from putting his Mark on Mika. He tied them together without knowing what he was doing or what the compulsion was. I have been able to resist," Adrik continued. Alarms began blaring in my head and I swallowed hard.

"Tie us together? You can do that?"

Adrik nodded slowly. "There are four parts of the bond to

complete. You and I have completed three," he answered.

My breath left me in an instant, and I felt as if the floor had disappeared beneath me.

"Explain," I demanded. Adrik nodded and indicated to the small lounge behind me. I shuffled back and sank onto it, my mind in a state of shock.

"To bind someone to another being who can virtually live forever, the process needs to be incredibly powerful and be able to stand the test of time. With very few exceptions, we are immortal, and so an enchantment that binds a soul to one of us needs to be incredibly strong, and able to withstand everything. From what we've read, the bonds that bind us only strengthen over time, making us almost addicted to one another, winding deeper over time so that we're happy and don't want to be without one another even after thousands of years. We have discovered there are four bonds to complete. We are to tie ourselves together through mind, body, heart, and soul," Adrik began.

"How have we completed three?" I demanded, panic beginning to sink in.

"When we first shared our minds, you trusted me not to take advantage of your moment of vulnerability and I did the same. That was the first. You felt the bond, although you didn't know what it was," Adrik answered.

I sucked in a sharp breath and nodded, remembering how it felt as though tiny but impossibly strong ties had wound us together, bound us somehow.

"Next, we bound ourselves by body. The first night we physically slept together sealed that bond," he continued. Again, I nodded, having felt that too. My gaze lifted to his, dread rising inside me. That left heart and soul, and I wasn't sure which one I preferred.

Adrik seemed to read my look and turned away from me, his jaw clenching so that a muscle ticked in it as he stood and paced away from me.

"The third bond was completed tonight—heart. I told you I loved you, and you said it back. It may have been said in anger, but the words were honest, and it bound us in that way."

I knew it, but I didn't want to accept it.

"You're wrong," I whispered, tasting the lie but refusing to acknowledge it.

"You don't want to love me… I get it. I am the thing you have been taught to fear, and tonight you have learned I have known something important involving our futures together and refused to tell you. You knew I was hiding something, but not what," he continued, and I noted the stiffness in his shoulders and the way his fists clenched.

"I don't want this," I whispered, feeling shock work its way through my body. I didn't want to be bound to anyone, never, much less a King of Hell. How was that supposed to work? I was mortal in the end, and he could live forever. He was darkness and I was light; the two were not meant to merge.

"I know," Adrik replied in a low voice, and as hard as I tried not to feel it, as hard as he tried to conceal it, I felt the whip of hurt that lashed at him. "But the reality is that we are destined to be together, and whether you like it or not, it is happening. I have resisted thus far in binding our souls because I wanted to wait for the right time and place to tell you, and hopefully bind us with your blessing."

"And I should thank you?" I snapped, happy to feel anger instead of fear or that numbness.

Adrik's eyes flashed in anger, but I welcomed the look. I didn't want to see things from his point of view, I didn't want to hear the pain in his voice or see the guilt in his eyes. I wanted to be mad at him and hate him for doing any of this without my knowledge.

Would it have made a difference, though?

That voice in my head sounded a lot like my AP. We'd had a lot of discussions about fate and destiny, and how one could never outrun it. Oh God, my AP was right. She had warned me against talking to him, warned me of his manipulations and trickery, and I had been so sure my intuition was right. It had never led me astray before... Was I wrong this time? Was Adrik really that good at being someone else, or was I just hurt and scared?

"Resisting our bond has caused me pain I hadn't expected, and has taken willpower I didn't know I had," he added softly.

I shook my head. "Despite any of this, you're wrong. You got the wrong woman. We did not meet the way the prophecy said we would, so it's not me," I tried, my voice almost pleading. Yet at the same time, my heart ached at the thought of not being the woman he was meant to be with. For heaven's sake, did I want him or not? This stark contrast in my feelings was making me dizzy.

"The binding would not be possible if you were not meant for me. You are my mate, Calixta," Adrik assured. I gritted my teeth and shoved up from the couch, turning my back to him. This was all wrong; this shouldn't be happening.

I needed to leave.

CHAPTER TWELVE
CALI

"I want to go home."

"You cannot leave here. It's not safe," Adrik answered.

"I don't want this, Adrik. You can't keep me here!"

"This is happening, and it doesn't matter if you want it or not.
You can't leave here unless I let you go, so sit down and listen,"
he snarled.

"Why? Because you demanded it? You may be a King of Hell,
Adrik, but I will not bow to you or your demands," I snapped,
beginning to panic, wondering if he really could keep me here.

"I have never asked you to bow to me, Calixta. I want you to be
reasonable and sit down," he gritted.

"Reasonable? You just told me I have no say in my own future.
You just admitted you've been lying to me for weeks,
manipulating me, slowly stripping away my freedom. And what?
I'm supposed to be grateful now that you didn't finish the last
bond out of some kind of guilt?"

"Sit down, Calixta," he warned in a growl.

"No! I want to leave." My breathing was choppy now, and I was
getting tunnel vision. The walls were closing in and the air was
getting too hot to breathe.

"Listen to me, Cali."

"I don't care! Am I a hostage here, or can I leave?" I shouted,
hating the feeling of tears stinging my eyes.

"Calixta, I understand you're angry at me right now, but you need to think about this. The Angels know your face, they surely know where you live, I can't just—"

"I don't want to be here! I wish we had never met!" I shouted. Adrik paused in his advances. "I should have known not to expect differently from a Demon King, and I would rather work with the Angels than be tied to your side for all eternity!" I screamed, fear and panic overwhelming me to the point where I had no idea what I was saying. I just wanted to hurt him; I just wanted him to let me go.

Adrik's face reflected the pain and shock of my words. I had the briefest moment of regret, but I shoved it aside. I could worry about my words later, I needed to get the hell out of here. Without waiting for him to give me his permission, I ran for the door we came from and yanked it open. He cursed behind me, but I was out the door already.

"Calixta!" he bellowed. I was down the hall, my heart hammering and eyes stinging with tears when I ran into another man: tall, tattooed, with dark eyes and a confused frown.

"Wha—"

"Calixta, come back!" Adrik shouted behind me.

"Lost your Witch already, brother?" The man smirked, steadying me.

Brother. He was another King of Hell.

Unwilling to let him capture me, I drew on my magic and threw the brother several feet away from me. He gave a shout of surprise and slammed into the opposite wall, the crack of his skull against it sickening. I was preparing to strike again, to knock them both out and find a way out of this place, but before I could, I felt Adrik's mind merge completely with mine.

Completely.

Pain hit me, mind-numbing pain that caused my knees to buckle and tears to sting my eyes. I screamed in agony, feeling as though a gaping hole was ripping its way through my center, acid and hellfire replaced my blood and my bones were now infused with the very essence of pain.

All at once, it vanished and I was left curled up in a ball, my breathing ragged and sharp, tears leaking from my eyes.

God, that was what he was feeling right now? All that pain, and he was standing there talking to me, giving me an explanation that surely could have waited until he was healed.

"Adrik," I gasped, my voice harsh. Despite the current situation, I wanted to heal him—I needed to.

He came to kneel beside me, his face was mere inches from mine. "I know you hate yourself for falling in love with a Demon King. Fine, I get it," he began, his voice a dangerous growl. "You can hate it all you want, you can hate *me* all you want, but I will love you anyway. I love you enough to put your happiness above my own comfort or joy. But your safety comes before all else. And if you *ever* do something so stupid as to give your position away when Angels are around or attack one of my brothers again, I won't give you a say in how this bond goes. I will Mark you here and now," he ground out. The deadly note of seriousness in his voice made me shiver, the words I wanted to say drying up on my tongue. I could feel his hurt that I was refusing him, feel that soul-deep pain of rejection in him, and I had no words to soothe it.

But I could heal his physical wounds.

I slowly pushed myself into a sitting position and as he moved back to his door where he leaned heavily against it, sweat glistening on his forehead. I finally noted the increase of blood seeping through his shirt and staining his hands.

"Let me heal you," I almost begged. Everything else could wait, but I needed to heal him now and get rid of the pain.

"I have already called for Mika," he gritted out. More pain hit me, this time my own, and it came from deep within my soul. He didn't want me to touch him. A flash of memory came back to me, the first night we'd met, and I'd healed him, that cocky grin and flirty glint in his eyes. I could feel his skin beneath my palms and was drowning in the scent of him, trying to resist the compulsion to kiss him.

And he wanted another woman to heal him.

I frowned, and I knew that pain was reflected in my face, but he gritted his teeth and turned away from me.

"What the fuck?" a voice groaned from across the room.

I turned to see the brother I'd hurt stagger to his feet, holding a hand to his head. There was blood seeping from between his fingers, and I winced.

"What's going on?" he demanded, looking between us.

"Malik, meet Calixta, my mate," Adrik introduced, calm and collected, as if he didn't feel like his insides were being shredded.

"Cool, hi... Why did I get hit?" he demanded.

"I was trying to escape," I answered, knowing I owed him that much.

"Right, again, I get it. But why did *I* get hit?"

"You were in the way," I continued. Malik blinked a few times and shook his head before he pulled his hand away and looked at the blood with a grimace.

"I'm sorry," I said quickly, getting shakily to my feet. "Let me heal you?"

My words hung in the air, unanswered and unacknowledged. At that very moment, rage and possession flooded the room so strong I almost choked on it. I turned to look at Adrik in surprise, knowing the flood of emotions were coming from him.

His blue eyes glittered in warning at his brother, his body unnaturally still, his gaze unwavering. Malik looked amused for a moment, but then the humor slowly died away and his gaze flicked to me. Something like disappointment shone back at me and then sympathy for his brother.

"Don't worry about it, brother. I'll heal fine on my own," Malik assured, and I couldn't help but feel a little rebuffed at his words. Malik wasn't looking at me anymore, and I got the sense he was… disappointed in me. But how? Why? He didn't know me. My gaze flew back to Adrik as the tension in the room slowly disappeared and he nodded slowly before sinking against the wall again. Then it clicked. He was talking to his brother via a mind-link so that I wouldn't hear. More hurt compounded on my heart. I had never felt more alone or isolated in my life.

Just then, the door across from Adrik's opened and another man stepped out. He too was tattooed and tall. His dark hair was short cropped, his jaw covered in a light amount of stubble. His eyes were black and filled with curiosity. He took note of all of us here and our positions. I was sure he could feel the lingering emotions in the room.

"I feel like I missed something," he voiced. Just then, a small woman stumbled against him, her jet-black hair was shoulder length and layered, sticking out at all angles, her eyes a bright green and her cheeks flushed. She was buttoning her shirt and looked a little disheveled. Her gaze roamed around the room and lingered on me for a moment before they flew to Adrik and she gasped, her hand pressing to her waist.

"Why haven't you had your mate heal you, you idiot?" she hissed, rushing towards him.

"Sorry to interrupt what I am sure was a very PG-13 moment, Tomika, but I could use a little of your magic," Adrik admitted, slowly sinking to the ground. I noted the lines bracketing his mouth now and the paleness of his skin. It was killing me that he wouldn't let me heal him.

"I repeat, you have a Witch right here. I can feel how desperate she is to heal you," Tomika reprimanded. The man who had come out with her was standing close and I felt how much he hated watching his woman peel the shirt from his brother or put her hands on him. But there was also concern for his family.

"Hi there," Tomika greeted, flashing me a quick smile. "I'm Tomika, but please, call me Mika. This here is my mate, Cole, ruler of the first circle of Hell," she introduced before turning her attention back to Adrik. I swallowed several times, my throat raw.

"I am Calixta," I greeted. Mika smiled softly again and closed her eyes, focusing on Adrik. Cole looked from his mate to Adrik and then suddenly whipped around to look at Malik, a frown on his face. When his gaze slowly slid back to mine, it was with understanding, but still that sliver of disappointment.

What the hell?

I continued to watch Mika as she healed Adrik, and I tried to touch his mind, to reach him, but he gritted his teeth and his guards remained up the entire time, refusing to let me help soothe him. I wanted to cry again, but I managed to hold it in check. It was a little while later when Mika finally sighed and stepped away from Adrik. Cole was there in an instant, his arms around her as she leaned against him.

"You'll be fine," she announced. Tension leached from my shoulders and Adrik slowly got to his feet, refusing to look at me. An awkward silence filled the hall as everyone tried to avoid looking at me.

"Uh… since you're here, I could use a little healing if you're able, Mika," Malik announced. Mika turned her gaze to look at him and she shook her head as she looked at the blood on his hand.

"What did you do?" she asked with a roll of her eyes. Cole sighed but let her out of his grasp.

"This wasn't my fault," he defended.

"Right," Mika said sarcastically, with a fond smile. I looked at Malik and wondered why he didn't just tell her that I was the reason he was bleeding. His chocolate brown eyes watched me with a little more understanding than I liked, considering I knew nothing about him.

Another door opened further down the hall, and a fourth man strode towards us. I wanted to shake my head and throw my hands up in exasperation. How were all these brothers so goddamn gorgeous?

This one wore sex like a second skin, his dark green eyes seemed to have a perpetual flirtatious glint in them, his mouth set in a smirk like he knew something we all didn't. I got the impression this was his usual look.

"Harkyn, this is Calixta," Adrik introduced roughly. The brother looked me over slowly from my feet to my head before he grinned and winked.

"Hey there, beautiful."

I raised an eyebrow, unimpressed. There was a low rumble from Adrik, and his blue eyes shot angrily to his brother. Harkyn's grin only widened, and he sighed with exaggeration.

"Fine, I won't flirt. Where are we going?" he asked.

"You and Malik will take Calixta back to the surface and watch her home," Adrik announced. I whipped around to look at him, shocked, upset, and disbelieving.

"What?"

Adrik didn't even look at me.

"She has warding around her home which has hidden her all this time. She will need to allow you entry before she puts the wards back up. I don't want her out of your sight unless she's in the bathroom. You can come up with a way to stay in contact during those moments, make sure every entrance and exit is guarded and surveilled," Adrik told them.

"Wait, what's going on? I'm not taking them back to my house," I argued, but Adrik continued talking as if I hadn't even spoken.

"She works every day at an animal shelter from nine in the morning till four in the afternoon. She can order food and have it delivered to her home, and since humans are the only ones who can find her home, you should be safe with whoever approaches her or it. If you are concerned, even for a moment, or need clarification on something, reach out to me, don't ask her. I don't trust her to tell you the truth," Adrik continued.

"Adrik," I tried again, unable to believe him.

"How long are we going to be with her?" Malik asked.

"As long as it takes."

"Wait just a damn minute," I snapped, taking a step forward, but froze when Adrik's icy gaze shot back to me.

"I cannot trust you not to give yourself away in order to help someone else. I don't know if you would ignore another of my orders if or when the Angels use a human's pain to draw you out. Now that you have given yourself away, they will hunt the humans you heal every week and hurt them until you give yourself up," Adrik told me. His eyes shuttered and expression turned blank.

I gasped, fear for my friends rendering me speechless.

"We have to help them," I whispered.

"And I will, because I know it matters to you, and whether you think so or not, your happiness matters to me. Just not as much as your safety. If you promise to cooperate and allow my brothers to guard you, then I will see to the safety of the people you heal. If you ignore their orders, try to lose my brothers, or run away, I will complete our bond and lock you away down here where you will see none of them ever again. Am I understood?" Adrik asked, his voice so matter of fact and devoid of any of the warmth and heat he usually spoke to me with, that I felt like I was looking at a stranger. Had all of it been a lie? An act?

My immediate reaction was to tell him to go fuck himself while doing what I wanted, but he had all the advantages here. I didn't know how to get out of here, I didn't know how to protect my people while keeping safe.

"I know you're hurt, Adrik. I know I hurt you... but please don't do this," I pleaded softly, hoping he'd see reason.

"Do you agree to the terms, Calixta? Or will you remain here?" he pushed, that muscle in his jaw ticking again.

Silence rang throughout the hall, no one even breathed. I watched Tomika take a half-step forward, her expression a mix of anger and sympathy, but Cole tugged her back shaking his head. She pressed her lips together and I turned back to Adrik who was watching me with that infuriatingly blank stare.

"Fine," I whispered.

Adrik stepped in close to me, his face impassive and that metal wall still up.

"You did this, Calixta. You didn't listen to me and stay hidden, and you caused this problem. You refuse to accept our bond and have made it crystal clear you'd rather be with my enemy than with me. Fine. I won't hold you prisoner here where you'll be miserable or subject you to my presence which you obviously find so repulsive now. I'll give you a chance to prove you can be safe on the surface. But I will not leave you without protection. If it's not me, then you *will* tolerate my brothers."

"He was going to kill you—" I tried to explain, my voice breaking, but Adrik shook his head and took a slow step away from me. I didn't take my gaze away from him, wanting to etch this moment into my mind. I felt like a fool, as if I'd been played. I didn't know who this man was, but it wasn't the Adrik I'd fallen in love with.

"Malik, Harkyn... I know you do not have mates yet, so you cannot possibly fathom what she means to me, but her safety comes above all else. You know what I'll do if she's taken from me," Adrik warned. His brothers stiffened and Harkyn actually lost that smirk on his face, his expression serious.

"You have our word, brother. She'll be safe with us," Harkyn agreed.

Both brothers stepped over to me, and I looked at Adrik again, desperate for him to say something, to show me a sliver of the man I thought I knew, to prove to me I wasn't crazy for loving him and that all these weeks hadn't been a lie and a manipulation.

"Remember your promise, red," he whispered softly.

My heart cracked open at the nickname, at the tiny breath of warmth in his voice and the minute moment of softness in his gaze. The man I loved was in there, somewhere. He was just hurt.

Nodding, I kept my gaze locked on Adrik as his brothers each took one of my hands and I was suddenly shrouded in shadow and whipped away.

CHAPTER THIRTEEN
ADRIK

I gently swirled the amber liquid in my glass as I stared at the flames in my fireplace. Calixta's words from days ago still circled in my head. I was torn between being mad at her and mad at myself. I knew deep down if I had told her in the beginning that she was my mate, she would have disappeared into the night, and I'd never have seen her again. At the very least, she would have run, and I'd have spent the next few years hunting her and being hunted by Witches who would have tried to protect her from me. And in her attempt to escape me, she likely would have wound up in the clutches of Angels, or dead at the hands of a Rogue.

I had been sure I was doing the right thing.

But she was right, in a sense. I had trapped her. I'd known she was mine, and so I'd manipulated every situation to bring her closer to me, to ensure she felt something for me and that she would want to be around me and therefore get closer to completing each bond.

I finished what was in my glass and set it down hard on the side table before thinking better of it and throwing it into the fireplace. I was angry, my mood had been volatile these last few days, and everyone had given me a wide berth. I'd spent some time in the Pit, going over torture techniques with my Knights and making sure everything was running as smoothly as it was before I met Cali. I'd even gone hunting a few times, taking out a few more Angels and a few more groups of Rogue Demons—

anything to lessen the rage in my mind.

I just wanted to feel her in my arms again, but every time I almost gave in, her words whispered in my mind, how she wished she'd never met me, that she would rather work with the Angels. I knew those words had been said in a moment of fear and anger, but they had been true in the moment. I knew she felt betrayed, but to go so far as to prefer the dick-bag Angels over what we felt for each other?

I'd never known someone's words to hurt me before, but hers had. Only because at the time, they'd been true. I could tell she regretted them, that she had hated that she'd said them the second they left her mouth.

She wanted to speak to me, see me. I knew that, and I wasn't staying away from her to hurt her. I needed time to process things and decide how we were meant to move forward.

"Brother." Malik's voice whispered across my mind.

"How is she today?" I asked immediately, sitting up in my chair.

"Miserable as ever and trying to pretend she's not. When are you going to end this and come see her?"

I scrubbed my hands over my face and sighed.

"Soon."

"You know this arrangement is unnecessary. Even if she doesn't want to, Cali loves you," he tried to console.

"We both need some space to see how we truly feel. She needs time, and I'm giving her that."

"That sounds like an excuse," Malik argued.

"When you find your mate, brother, I'll be happy to tell you how to handle it. In the meantime, watch over her and contact me if there is any danger."

"You won't need to give me advice on handling my mate because I'm not going to give her the choice like you did. We'll get the shit stuff out of

the way first and then we'll move past it and be happy," Malik
explained, his self-confidence almost enough to make me crack a
smile.

*"Mates don't work that way, brother, but I can't wait to see how you
handle yours."*

"Coward."

"Dickwad."

Malik's humor was instant, and I shook my head, groaning into
my hands. The temptation to see Cali was growing, and I knew
I'd have to give in sooner rather than later. Neither of us could
truly move forward until we put this behind us, but I'd give her a
little longer to examine her true feelings before I saw her again.

~

CALI

"Will you *please* go away?" I begged for the umpteenth time as my
two shadows continued to dog my every step.

It had been four days since Adrik had sent me away with his
brothers. Neither of us had spoken to one another, and I felt how
hard it had been for him to refuse to allow himself to sink into a
dream with me every night. It hadn't stopped him from checking
on me in other ways. Sometimes when I really needed him, he
was there. At night, I'd feel his body wrap around mine even
though he wasn't there. During the day, his mind would brush
mine often and soothe me when the separation began to get too
much. I wanted to do the same for him, but he kept his mind so
tightly guarded that it was almost impossible for me to get to
him. I knew he was hurting still, my rejection had wounded him
greater than I had thought was possible. I wasn't sure if he was
refusing me entry to his mind to save me from feeling it, or

because he was still mad. It was probably a combination of both. I glared over my shoulder at Harkyn and Malik, and both gave me identical grins of mischief.

"Not a chance. I'm waiting for you to fall in love with me, *mi amore,*" Malik answered, throwing in a little bit of an exaggerated foreign accent.

"You can't make someone fall in love with you," I mumbled, glaring at the footpath when I remembered that the first time Adrik and I had said we loved each other was in the middle of an awful argument which resulted in not seeing each other for days and me getting stuck with the two most annoying Demon Kings in the world.

"Exactly, gorgeous. So, we'll just have to continue stalking you and hope for the best," Malik continued as if he hadn't a care in the world.

"You're not my type," I pointed out.

"Ah, darling, you are in love with my brother. I would argue that a Demon King is *exactly* your cup of tea," Malik grinned.

"Too bad I drink wine now," I muttered and pushed open the doors to the shelter. I heard muffled laughter behind me and rolled my eyes. There was no insulting these two: they took it in their stride, made a joke, or loved the sass. What was wrong with them?

"Come on, gorgeous," Malik said, moving quickly to step in front of me, forcing me back against the desk. "You know you can't stop thinking about me."

I blinked and licked my lips and smiled. Malik's eyes followed the movement of my tongue and I leaned into him, placing my hand on his chest.

"You're right... Speaking of having thoughts of you in my head... It's Thursday. Would you please take out the trash?"

Harkyn choked on a laugh, and I turned to see his shoulders shaking. Malik looked momentarily disappointed before he shrugged and smiled.

"Anything for you," he agreed with a dramatic bow. I rolled my eyes again.

"You know I'm supposedly mated to your brother, right? Why are you even attempting to flirt with me?"

"Because it's fun," Malik answered, grabbing the trash by the desk and tying it off. I watched him take it out the front door and turned to Harkyn.

"So, it's his turn to be a pain in the ass today and your turn to be silent?"

"We don't want to overwhelm you or let things get boring," Harkyn replied with a shrug, looking around.

"And you have nothing better to do? No souls to torture?" I asked, looking over the books to see if we had any appointments today.

"I don't really do the torturing unless someone needs a real lesson in pain. I have Knights to take care of that stuff for me. And my circle of Hell is running just fine at the moment," he explained.

"And you don't have a woman to help pass the time with? Perhaps someone who can stand you for longer than a few hours without needing to find an excuse to leave the room?" I asked, part teasing. Harkyn chuckled, and I'd be lying if I said the sound didn't make me squirm a little. All the brothers had that ability, no matter how crazy I was about Adrik, they were all too sexy to be allowed around women. As Harkyn's chuckle died away, his eyes flickered for a moment, a more serious expression crossing his face as his thoughts turned inwards. I watched him for a moment, interested in what had caught at his thoughts.

"There is someone… isn't there?" I asked softly. Harkyn jerked his head back as if trying to wrench himself out of his thoughts and shook his head.

"No… not really. It's… complicated," he supplied with a small, forced smile.

"As in she doesn't know who you are? Or that she does know and is trying to run in the other direction?" I pushed.

"You ask a lot of questions," he muttered, clearly not wanting to continue with this line of conversation.

"What can I say? I like to know things," I smiled. Harkyn shook his head at me, and I searched for something else to say, something to break the awkwardness. I got the impression Harkyn hadn't mentioned this woman to anyone else, and I didn't think he'd appreciate me outing him to his brother. Malik pushed through the front door and I drew in a quick breath, deciding on a topic.

"Can you guys explain all this Hell stuff to me a little more? How exactly does Hell work?" I asked, leaning forward on my elbows. Harkyn's eyes warmed slightly in appreciation and he slid onto a chair by the door. Curiosity was getting the better of me anyway, and I wanted to know more about Adrik's world.

For the next hour, Malik and Harkyn explained to me how the different circles worked, their Knights, and why Angels and Demons were fighting one another. They went through and detailed each of their brothers too, although interestingly, both seemed a little uneasy when talking about Corvin, the King of the ninth circle.

Both brothers did extremely well not to talk about Adrik or mention his name to me, for which I was grateful. I was still mad at him for hiding what he knew about the bond, but that stupid part of my head understood his fear of telling me. Because he was right: I would have vanished within the hour, and he'd never have found me again. But I was still mad that he'd never told me, and I was mad that *he* was mad. What, he was the only one allowed to risk his life for the person he lo—cared about? I shook my head. I knew what my feelings for Adrik were, but thinking about them when I'd only ever said them once aloud, and in the midst of an argument made me not want to even think the word, much less utter it again.

More than anything, though... I missed him. My body missed the feel of his, my heart missed knowing he was close, my mind was constantly tracking back to him, hoping he'd reach out. It was a torment I wasn't prepared for.

As if he felt my pain, Adrik's mind brushed mine gently, almost feather-like. My eyes filled with tears at the contact, and for the briefest moment, I felt his fingers stroke my cheeks and then he was gone.

"Cali?" Harkyn whispered softly, as if he were worried about upsetting me. I cleared my throat and shook my head.

"I need to wash the dogs," I announced, blinking quickly to rid myself of the tears. Neither brother spoke, they just looked at me, full of awkwardness, and nodded. Forcing a smile to my lips, I spun on my heel and marched towards the washroom to prepare the bath.

We had over thirty dogs here, waiting for their forever homes, and more than fifty cats. There was also an assortment of other animals from birds to mice and hamsters and even a few horses. The shelter was on several acres, so we had the space to keep so many animals. All the animals were on a schedule for bathing and exercise, and it was important to stick to it or the animals became antisocial and dirty. The shelter didn't have a no-kill policy, but I had influenced the owner enough that it hadn't ever happened while I was there and had even taken it upon myself to foster some until a home was found. I usually gave potential buyers a little extra something to make them more determined to give an animal here a forever home and a great life. I hadn't ever had a single return, and everyone went home with an animal that truly matched them and their lifestyles.

Apart from rehoming a one-year-old Labrador and two kittens, my day went by without anything interesting happening. Malik and Harkyn continued to be smart-asses, I sassed back, and they laughed, even when I wasn't feeling it. They helped me with the animals and tried to appear non-threatening when we had potential clients come in looking for a pet.

And still… that deep, aching hole in my chest refused to go away.

~

ADRIK

"You messed up, didn't ya, son?"

I turned to find Sol glaring at me, his wrinkled hands on his hips.

"What makes you say that?" I asked with an inner sigh.

"Because our girl hasn't been here for a week, and you're tellin' everyone who comes lookin' for her that she's gone," Sol explained.

"And for now, she *is* gone," I replied, looking around us. Over the last several days, I'd come here to the underpass, warning all her regulars not to come, that Cali had been forced into hiding for the time being and that they were all in danger. Most of them had spread the word so I'd had very little people to warn over the last few days. I searched for them and found them doing well enough, so I let them go. The do-gooder charity people stayed away too, understanding that Cali was in some kind of trouble and that she was protecting everyone by remaining in hiding.

"What did you do?" Sol demanded, poking me hard in the chest. I blinked at him in surprise and a small smile slipped out at the old coot's audacity.

"I didn't do anything. Some people found out what she can do and they're after her… she's in hiding," I explained, knowing that if any of them got most of the real story, it should be Sol. The old man's face cleared, and he shook his head.

"Some of your people, or mine?" he asked, squinting.

"Not exactly my people, but more mine than yours," I admitted.

"Is she okay?"

"She will be. Right now, she's upset and feels trapped. I came here to warn all the people she heals to stay away so that those looking for her won't try to hurt any of you in an attempt to find her or lure her out of hiding," I explained. Sol studied me a little longer, and he sighed heavily and shook his head.

"Is this your fault?" Sol asked. I frowned and thought about his question. Was this my fault? Would Cali have still been discovered had I not been fighting the Angels? Would she have been safe if she hadn't feared for my life and therefore revealed herself? The Angel I'd spoken to had said he and his group were there because they'd heard a rumor of a Witch healing in the area. Either way, they would have shown up, and if they'd hurt any of her people, Cali would have sacrificed herself to save them.

"No," I answered and shook my head. "No, it wasn't my fault. I think it was lucky I was here because I have the resources and ability to hide her and protect her."

Sol seemed to take in my words but made no comment. Neither of us spoke for a time until the old man sighed and shook his head.

"None of us are meetin' here anymore, but we're gettin' together somewhere else. We still need to eat, and those people in vans still want to help us get clean clothes and warm food. It's too cold out to refuse their help," Sol explained. I frowned, not liking that idea, but Sol was right. These people still needed help, and there would be more than one group of do-gooders out at night helping transients like these people.

"Fine," I answered and nodded. I'd have to come out again and look out for them. At least if I kept Sol and the usuals safe, Cali should be happy with that. I wasn't going to track down every human she healed and be sure of their safety, but the main group seemed to stick together at nights, so I'd look after them.

"Have you seen Sky and her mother?" I asked, just remembering the little girl Cali had been making progress with.

"She's been around lookin'. I told her to stay away since you were warnin' everyone Cali was in danger," Sol answered.

"Do you know where I can find her?"

Sol frowned at me suspiciously and I waited. I wasn't going to explain myself to him, my patience was basically non-existent these days. My chest was constantly aching, my body was tight, full, and desperate for my mate. My mind was a chaotic pit, unable to be soothed, and my palm was constantly itching, my soul urging me to complete our bond and claim my woman.

"I don't know exactly. I know her Mama works for that real-estate on Bourke street," Sol finally answered.

"Thank you. Stay safe, Sol. Cali would be furious with both of us if anything happens to you," I warned.

"I can look after myself just fine. You look after our girl," he returned. I nodded, reminded once again why I liked the old man. I watched as he turned around and started away from me before I wrapped myself in shadow and went in search of Sara, Sky's mother.

I found myself in front of a fancy looking real-estate agency that had several large windows showcasing the offices inside. I searched the desks and stopped when I found Sara. Hopefully this worked.

A little bell chimed in the door as I entered, and I straightened as several pairs of eyes swung towards me.

"Oh, hello," a woman with black hair greeted, her dark eyes looking me over from the tips of my boots to the top of my head. I didn't need to be a millennia old Demon to see the desire on her face; however, it did nothing for me. I got the feeling no woman would ever make me want them like that again.

"Can I help you?" she asked, and the innuendo in her voice was thick. I smiled, turning on the charm because I knew it would work better than being my bitter self.

"Actually, I'm here to see Sara," I answered, looking past the dark-haired woman to Sky's mother. Her eyes widened, and recognition flashed on her face.

"Oh, hi, Adrik," she greeted, looking a little uncertain.

"Oh. Well, I am senior saleswoman here, and I would be more than happy to assist you in all your needs," the woman tried again, her smile full of sin and sex. Again, nothing.

"Thank you, but I made an appointment with Sara, and I'd like to keep it," I assured with a wink. Sara stood up and stepped towards us.

"Right, I'm sorry, Monique. I forgot that I ran into Adrik here yesterday," Sara began, looking uncertain.

"Yes, she promised to show me some properties she thought I'd like," I continued, needing to get Sara out of the office for a few hours. Sara's eyes widened and she hesitated a moment before nodding.

"Oh… well. If you need anything else, you know where to find me," Monique continued, flashing me that smile again before sauntering back to her desk. I turned back to Sara as she stepped in close.

"What's going on? How did you know where I work?" she whispered.

"Sol told me. Cali wants to see Sky for another session, but she can't be out in the open right now, it's too dangerous. Will you come with me?"

Sara's eyes widened again, and she sucked in a sharp breath, hope sparking.

"Yes, we can go get her right now," she agreed, her face brightening. I tipped my head towards the front door and waited as she grabbed her bag and jacket.

"I'll be back before closing, Monique," Sara called. Monique nodded, but I could see the dislike on the woman's face. Some people just couldn't stand to lose out.

We stepped out onto the bright sunlit street and Sara turned to me.

"Can I meet you somewhere?" she asked.

"Do you know the animal rescue shelter off the highway?"

"Yes."

"Go get Sky and meet us. Cali will be there," I explained. Sara sucked in a shaky breath and let it out, her eyes shiny with unshed tears.

"Thank you. I know you said she's in danger and the others told me it was because someone found out about what she can do. I thought she'd be gone for good, and she is my only hope for Sky. Thank you so much for coming for us," she choked out.

"Cali hates that she's in hiding, but she refuses to stop what she was born to do. Just go get Sky and meet us there," I replied, a little overwhelmed at the force of this woman's relief. She nodded and brushed away a wayward tear.

"I will. Thank you," she said again before hurrying to her car. I looked around and ducked into a small alleyway before shadowing myself to the shelter.

I appeared outside the building and took a moment to try and figure out what I was going to say. Cali could still be mad at me, still feel trapped and manipulated. I didn't want to fight, but I was so desperate to see her again that I would even take fighting with her over not seeing her at all. I could feel her close, and every cell in my body screamed at me to go to her.

"Finally pluck up the courage, brother?" Malik asked, his smug tone setting my teeth on edge.

"Go fuck yourself, Malik. I need to see my mate in private, you and Harkyn can take a small break," I replied.

"You really think she's going to let you in her pants that easily?"

"Like I said, Malik, go fuck yourself. There is a woman and her daughter on her way here, let them pass and remain hidden, they're here to see Cali," I explained, showing him an image of the pair.

"Good luck."

I sucked in a steadying breath and marched towards the door, hating that I'd likely need all the luck I could get.

CHAPTER FOURTEEN
CALI

The bell at the front door sounded and I looked up from the paperwork on my desk. I waited for Malik or Harkyn to call out to me, but the building was quiet with the exception of the animals. Unease pricked at me, and I stood slowly, preparing to strike out with my magic if I needed to. I edged around my desk and was taking slow steps towards the office door when it was pushed open suddenly. I raised my hands to throw my magic, but paused when my eyes landed on Adrik.

Adrik.

He was here.

Something inside me broke at seeing his face for the first time in days and I sucked in a sharp breath.

"Hi," I whispered, my voice cracking.

"Hi," he returned, his expression one of uncertainty. We both stood in heavy silence for a moment, neither of us quite sure what to say.

"Where are... uh... where are Malik and Harkyn?"

"I asked them to give us a moment," he answered and stepped further into the room. My body instantly responded to his nearness, and I swallowed hard, backing up to my desk. How did I want him so much?

"Are we talking again?"

"I'd like to," Adrik answered without pause. I nodded and couldn't stop myself from looking him over, my eyes devouring the sight of him. I'd missed him so much, my arms ached to hold him, my body was urging me to fling myself into his arms and let him keep me close, to make me feel safe again.

"I have been looking out for your people," Adrik began.

"They're okay?" I asked, dragged back to the conversation.

"Yes," Adrik nodded. "Sol had something more to say about it all, but he's just worried about you."

I smiled softly, my heart hurting at the idea of never seeing him again.

"Are they staying away?" I asked, watching as Adrik seemed to move in closer, but I never actually saw him take a step.

"Yes, they understand why you're not there." His voice was set low and intimate, and I shivered, barely restraining myself from lunging at him.

"Are... are Malik and Harkyn coming back?" I asked, my voice nowhere near as strong as I wanted it to be. I was mad at him, and I had every right to be mad at him. So why did staring into his beautiful blue eyes make me want to melt at his feet and forgive him for everything? I knew he wasn't influencing me; he had kept that damn wall in his mind between us for days now.

"When I ask them to. Are you done trying to make small talk?" he asked. I nodded, not knowing what else to do.

Adrik took a slow step forward so he was only a few inches from me.

"I miss you," he admitted softly, his eyes never leaving my face. Well... shit. How was I supposed to say something snarky after that?

"I... I missed you," I admitted. Relief shone in his eyes for a moment, and I refused to allow the small smile I could feel to break free. He reached out with one gentle hand, and I closed my eyes as he cupped my cheek. My skin beneath his touch felt alive and warm. I leaned into his hand and tried to guard my heart, but every part of me was begging him to come closer, to erase this space between us.

His other hand cupped my other cheek, and he tipped my head back, dark eyes searching.

"I hate being apart from you," he rasped, and I could feel my defenses shudder.

"Me too," I managed to admit. He stepped closer, his hands sliding through my hair. I tipped my face up so that I could look at him properly, and he leaned down to press a kiss to my forehead.

More!

My body was screaming, but a small part of me held back, unable to fully forgive him yet. He pressed his forehead to mine, his thumbs brushing my cheeks and I reached up to wrap my fingers around his wrists, holding him there. I'd missed him so much. Neither of us spoke for the longest time, both of us seemed to just need to be in each other's presence, soak in the other person. It was hard to believe how much I missed him, and how much I'd gotten used to him in the few short weeks we'd known each other. I guess I had the mate bond stuff to thank for that. It was intoxicating.

After a moment, he stiffened and sighed.

"I... I bought you a present," he finally said. I frowned.

"A present?"

The bells to the front door jingled.

"Hello?" a familiar voice called. I gasped and looked back at Adrik who smiled gently down at me.

"You brought her here?" I gaped.

"I knew you were worried about losing your progress and you really are that girl's only hope," Adrik explained. Without another word, I threw my arms around his neck and pulled him close to me. Parts of me stood up and screamed at me to do more, other parts were simply soothed at having him here in my arms again. Adrik wasted no time in wrapping his arms around me, and I soaked in the feeling. It was like I was drying up without him, and now that he was here where I could touch him again, I was finally coming back to life.

"Miss Cali?" Sky called.

"You better go to her," he whispered against my ear.

"Thank you," I returned, pulling back to look up at his face. "Thank you, so much."

His blue eyes were smiling down at me, and I watched as he pulled away reluctantly and indicated to the door. I hurried past him with a smile and laughed when little Sky's face lit up and she ran for me.

"Miss Cali! I was so worried about you," she cried, throwing herself at me. I wrapped her up and smiled, grinning at her mother over her shoulder.

"I was worried about *you*. Thank you both for meeting me here, I know it's a little different."

"Honestly, Cali, it's not even an issue. I'm just so glad you're able to keep seeing her. Are you alright? I don't really know what's going on, but Adrik here said you were in danger, and we couldn't meet at the underpass anymore," Sara answered, stepping up to take Sky's hand.

"I'll be okay. I just need to lay low for a little while," I assured. The bell jangled, and Malik and Harkyn walked in. Sara gasped and backed towards me, and I placed a soft hand on her arm.

"Sara, this is Malik and Harkyn, they've been helping to keep me safe," I introduced, hoping to put the woman at ease.

"Oh... hi," she greeted shakily.

"Hi there, beautiful," Harkyn greeted with a wink. I watched

Sara's face flush and rolled my eyes at Harkyn.

"Hello, sweetheart," Malik said to Sky. She waved shyly and I looked at the guys.

"Would you mind going and collecting the things I need for a healing session? They're in my bag by the front door," I asked, making sure not to mention that it was at home. The guys would know.

"On it," Harkyn agreed and strode through a side door.

"Why don't you two follow me down here, and we'll get a room prepped," I suggested, indicating to an exam room. It wasn't ideal, but it was better than nothing.

I glanced at Adrik over my shoulder and smiled my thanks. His smile was slow, but it lit his eyes and made my heart pound harder. Could we mend our relationship? Was there a way for us to patch how horribly we'd messed it up?

I spent hours with Sky and Sara. I'd missed our last session, and so I wanted to make up for it, and then some. Adrik was in the room the entire time, his presence almost impossible to dismiss as I concentrated on the girl lying on my table. Sara was a ball of grateful energy, too overwhelmed with the fact that we came back for her daughter to do more than watch with her hands clasped and blinking away tears. It made my heart clench to know I was able to help these two.

I'd gotten to know the two of them since I'd first started healing Sky, and they were all each other had. Sara and her parents didn't talk, they'd disowned her when she was seventeen and refused to see her again, despite her earlier efforts. Sky's father had been in the same boat with no family. The two of them had been deeply in love, but he'd been killed in a neighborhood shooting when Sky was three. It had just been the two of them ever since, and Sara was petrified to lose her daughter. Any mother would be terrified to lose their child, but this little girl was literally the only person Sara had left.

I concentrated hard, using herbs that would aid Sky in her healing, and decided I had to make this girl an amulet. It wouldn't cure her, but maybe it would help hold off her illness in between our sessions and give me a greater chance at curing her altogether. No one had ever told me if they'd cured a disease like this in its entirety, although I was sure my Aunt could, but I could heal a human from injuries that would have otherwise killed them, I had to be able to do something about disease as well.

"Red, you need to stop now. You're swaying on your feet and are too pale." Adrik's voice in my head after all this time was enough to shove me from my trance, my mind calming suddenly, the burning I'd grown used to instantly soothed. I blinked my eyes open and staggered slightly. Adrik was there in an instant, his arms around me as he propped me up against him, his front to my back.

"Are you alright?" Sara asked, hurrying to her daughter's side.

"Yes... sorry. I think I just pushed myself a little too hard tonight. How long was I out?" I asked, looking at Adrik over my shoulder.

"A little over three hours."

I nodded and sucked in a slow breath, hoping to steady myself quickly.

"Are you okay, Miss Cali?" Sky asked as she carefully sat up, looking a little stiff after lying still for so long.

"I am, honey. I want to make you a special necklace to wear between our sessions," I told her, straightening up properly.

"Is that a good idea right now?" Adrik asked, and I knew he was frowning without looking at him.

"It is. Every time I heal Sky, I have to repair the damage that's been done since our last healing and try to do some more. It's two steps forward, one step back. If I can give her an amulet that will stop, or at the very least slow, the progression of the disease in between sessions, I think I have a much greater chance of *really* helping her," I explained.

"You think you can heal her completely?" Adrik asked softly.

"I really do. And even if I can't, I need to try. They're all each other has," I explained, closing my eyes on the way it felt to touch his mind again, to have him in mine. We had a lot left to talk about, some bridges to mend and wounds to heal, but this was a start. If a few days of distance and silence had taught me anything, it was that this mate bond was *real* and it was entirely too powerful to fight. I may be mad at the way it came about, but I couldn't deny that it was happening.

"I will wear anything you ask me to, Cali. I want to get better," Sky answered, bringing me back to the matter at hand.

"Good. I'm going to make you something, just rest here a moment," I replied with a smile. I stepped out of Adrik's embrace—I'd missed it entirely too much—and proceeded on shaky legs to my bag of supplies.

I listened to Sky and Sara talk to Adrik as I mixed my herbs together and came up with a spell in my head. Angelica, Tulsi, Neem, Anise, and Mugwort. These herbs would grant her not only protection, but also aid in her healing. While everyone was distracted, I drew my blade and, bracing for the pain, drew it across my palm. The sting was immediate and sharp. Adrik paused in mid-sentence and spun to look at me, his mind pushing further into mine.

"What are you doing, red?"

"A spell. Keep them talking," I replied, holding my palm out over

the bowl so that several drops of my blood splashed to the bottom. When I was sure there was enough, I pressed a handful of tissues into my hand and dropped a clear quart into the mixture and centered myself. Sara and Sky knew I could heal, but they didn't know I was a Witch. The word had too many negative connotations attached to it thanks to humans, and I didn't want them to start distrusting me. When the herbs and blood were well mixed, I tipped the mixture into my hands with the quartz and centered myself. Drawing from my power, I transferred it into the quartz using the spell I'd just created.

By my blood, I bind to me,
The powers of Earth & Fire.
Let my blood be the tie,
My need of you is dire.

With my lifeblood, I spell you to me,
Water and Air, hear my call.
Bound by me, I thrice encircle thee,
Elements four, tied to my Soul.

By my blood, tie your powers to my need.
Mighty Hekate, you are the key,
Grant me your aid, let me heal,
Elements Four, my words conjure thee.

Protect, heal, shield, and mend,
I call on you, your powers send.
By the elements and the mighty Goddess,
My will is nigh, my blood the tie.

A hush fell over the room, and when I opened my eyes, the blood and herbs were gone, infused into the crystal, and the quartz remained in my hand. I could feel it pulsing with power, but I knew none other than a Witch would feel it. The herbs I used would cloak the magic in it, so Sky would not be the target of any supernatural beings looking for a Witch.

I turned to look at Sara and both she and her daughter were watching me with wide eyes.

"What is that?" Sky asked, her eyes on the crystal.

"This is a quartz. It may seem impossible, but it will protect you and aid in your healing. Do not take it off until I see you again," I instructed, slipping it into a stringed necklace that would cradle it but still allow it to do as it was meant to do. I adjusted the length of the necklace and then slid it over Sky's neck.

She gasped and looked down at it, her eyes wide.

"I can feel it," she whispered in awe. I smiled and patted her arm. "Good. It should do the trick. It's bound to me, so the stone will continue to draw healing ability from me as long as you are wearing it. It should keep our progress where it is or maybe even help increase it. It'll be fine in the shower, just don't take it off," I pressed, needing her to understand that. It was tied to me by blood. No matter where it was, it was going to draw from me until it was crushed. I would rather my magic be going to someone and not left to spill out on a table.

"Calixta," Adrik growled low in my mind. I knew he had just realized what I'd done, but this was not the time to discuss it.

"Thank you, Cali. You are a miracle, and I'll never be able to thank you for what you've already done for my daughter," Sara whispered, leaning forward to hug me. I smiled and hugged her back. Being this tired was worth it.

"You guys should go now. I am so happy to have been able to help. Please don't mention to anyone that I was here or that I helped you some more. I don't want to risk being found again," I pressed.

"Our lips are sealed," Sara promised.

"We'll find you again if we are able to do another session next week. Until then, just keep the necklace on," I instructed.

"I will," Sky promised.

With one last hug to both of them, I watched as they left the shelter. When the bell jangled over the door, announcing their departure, I leaned heavily against the exam table.

"What were you thinking?" Adrik growled darkly. I closed my eyes and sighed heavily.

"I was thinking that I want that girl healed and on her way to a normal, happy life. And if she is the only one I am able to heal for the time being, then I am going to do everything I can for her," I answered. I opened my eyes, looking around for a chair to collapse into. Adrik snarled and stomped around to my side of the table. I barely opened my mouth to protest before he scooped me up into his arms and carried me out of the room and towards my office.

"I can walk," I protested, but I was exhausted, and I knew my voice reflected it, no matter how hard I tried to hide it.

"Barely," he muttered under his breath, and I could feel how upset he was with me. He'd learn though, that it didn't matter how mad he got at me. I needed to heal, it was my nature, it was me at my core, and it didn't matter to me if I was left weaker than normal. I would recharge and be fine in a few hours. Sky now had a chance at *real* progress.

Adrik took a seat on the small couch and held me close to his chest. I smiled and snuggled in closer to him. I really had missed him—every part of him. His scent, his heat, the way his body moved with such lethal grace. I missed the way his eyes darkened with desire, the way his smile screamed sin and sex. I'd definitely missed the feel of him in my arms and how safe I felt wrapped in his. He was a King of Hell, he was a Demon, he was everything bad I'd been told about Hell's creatures… but he wasn't. Not to me. Was it possible everything I'd been told was wrong? Was there more to Heaven and Hell than what we all knew?

"I'm sorry," I whispered, my voice cracking. Adrik's hand stopped running up and down my back and he stilled beneath me. I took in a steadying breath and pushed myself up so that I was looking at his face.

"When you told me… I was angry, hurt, and upset. I felt betrayed and like you'd played me for a fool. I felt your emotional pain, your physical pain, and then the truth… all of that combined with everything I'd ever been told about you… The doubt I suddenly had in myself and my ability to distinguish the evil from the good was near debilitating," I explained, scrubbing a hand over my face.

"I shouldn't have said what I said. I was feeling trapped because I was down there with no clear way out and suddenly told I have been irrevocably bound to another being for all eternity. It's just… I was angry and scared. I'm sorry for what I said—I'm not sorry I met you. I don't regret spending time with you or falling for you," I continued, hoping he could *feel* what I meant rather than focus on my words.

"I am sorry, too," Adrik responded, his voice low and deep. I dragged my gaze back to his sapphire eyes and he smiled gently. "It seems we were both scared. I was scared to lose you once I found you. Cole messed up with Mika, but we didn't know what was happening; I didn't want to mess things up with you the way he did with his mate, so I tried to get you to know me first, and things progressed naturally but with consequence you weren't privy to. If I told you what was going on, I felt that you'd be gone from my life before I could blink, and I didn't want to risk you falling into the hands of the Angels," he explained.

"When were you going to tell me?" I asked, my voice soft and unsure. Adrik sighed.

"Honestly, it would have been by now. I didn't want to bind us completely without you knowing. When our minds were bound, I didn't know it would happen then. It was different for Cole and Mika, but I guess the underlying factor was giving each other trust. Bodies... well... okay, I knew what was happening there, but I'd been aching for you since the night we met and I was beyond help at that point," he continued. I smiled softly, remembering how we'd been teasing each other for weeks.

"I was too," I admitted. Adrik's smile was small but appreciative of my honesty.

"Then the heart bond? That was an accident. I mean, I knew I was falling for you and made no attempt to stop it, but I wanted to tell you I loved you in a different way. And soul? Well... I wanted to tell you everything and wait until you asked me to bind us to do that. I wanted it to be your choice," he admitted. My heart clenched. I knew in the end it would happen anyway, and it didn't matter that three of the four bonds had been completed. Having completed any of them had given us a permanent link to each other, but it meant a lot to me that he wanted me to be aware and agree to our souls being bound for all time.

"I'm sorry I scared you," he added.

"I was scared *for* you, more than *of* you. And I was hurt that you wanted Mika to heal you and not me," I admitted. Adrik sighed and shook his head.

"I was hurt and angry. I was afraid if you touched me, I'd hurt you, and I could never forgive myself for that," he answered. I nodded slowly and gently stroked his cheek, my gaze drawn to his full lips.

"Are we okay?" I asked, dragging my gaze back to his. Adrik studied me carefully, searchingly, and then nodded.

"I think we can move past this. Do you?"

"These last few days have sucked beyond the meaning of the word. I don't want to do it anymore," I admitted. Adrik smiled and dragged me closer to him, his hand tipping my face up.

"I promise to be a good mate to you, Calixta Cane. I will do everything I can to make you happy, to make you proud, and to keep you safe. I don't want to be apart from you like this again," he admitted. My heart pounded hard, and butterflies let loose in my stomach at the fierceness in his eyes.

"I love you."

The words from his mouth were like music to my ears. My heart leapt, and I couldn't have prevented the smile on my face had I tried.

"I love you, t—" I didn't get to finish my sentence before his lips were crashing down on mine, his hands threading through my hair. I sighed against him and parted my lips, feeling his tongue stroke mine. His hands slid to my hips, and I laughed when he lifted me and turned me so I could sit with my legs either side of his. I wound my arms around his neck to pull him closer, my body singing with the pleasure of holding him close.

No, we weren't out of the woods yet. We had a lot of things to talk about, boundaries to put in place and a discussion about our future would have to happen soon. But for right now?

I didn't want to be anywhere else but in his arms.

CHAPTER FIFTEEN
ADRIK

Pulling myself away from Calixta after so much time apart was one of the hardest things I'd had to do. All I wanted was to be with her, inside her, hold her to me and never let her go again. But I could feel her hesitation, her uncertainty, and that small sliver of fear. She didn't know what to expect, what it all meant, and I wasn't going to continue to manipulate situations for my own gain. This was a fresh start, and as much as it pained me to leave her warm embrace, there were other things I had to do. Night was falling, and I had to check out the new spot Cali's homeless people were gathering to make sure they were safe, and all accounted for. Cali had been happy to know I'd spoken to Sol and that he was doing well. She wanted to make him a healing necklace too but not tell him what it would do. I wasn't too keen on it. I liked the old man and all, but I hated that she'd bound herself to a stone by blood. It would constantly drain small amounts of her energy until it was destroyed.

I left the shelter with another warning to my brothers to look after her. I hated them being anywhere near her, but she needed protection, and I had work to do. Tonight, though, they could go somewhere else, and I'd take over protecting my mate. My cock throbbed at the thought of it.

I shadowed to the secluded area I'd found Cali's people in before and took a moment to sense around me for Rogues or Angels. It seemed clear, and I cautiously stepped out of the shadows to look around. The human charity people were here, their van that offered showers had a line outside it. Someone was dishing out hot food and there was another table further down with small food bags. They could each take one and it would have a meal in it for tomorrow as well.

Some of the familiar faces stood out, people giving me a quick nod or wave, others frowned as if they couldn't place my face. I did a mental checklist of all the ones I could remember and searched harder when I couldn't find Sol. Where was that old man?

I felt Cali brush my mind and I kept my smile to myself. It hadn't been pleasant keeping her from my mind for the past few days, but I had been worried I'd make things worse in my angry state, and I didn't want to risk hearing more truths about how she didn't want to be with me. But now, it was a welcome sensation to have her comforting me.

I brushed a kiss across her cheek, even with the distance between us, and triumph bloomed when I felt her instant reaction.

Dragging my attention back to where I was, I started looking through tents and under makeshift shelters. There were several barrels scattered around with fires lit in them as the nights grew colder, people lining up to grab jackets or have their clothes mended. I opened my mind to search around me, hoping to catch the thoughts of some of these people, to someone who might be talking to Sol or know where he was. I waved to a few of the people who waved to me and nodded to some of the charity workers who called out. Who would have thought that me, a King of Hell, would have been so welcomed by these kinds of people? Truth be told, I'd never given these humans much thought. They were just like the rest; they had never been of much concern to me until they were down in Hell. Yet, here I was, walking among them, I knew a lot of them, their names, their dreams, and their situation. I didn't care for most of them, but there was the odd few I wanted to keep an eye on and whose deaths I would be at least angry about.

Progress.

"I don't know who you're talkin' about," a pained voice cried, followed by the sound of a heavy punch. I stiffened, my whole body tensed and ready to run. Where had that come from? That had been Sol's voice.

"You know the Witch, human. Where is she?" someone snarled.

A hiss escaped through my gritted teeth, and rage filled me as I heard Sol take another physical blow, the old man's cry of pain scratching at my mind like claws. I wrapped myself in shadow and disappeared, not bothering to first conceal myself from the eyes of watching humans. I followed the sound of the voices two short blocks away and found myself a few feet from a group of Angels who crowded around a man on the ground. My gaze caught on Sol's face where bruises already discolored his skin and fury bubbled in my veins. The old man's eyes opened slowly, his entire body ridged and preparing to take another blow when his gaze landed on me. His eyes widened and he suddenly looked scared.

"No! It's a trap!" he shouted. I felt a presence behind me and ducked quickly, spinning out and swiping at whoever was behind me with my leg. An Angel crashed to the ground, her face a mask of fury. I kicked out again, getting her square in the face before I was on my feet, throwing hellfire at another. He shrieked in agony as another came towards me. I dragged my blade from its sheath on my hip and struck out, nicking one of the Angels who got too close. He slid sideways, shouting something at me, but I didn't bother to listen. Another two Angels rushed me, and I blew more hellfire in their direction—the sounds of their screams was music to my ears.

Fucking fuckers.

It didn't seem to matter how many Angels I put down, more kept on coming. I needed help, especially if Sol was going to make it out of this alive. I drew fire from deep within me and blew it at a group of the Angels, setting four more aflame. Sol was still on the ground, but he was crawling painfully to an alcove in the alley, trying to stay out of the way.

"Adrik, what's going on?" Cali's voice in my head forced me to take a deep breath. She could feel my anger and my hate towards the Angels, but also my fear for the old man. I reached for my brothers, about to call them for aid when pain shot up my chest from my waist.

"Fuck!" I roared, snapping off all contact with Cali to protect her from feeling my pain. I wrenched at the Angel Blade in my side and threw it at the Angel it had come from. It hit him right between the eyes and he fell screaming to the ground. I manifested my sword from thin air and used it to remove his head from his shoulders. Blood spurted powerfully from the place where his head had been, and I cupped a handful of it in my hands before pressing it to my wound, my eyes scanning the mass of writhing and screaming bodies around me. I hissed as the Angel blood hit my skin. It bubbled painfully over the wound, and it took a few seconds for it to start healing.

Besides a Witch, the only thing to heal a Demon King from an Angel Blade was the blood of the Angel who stabbed them. I didn't know how or why it worked like that, and I didn't much care right now to ponder it.

I gripped my sword tighter and hurried to dispatch a few more Angels who were too distracted by hellfire to pay much attention to me. One by one, they all fell until I was standing in an alley with twelve dead Angels. A deep, rattling breath dragged me from my musings, and I rushed towards Sol. He tensed when I reached his side, but relaxed when he saw it was just me.

"How bad are you hurt?" I demanded.

"Y-you... I knew you weren't... human." Sol panted, his eyes wide with fear.

"You can say I told you so later. Where are you hurt? I need to get you help," I demanded, panicking at the thought of how Cali would react if Sol died.

"It's too late, son. You need to go, *now*. It's a trap," he warned, pushing feebly at my hands.

"I already killed them all," I reminded, opening his jacket to look at his wounds. There was no blood, but I had a nasty suspicion he had internal bleeding.

"That was just... th-the welcoming party. There are m-more coming," Sol warned, coughing. The sound was wet and alarming.

"Then let's get you out of here," I said, scooting closer, preparing to pick the old man up. He shook his head, holding out a hand to keep me away.

"They're gonna kill them all. All the people Cali loves, they're goin' after 'em," Sol warned, coughing hard again. I grimaced when his palm came away smeared with blood.

"I'll get you to Cali first so she can heal you, then I'll save the others," I explained, ready to knock him out to shut him up.

"They need you to protect them, Adrik. And so does Cali," he groaned, his breathing labored and face deathly pale. I could hear the rattling in his chest and the wet sound that accompanied it. A curious wrenching tugged at my heart, and I found myself desperate to save him, unable to accept the old man's death. I had been alive for eons and seen more death than it should be possible to witness. I'd formed friendships with humans before and lost them to the inevitability of death. But none of them had affected me so strongly.

Sol opened his mouth to protest but he was cut off when we heard screaming. He groaned, and his fear battered at me.

"Go! Go, you have to save them," he shouted, his face a mask of fear and pain. But it wasn't fear of death, it was fear for the others.

"Just let me——" I tried again.

"No!"

Gritting my teeth, I reached for my brothers, trying to block out the sounds of screaming from a few blocks away. I staggered back when nothing happened. There were no lines of contact, no way for me to reach any of them. It was like there was a wall and I couldn't breach it.

Fuck.

~

CALI

I stiffened in my seat when Adrik suddenly cut off all contact. I tried to reach out to him again, but that damn wall was back in place. I could probably push through it if I was desperate, but I was worried about distracting him from whatever had made him so angry.

I glanced down at the new amulet in my hand, the one I'd made for Sol once Adrik had left. I knew he didn't want me to waste my magic on another one, but Sol mattered to me. I just wanted to keep him safe.

I took a few minutes to breathe when the echo of Adrik's pain pricked my chest, and my heart pounded hard in the silent room.

Something was wrong. Adrik had been beyond mad. He'd been livid and I'd caught the flash of pain before it all went silent.

"Malik! Harkyn!" I called and got up from the lounge. I swayed slightly but regained my balance and hurried for my office door. Both brothers appeared before me in an instant, weapons drawn.

"What is it?"

"Are you okay?"

I took in a steadying breath and shook my head.

"Adrik is in trouble. I was in his mind, he was okay, then I felt him get worried. I stayed quiet, but then he was angry, angrier than I have ever felt him, and then he cut off all contact with me. I felt pain before he did that, and he's got a block up between us again. I could break through it, but if he's in a fight, I don't want to distract him."

Malik looked at Harkyn and both brothers frowned.

"Are you sure?" Harkyn asked.

"Positive. You need to go to him, he could be in trouble."

"You need to come back to Hell with us and wait there," Malik said.

"No." I shook my head. "There's no time. Just go. I will wait right here, no one knows where I am. You need to go to him; something is wrong."

"We can't just—"

"Try to reach out to him. Both of you. See if he will answer you," I suggested urgently.

Malik sighed heavily and silence fell. I watched as both brothers frowned at each other again and Harkyn shook his head.

"Does that remind you of—" Harkyn began.

"When Cole was attacked with whatever it was the Angels put on their blades to make it impossible for him to reach us? Yes," Malik finished for him; his tone grim.

"Go to him," I urged and quickly described the neighborhood he was in.

"We can't just—"

"Yes, you can. Now go!" I shouted, beginning to panic now. If Adrik was in pain and angry, and there were Angels around, then he needed help. I didn't want to sit here and discuss if I should be alone or not.

"Stay in that room. Sit down and do *not* go looking for us," Harkyn growled, marching me back to my office.

"I will. Just go!"

The brothers looked at me uncertainly again and I was fully prepared to knock them both down and go after Adrik myself if they didn't get a move on. I was sure that showed on my face as both brothers shadowed out of there quickly.

Like Hell I was staying put. The second they were gone, I ran for my bag and yanked out my keys before I jogged out the door. I only paused long enough to lock the shelter door before I was in my car and racing towards the other side of town. Adrik was in danger, possibly injured, and I had a feeling so were my people. He'd gone looking for them, after all.

The sun was down, the night was cooler, and there was fog on the ground. Clenching the steering wheel tightly, I gritted my teeth at every stop light or tight bend. I couldn't feel Adrik anymore, but I knew he was still alive. I replayed the last moments I was in his head, frowning. He'd been looking for Sol, I knew that much. He'd been worried because he couldn't find him with the rest of the group. Then he'd gotten mad. I hadn't been paying enough attention, too tired from healing Sky to really see what he'd been seeing. I'd been relying on his emotions to tell me when something was wrong, and it had all happened so fast that I was playing catch-up.

Was Sol okay? Has he been hurt? Who had hurt Adrik?

I glanced at the next street sign and cursed under my breath. I needed to move faster, but there was no hope of it if I wanted to get there in one piece. Unable to sit here any longer, without any clue as to what was going on, I pulled over for a moment and focused on the wall Adrik had put in his mind. When he'd been mad, this wall had been impenetrable. I was counting on the fact that he was too busy to pay much attention to keeping it up. Gritting my teeth, I pushed carefully, easing it down and lowering it until I had full access to him again. My heart thumped hard as time ticked on, but I had to know, or I was going to go mad.

As soon as the wall was down, I was careful to keep my own emotions locked up tight so I didn't distract him, and almost gasped at the blood and violence before me. Angels were strewn all around, some of them on fire. Blood coated Adrik's hand as he wielded a sword, a thin burning sensation on his body told me he'd already been injured.

I hurriedly put my car in drive and shot off, tearing around corners. I was less concerned with running into police and more concerned with getting to Adrik on time. And Sol... where was Sol? It was disorienting driving and still seeing through Adrik's eyes, but somehow, I was able to stay on the road and not run into any other cars.

Another burst of anger, and I saw Sol through Adrik's eyes. A cry of alarm escaped my lips, and I tightened my hold on my emotions, so they didn't bleed over into Adrik's mind. Sol was lying there, broken, and bloody, he was pale and far too still. I could tell he was alive, but Adrik gave the impression of not holding out much hope for my friend. He wanted to call me to heal the old man, knowing how much I loved him and that I would do everything in my power to save him. But a part of him, old and powerful, refused to ask me to join a situation where my life would be in jeopardy. My safety came first to him always, second to nothing.

I wanted to be mad at him for making decisions like that for me. Sol was my family; he was important to me. If I wanted to risk my life for his, then it was my prerogative. But I knew that feeling deep inside him, that part that was abhorred by the very thought of seeing me in a place like that, surrounded by the enemy and likely to be taken from him or killed. I couldn't hate him for not being able to ignore an instinct as old as time to protect his mate.

Adrik turned around and snarled at the group of Demons who appeared. At least twelve of them stood there, scars and ink etched into their thick skin. Something about these guys looked wrong, but I couldn't understand why seeing them pissed Adrik off so much. They were just Demons. I could hear more screaming and crying where Adrik was, glass smashing and fire licking the sides of buildings.

"Care for some help, brother?" a voice called. I gasped in relief when Adrik turned, and Malik stood to his left.

"We weren't going to let you have all the fun," Harkyn added, appearing on his right.

"Where is Cali?" Adrik growled.

"Safe," Harkyn assured. Adrik wanted to ask how, where, but at that moment, the other Demons raced forwards, daggers and swords raised and a war-cry sounded.

"Let's lead them out of here, there is a human to protect," Adrik shouted.

"We'll follow your lead, brother," Malik agreed, his voice grim and expression murderous.

CHAPTER SIXTEEN
CALI

I leapt from my car and hurried to where the fight was. How no other humans had come running to this area was beyond me. There was so much noise, screaming, and fire, that at least the authorities should have arrived by now. I skidded to a halt when I saw the first body. Patty, one of the homeless women I'd known for the last few years, was lying in a bloody mess on the ground, her eyes frozen open and glazed with death. A sob escaped my throat, and my gaze followed the small trail of bodies behind her, each of them as dead as the last.

Angels did this? I'd always known I never wanted to be in their care, but to see the kind of pointless and malicious killing they were capable of made me wonder if Demons really were the evil ones.

Stumbling forward, I tried not to look at the faces of those I'd been healing for the last few years, tried not to remember what it sounded like to hear their voices or see them genuinely smile. They were gone, and I couldn't save them now. I gasped at the sound of wings and watched as several Angels swooped downward to where the main fight seemed to be taking place. I was terrified for Adrik, but I also knew he had his brothers to back him up. I needed to find Sol.

Centering myself, I tried to push past all the pain and death around me and find my friend. He was more than a friend to me, Sol was family. He had taken to me quickly, showed me the safest places to heal people, and those I could trust and those to be weary of. He'd told the other transients that they could trust me. He was like the grandfather I never got.

I felt him then, a block away, his life force flickering.

"No," I whispered brokenly, my eyes flying open. *No, not Sol.* I spun in his direction and ran toward him, desperate to save him. I dodged behind a burnt-out truck when three heavily muscled men came marching around a corner, their eyes glowing with fire, their bodies scarred with odd symbols. Demons. I barely bit back a gasp when I noted the human they were towing behind them, her hair gripped in one of their hands as they dragged her. She sobbed and tried desperately to get her feet under her.

Drawing magic from within myself, I took a moment to prepare, knowing I'd only get one shot at the surprise. The woman screamed as the Demon holding her let her go so that she hit the ground hard but stepped on her hand to prevent her from running.

"Let's just take her heart here," one of them said, his teeth sharp and voice guttural.

"I agree," said the second one. The last Demon nodded, choosing not to speak.

"Please, no!" she sobbed, tears streaking her dusky skin.

"Shut up," the first one snarled, yanking a wicked looking blade from his belt. Sucking in a steadying breath, I stepped out from behind the truck and threw my magic at them. Two of them flew backwards immediately, and the third turned to look at me in surprise. He barely opened his mouth to shout when he joined his friends. I used my magic and tied it to their life forces and pulled. My soul wept at the way I was using my power—to hurt, to kill—but I stayed strong, dragging the life out of them. Their energy was sent out into the universe.

I staggered forward, my knees shaking and threatening to give out, but I held on, needing all three gone or this was for nothing. I was still weak from all the work I'd done on Sky earlier, and then creating two amulets for healing and protection. This was not easy magic, and it was only to be done when absolutely necessary.

When the last one gave a wheezing breath, I let go and fell forward onto my knees, my hands bracing me so that I didn't faceplant.

"W-what... what are you?" the woman who had been about to die asked.

"Nothing. Just... run. Get far away from here before another Demon finds you," I muttered, wiping at my forehead with the back of my hand. Sweat coated my forehead and spots were flicking in and out of my vision.

"Let me help you up," the woman demanded, hurrying to my side.

"You have to leave," I tried again.

"I'll leave when I know you're not going to die for saving me," she argued, her hands gentle as they gripped my forearm. Her beautiful corkscrew curled chocolate brown hair had been pulled half out of the tie she'd had it in, and she took a moment to shove it out of her face.

"Thank you," I mumbled, making an effort to keep my legs locked beneath me this time. I swayed slightly and forced myself to steady.

"Come on, you're coming with me. I need to get you out of here," she warned.

"No," I mumbled and then stiffened. "No! I have to find Sol. He's hurt," I remembered, staggering away from her.

"You'll die," she warned.

"I won't leave him there." I fought her grip and kept jogging,

weaving slightly as I attempted to stay upright. My head kept
spinning and I felt my magic struggling to replenish itself.

"Shit," I heard the woman hiss before she jogged the short
distance to catch up to me. She took my arm and I started to
struggle.

"I'm not taking you away from here, I'm coming with you. Lead
the way to your friend," she assured when I kept fighting her.
Grateful that she was there, I nodded and kept walking.

"I'm Keira, by the way," she introduced as we kept an eye out for
any other unwanted visitors. The majority of the fight was several
blocks away, but the noise was loud and scary.

"Calixta," I returned tiredly.

"That's an odd name."

"My friends and those I save call me Cali," I offered. She smiled in
appreciation and nodded. I searched for Sol again, beginning to
panic when it was hard to find him.

"Left!" I shouted, reserve energy pouring into me from the need
to save my friend. Keira stayed close to me as we worked our
way down an alley. It was littered with the bloody and charred
remains of Angels, but I ignored them and searched for Sol.

"Are those..." Keira gasped, her face awash with amazement as
she saw the wings broken and bent in front of us.

"Angels, yes. But they're not what you've been led to believe," I
answered, jumping over an Angel with his throat torn out.

"Considering I was an Atheist up until twenty minutes ago, I
didn't think anything about them," she admitted in wonder. I
almost smiled.

"Sol?" I called out, feeling no one else down here. I was sure this
was the direction I'd felt his energy in. I looked around; it
certainly looked like the alley Adrik had been in. A small sound
caught my attention, and I snapped my head in that direction,

trying to discern his shape in the dimly lit alley.

"There!" I cried when I saw his foot sticking out from a small alcove. I wrenched from Keira's grasp and staggered towards him, my eyes already filling with tears at the flickering and fading life force he gave out.

"Sol," I whimpered as I fell to my knees beside him, taking his hand in mine. He blinked and frowned, a small trail of blood leaking from his mouth. His skin was pale, almost gray.

"Sunshine?" he whispered. The sound that escaped me was half laugh, half sob, and I inched closer to push back a lock of gray hair.

"I'm here. Just hold on, okay? I'm going to heal you," I whispered.

"It's too late, sweetheart," he murmured, and it was obvious how much talking hurt.

"Don't say stupid things, Sol. Now lay still, I'm going to work on you," I demanded sharply, and took a moment to think. "The amulet!" I cried, remembering that I'd thrown it around my neck on my way out. I tugged it free and hurried to slip it around Sol's neck, making sure the crystal rested on his chest.

"Let me help. What can I do?" Keira asked. Gratitude for her was fleeting, pushed aside by my desperation.

"Just hold his hand," I told her before I closed my eyes.

"*AP?*" I called, desperate.

"*Why are you so weak, Cali? Is it that Demon King? What is going on?*" my aunt demanded at once.

"*Please, I need you. My friend is dying, and I have expended too much energy today already. Help me?*" I pleaded.

"*Where is your Demon?*" she asked sternly, but I could tell she was hurrying to find somewhere safe and private.

"*Fighting. Angels came and they were trying to lure me out. They attacked my people and he's trying to save them,"* I answered, squeezing Sol's hand. I could feel the talisman working. It was taking energy from me, but only small amounts. It would help stabilize him, but it wouldn't save him. Nothing would unless I worked quickly.

"We're going to have a long chat soon about your responsibility to yourself," AP warned, but even as she spoke, I could see she was casting a circle to give herself protection in preparation to heal. Gratitude for my aunt warmed me, and I tried to hold back my tears at the thought of losing Sol.

"Ready?" she whispered, and I felt her hand grip mine, even from the other side of the world.

"Ready."

Drawing in a deep breath, I pressed both of my hands gently over Sol's stomach and chest and let my aunt's magic join mine and flow through me. Strength flooded me, filled every malnourished cell, every part of me crying out for energy. It boosted my own power and together, my aunt and I sent out healing energy to the man beneath my hands. My breath was uneven and shallow, and I had to concentrate twice as hard where to direct the magic. Power could be addictive, seductive, and I couldn't let myself get hooked on the feeling.

I focused on Sol and almost faltered in my work. His injuries were horrific. Several organs were ruptured and bleeding. His spleen was lacerated, causing him to bleed out faster. Several ribs were broken, others fractured. His right arm was ripped from its socket and dangled uselessly at his side. Sol's hips were cracked, and one knee shattered. He was a complete mess.

Anger at the Angels tried to invade, but I had to ignore the emotion. Healing was purity and light; I couldn't afford for darker emotions to creep in. I could feel the tears drying on my face as I ignored my own pain and weariness and channeled everything into Sol.

Time meant nothing when healing. I was outside my own body and repairing someone else's. It was a process difficult to describe unless you knew how to do it too.

"Angels did this?" AP asked, horrified as she helped me to mend broken bone, tissue, and torn muscle. We soothed scarring and tearing and put Sol back together again.

"They want me, and I refused to go to them," I admitted.

"Your Demon is really helping you?" I could hear AP's hesitancy. She had grown up like me, told that Demons were bad, Angels were good, but that a Witch didn't want to belong to either side. I felt her hope, and knew it was for me, that Adrik wasn't a charlatan and that what I felt for him and knew he felt for me was real.

"He will die protecting me, AP. And he knows these people matter to me." My aunt didn't respond to that, and I left it alone. She would learn to trust Adrik, or she wouldn't, but there would be no influencing her either way. She'd have to come to a decision on her own.

Something was trying to drag me back to my own body and away from healing. I frowned and tried to ignore it.

"Cali! Come back!" a woman begged, her voice panicked. I fell out of my trance and blinked several times to bring the situation back into focus. Keira sat on the other side of Sol, her wide eyes staring behind me. Slowly, I looked over my shoulder and found myself looking at three Angels.

"Well, well... we found the Witch," the one standing in the front of the group drawled smugly.

Shit.

"Come with me now, Witch, and we'll leave this place and all those who survive alone. Fight me, and I will make sure that man at your side is punished for it," the leader threatened. I wanted to throw my magic at him, but I knew I had little to spare.

"How could you do this? How could you hurt so many innocent people?" I asked instead.

"Humans are of no consequence to us. They act as a currency, and we are bored now. We want Witches to finally put the Demon filth back where they belong: in Hell," he explained, stepping forward. My gaze flicked to the other Angels who stepped with him, and my eyes lingered on Hariel. He'd helped me before; he'd insinuated he had a mate. His gaze found mine and he gave a slight shake of his head.

"How does that justify what you've done here tonight? These people didn't deserve any of this."

"Witch, I grow tired of your questions. Let us leave this place now, or the humans before you will suffer," the Angel snapped. His face was too symmetrical, and far too smooth to be mortal. All of them were devastatingly handsome, but where the Demons were more on the rugged side, the Angels were more CEO office types. Each side attractive, but the Angels definitely didn't blend in well with the human population.

I got slowly and unsteadily to my feet, trying to keep Sol and Keira protected behind me. AP was still there, still lending me her strength even though it would wane soon. I didn't want to drain her so much because she would be left alone and shaken, too far away with no one to care for her as her energy slowly returned. I also knew she wouldn't leave me here alone to face off against three Angels.

I summoned magic and let it grow inside me, preparing to defend myself and the two humans behind me.

"Stupid Witch. I don't need to refrain from hurting you when I capture you. If you insist on doing this the hard way, I *will* hurt you," the Angel snarled, inching forward, his hand going to his blade.

"Cali, where are you? What are you doing?" Adrik's voice filtered through my mind, and I felt relief at hearing his voice, at knowing he was still alive.

"Oh, you know... shopping," I lied, knowing he'd try to protect me, but I didn't want to risk his life again,

"Cali, whatever you're doing... stop it. I can feel your magic, you haven't properly warded yourself!" he ordered.

Shock shot through me, followed by anger and annoyance at myself. I hadn't ever made a mistake like that, not even when I'd been a child. No wonder the Angels had found us.

"What do you choose, Witch? If you make me fight you, I will kill the two behind you to remind you of what happens when you disobey an order," the lead Angel asked, his expression so pompous and superior I had the urge to drag my nails across his too-perfect face.

"Cali, I cannot protect you; I am pinned down. Whatever you are doing, stop, and get to safety," Adrik growled, and I caught the way speaking to me caused a set of claws to rake down his chest. I winced at the momentary flash of pain I felt and glowered at the Angels, lifting my chin in defiance.

"Go fuck yourself," I spat, clinging to my courage and my anger. Then several things happened at once.

"Cali!" Adrik shouted, his fear and denial ringing clear as day in my head.

"No!" Sol shouted behind me, his words coupled with Keira's gasp.

The lead Angel threw something, and I noticed too late that it was a blade. It would have hit me square in the stomach, a pain that would have dropped me...

If it hadn't been for Hariel.

I had barely raised my hands to defend myself when Hariel was there, knocking the blade to the side, his back to me. He faced off against his leader and a deadly silence followed. Thunder boomed ominously overhead, and I found myself holding my breath.

"Hariel... what are you doing?" the lead Angel asked, his tone low and deadly.

"You cannot hurt the Witch. She is right, Turien, we have allowed our actions to stoop to depths our enemies would take. We don't hurt humans; it is not the way. And yet for centuries we have allowed our standards to lower so much that we are hardly better than those we have vowed to defeat," Hariel explained.

"You stand against me?" Turien questioned.

"I do not want to stand against my brothers, but we have turned our backs on our true purpose over the centuries, and we have gone too far. We are better than this," Hariel urged, stepping forward to emphasize his point.

"The Witch is coming with us, Hariel. If you stand in my way to acquire her, you will be a traitor to the Garrison, and the punishment is death," Turien ground out in a hiss, his arctic eyes deadly.

"Turien—"

"Step aside. That is an order," Turien interrupted, stepping forward and drawing his sword, the scraping sound of metal sending a shiver down my spine.

"Do not do this," Hariel whispered, the plea in his voice so filled with pain and regret.

"One last chance. Choose your path, but be prepared for the consequences," Turien warned in a low growl.

A pause, a shivering moment of contemplation where my fate and the fate of the two behind me was tossed into the air, the decision of one Angel deciding the outcome.

"I am sorry," Hariel whispered. I closed my eyes, fear clawing at me, and I prepared to strike out, refusing to go down without a fight. But instead of stepping aside, Hariel drew his sword and straightened in front of me.

"Traitor!" Turien roared before he lunged forward. The sounds of blade clashing against blade was loud, and I stumbled back, my heart pounding hard and my mouth dry.

"Calixta!" Adrik roared in my head.

"I'm with Sol. Hurry! Hariel needs our help," I cried, pushing Keira down beside Sol to help protect her.

"You need to run, Sunshine. They're gonna keep comin' for you," Sol urged.

"They'll kill you to punish me. No," I shot back with a hiss. Sol took a moment to study me, and he swore under his breath. He wasn't fully healed yet, but he was healed enough to move if he had to. At least he was in no immediate danger of dying.

Hariel shouted in pain as a blade slashed at his side, and I felt more than heard the feminine gasp of pain that accompanied it. I glanced at Hariel and remembered he had a Witch with him. She'd been in his mind last time, watching them, I was sure of it now even if I hadn't been the last time we'd met.

He had a mate.

I threw magic at Turien when he moved in to impale Hariel on his blade, and the Angel hit the wall with a loud crack. Hariel spared me a grateful smile and fought the other Angel, taking him down easily. There was a rush of wind and when I turned to look, Adrik stood in the alley way, his sharp eyes taking in the situation in a second.

His gaze strayed to mine, and he looked furious, but I could deal with that later. We needed to protect Hariel.

"Cali," Adrik growled.

"Help Hariel. He is protecting me… he has a mate," I explained. Adrik hesitated a moment, and I knew he was considering how this changed things. *"Adrik,"* I pleaded.

Snarling, Adrik joined the fray, slashing out at Turien as he regained his footing. More movement caught my eye, and I gritted my teeth at the sight of three scarred Demons. Why were they here but not helping their Kings?

"They are Rogues, they live outside the rule of my brothers and I. Stay away from them," Adrik warned. No problem. As long as they stayed away from me and mine, I had no reason to confront them. Where were the other brothers? Why weren't they here yet?

The Angels have something on their blades that mutes our mind-link with one another, but it does not seem to work between mates. Malik and Harkyn have been cut and cannot reach out. I left them to fight the other Angels, I needed to come to you. Adrik's voice was sharp and to the point, but even as he spoke, I could tell something was wrong. He was weaker somehow and getting weaker as the minutes wore on. Was that from the Angel Blades, or that extra something on them he'd mentioned?

Hariel attacked the Demons, his blade glinting in the pale moonlight, his face a mask of fury and disgust. He was one of Heaven's warriors, and it showed as he fought the beings he was meant to kill. Adrik had taken over fighting Turien. The new Angels began teaming up against Hariel, and they got closer and closer to us. I had to help; he wouldn't survive with five against one.

"Cali, no," Sol cautioned, grabbing my hand.

"Stay down," I said quickly before getting to my feet. Keira was still sitting beside Sol, her gaze locked on the bloody and brutal battle before us.

I shot more magic out, hitting my targets every time, sending the other two Angels backwards so that they hit the building beside us. Adrik delivered a particularly brutal punch to Turien's throat and then turned to the three demons and raised a hand. I watched as he slowly closed it into a fist and the Demon's halted their advances. They choked and stumbled, gripping at their necks as if an invisible force were trying to strangle them. I touched on Adrik and pulled back immediately, when I realized he was draining them of their life and using it to boost himself. As distasteful as I found the act to be, I couldn't bring myself to care, as long as Adrik got the energy he needed to stay alive. Hariel was up again, striking at the two Angel's I'd sent flying as the Demons fell lifelessly to the ground. Adrik turned back to Turien and missed being stabbed with an Angel Blade by a hairs breadth.

I was torn between both fights, my soul screaming at me to do whatever it took to protect Adrik. But my core, my Witch-side, urged me to save Hariel, to help him as he had helped me.

"Don't interfere," Adrik snarled.

"Cali—" Keira called when I got up and ran towards Hariel. I shot a blast at Turien as I went past, causing him to stumble and take another slice from Adrik's blade. I knew the Angel would die without a Witch healing him, so I continued on. Hariel dodged a strike, and I sent magic flying at one Angel's face, momentarily blinding him. My own power was waning, but I couldn't think about it, if I did, someone would die.

"Calixta!" Adrik shouted again. He was going to be so mad when we came out the other side of this, but I was willing to risk his

wrath and silent treatment again if it meant saving those who needed help. Adrik and I had a lot to sort out, but one thing he would need to accept is that I would *always* help those who needed it, regardless of the risk to myself. It was me at my core, and it would not change.

Hariel kicked out at the Angel he had been fighting, and sent his blade slicing through his neck, his head toppling to the ground. I ignored the gory sight and watched as Hariel spun in one smooth motion and struck out at the blinded Angel, running him through with his blade. I quickly shrank back from the momentary pain the now dead Angel had felt, ignoring the way my stomach rolled in protest. I felt Hariel's emotional pain and despair at killing one of his own, but my sympathy was quickly replaced with panic when another Angel materialized behind him.

"Hariel!" I cried out in warning, running for him, but I was too late.

Hariel turned in time for the Angel to run him through with a blade, but it wasn't one of theirs. It took me only a moment to recognize the weapon as a Demon Blade, guaranteed to kill Hariel unless I was able to heal him. As focused on Hariel's as I was, I felt his mate's scream of agony and I continued to rush forward, scooping up a sword as I ran, raising it above my head. The new Angel yanked his sword free of Hariel's body and let him collapse backwards onto the ground.

Another Angel appeared at my side, and I changed course, screaming in a wordless rage and grief and closed my eyes as I struck out at her. The new Angel barely had time to widen her eyes in surprise as I aimed the silver blade at her neck. My stomach heaved as I felt it slide clean through it, and I watched with horror as the Angel's body fell to the ground, her head rolling away from the rest of her.

I'd just killed an Angel.

Shock at my actions was shoved aside when the echoing of the Witch's grief hit me. I dropped the sword and then gasped as pain lanced through me. I glanced down to see a dagger sticking out of my stomach. It took my mind several precious moments to process this, and my breath was yanked from my lungs once again when the Angel who had stabbed Hariel yanked the Dagger out of me and struck again.

"We can heal you back in Heaven," he ground out, his breath hitting my face.

"Calixta!" Adrik roared, and I glanced up, my hazy gaze coming to focus on him some distance behind the Angel. His panicked gaze was on me, too distracted to prevent the punch he took to his face or the blade that tore up the side of his arm and shoulder. Two more Angels appeared, converging on Adrik. Fire wrapped around my mate and the Angels, and they shrieked in pain, but more Angels descended, Demons hot on their tail. Despite my injuries, Adrik's fear for me was overwhelming and I worried at the decrease in his power, in his strength.

I had just been stabbed… twice. But my mind was only considering the danger my mate was in.

The Angel before me gripped my wrist hard and I was pulled back to my current situation.

A feminine, wordless cry sounded, and my attention was drawn to Keira as she rushed us, a broken pipe in her hand. She brought it crashing down on the Angel's head, and he stumbled back, more out of shock than pain, I was sure. His face contorted into an expression of anger, and he lifted his hands to grab Keira.

"No!" I cried and reached the Angel first, my hands wrapping around his forearm as I focused my magic on him. It wasn't me who directed the magic this time, it was my AP, and it turned his blood to acid.

An inhumane scream filled the air and he staggered back, falling onto the ground in a painful heap. My knees gave out and I slumped to the ground as I watched Sol stagger over with a discarded sword. With a shaky but powerful strike, he took the Angel's head and his screaming stopped. Sol almost fell over as the blade came free, but my worry for my friend was pushed back when Hariel wheezed, and I felt his mate's pain as if it were my own.

"I'm coming," I groaned, dragging myself over to him when my legs decided they no longer wanted to hold my weight.

"Cali," Sol called, limping to me.

"I need to get to the Angel," I cried, gritting my teeth against the pain in my abdomen. I refused to look at the mess, refused to pay the wetness on my stomach any attention. The Witch bound to Hariel was in pain, her terror at losing her mate was all-consuming and I was feeling it through him. I used their need as a barrier between me and the pain I was in.

"Hariel," I whispered as I reached his side. Hariel swallowed convulsively, struggling to breathe.

"Are you... okay?" he choked, his body beginning to shake.

"I'll be fine," I lied, astonished that his first question was about my safety.

"Good," he shivered, his breathing choked and labored.

"You saved me," I whispered, brushing his hair back from his face.

"You're a W-Witch... you should be... protected," he forced out, groaning painfully.

"I can feel your mate. She is with you, you have to hold on until she gets here," I told him, pressing my hands over his wound. Blood gushed and I bit back my need to gag as the metallic taste of blood hit me.

"Sh-she can't," he groaned. "L-locked in Heaven. Prisoner."

"Adrik! I need Mika," I called desperately.

"You are hurt," Adrik said instead, his tone bordering on animalistic.

"Hariel needs her. Now!" I sobbed.

"Tend to your own wounds, mate. I will not lose you," Adrik warned, his tone one of absolute resolve. I could see him still fighting, more Rogues and Angels flooding the alley from the only opening.

"Shh, it's okay. I am going to heal you," I whispered brokenly to the fallen Angel, closing my eyes, and reaching for my aunt again. She was weak but stayed connected.

"I need you, AP," I begged.

"I am not strong enough, Cali. I am so sorry, sweetheart. I would rather you save yourself than the Angel," she advised, her voice weak.

"Someone, help!" I cried, tears blurring my vision. I could feel his mate's pain as if it were my own, her heart breaking and fear of losing him suffocating me. My hands shook and my body throbbed and screamed in pain, but I had to work, I had to finish this.

"Y-you can't…" Hariel trailed off, gasping for breath.

I closed my eyes and tried to focus on healing him, but my magic would not surface. It was as if there was nothing left to conjure, nothing left to draw from.

I was empty.

"Please, stay," I begged. Through his mind, I could see his mate in a dank cell, her ankle chained to a wall, her dark hair falling around her face and her tears wrenched from somewhere deep inside her.

"I am so sorry," I whispered to her. Her cry of denial ripped at me

in a way that was more painful than the two Angel Blade wounds I'd suffered. I was dying, I knew I was, and yet this woman's pain at losing her mate had my complete focus.

"Please," she begged. I closed my eyes, gritted my teeth, and tried again, summoning magic from deep within, yanking on it, pulling harder and harder, hoping *something* would come of it.

But nothing.

Her sobs increased when she felt my hopelessness and I looked down at Hariel. Sol was at my side, pressing something into my abdomen and trying to say something to me, but I couldn't hear. Keira was at my other side, her hands on my shoulders as she tried to make me lie down.

"I am so sorry," I whispered to Hariel.

"You are my world, Shaye, and I am better for having known you," he whispered to his mate.

"No, wait! Come back to me. Stay with me," she pleaded.

There was a heavy, deafening boom of thunder I knew only too well. Air hit me hard, tossing my hair over my shoulder. I looked up as Zarak stood before me, his massive black wings tucking behind him. He was littered with cuts and burns—proof that he had been in this battle—and his black eyes searched me.

"Stay back!" Sol shouted as he scrambled unsteadily to his feet and grabbed the sword he'd discarded, pointing it at Zarak.

"Leave us alone!" Keira shouted, brandishing her rusted pipe again. I didn't get a chance to tell her to stop before she brought the pipe crashing down on his shoulder. The metal rod bent with the force of the impact, and she cried out, releasing the weapon as shock waves vibrated up her arms. Zarak frowned down at her as if he hadn't even felt the strike. Keira launched herself at him, kicking and punching, doing her best to injure him. Zarak shackled her wrists with no problems and set her aside, frowning at her with curiosity and confusion.

"Let her go!" Sol cried, limping towards Zarak with a sword. I wasn't worried my friend would hurt the Nephilim, I was worried Zarak's counterattack would kill Sol.

"Sol, no!" I warned, and was grateful when he stopped and looked to me with confusion.

"Amazarak... help me," I sobbed.

"You are injured, Calixta. You are human, you need healing immediately," Zarak informed me, setting Keira aside when she stopped struggling and moved closer to me, ignoring the two at my side threatening him harm.

"Hariel is dying. Please, you have to help me," I pleaded, my physical pain and guilt mixed with the grief of the other Witch was drowning me.

Seeing that we were friendly, Sol and Keira came back to my side. Sol pressed his hand once again to my abdomen, but I couldn't feel it. I was going numb. I knew that wasn't a good sign, but I didn't care right now.

"Where is your mate?" Zarak asked with a frown as he looked over Hariel and then behind us. I turned too, seeing a staggering number of Rogues and Angels crowding them, preventing them from getting to me. I would have wondered why they didn't shadow themselves out, but I had to assume it had something to do with whatever was preventing them from reaching their brothers and calling for aid. I caught a small glimpse of Malik and Harkyn were there too, evening the odds a little more.

"Zarak," I pleaded, needing him to tell me he could do something.

"Cali... he cannot. You must... free her. Find a... way. Save my mate," Hariel begged, his eyes beginning to close.

"I will, I promise," I said immediately, praying to the universe that I would survive to do as I'd sworn to do.

"You will be free one day, sweet Shaye. I will wait for you on the other side. This is not goodbye for us," he whispered to his mate.

"She will not need to free me, mate. I will end my existence to be with you long before then," Shaye promised.

"Do not give up hope, my love. There is more to live for than me, and you have never gotten to experience any of it. Be strong, for me," Hariel whispered, his voice getting softer.

"Please hold on, Hariel," I begged.

Zarak knelt beside the fallen Angel and frowned. "I have never liked your kind," he muttered.

"Nor I, yours," Hariel whispered with a twisted smile. "Protect the Witch...please," he added so softly it was almost inaudible, his eyes falling closed.

"I will be with you, always, Shaye," Hariel whispered to his mate, and I felt him slip from her mind. Her cry of denial was so strong, I was sure everyone could hear it.

Zarak made a grumbling, growling sound in his chest and closed his eyes before pressing his palm to Hariel's chest.

"Can you save him?" I whispered.

"No. But I can do something else," he answered as if even voicing the option went against his better judgment. I waited and watched, pain beating at me from deep inside, my eyesight getting blurry, my skin cold.

I had to blink several times as a bright tear seemed to appear in the air beside us. The tear widened more and more, and I gasped. Hariel gave a last, rattling breath and Zarak fisted his hand on Hariel's chest and pulled. I staggered backwards when an almost transparent Hariel was lifted from his body.

"Y-you're..." I breathed.

"I have Hariel's soul. I can keep it safe here in this dimension where he can wait to be reconciled with his mate," Zarak answered, gritting his teeth as if the effort to open the dimension took a great amount of power.

"Hariel?" I whispered. Transparent Hariel smiled down at me. "Save my mate, Cali. And then we are even," he reminded, his voice a little echoey. I nodded, watching with a slack jaw as he stepped into the doorway. There was a bright flash before the doorway closed and Zarak opened his black eyes to look at me.

"He's safe?" I whispered.

"Yes."

"You just created a whole other dimension," I mumbled, dizzy.

"Yes. You need to heal," he pointed out, frowning at me.

"No more magic," I explained with a small sigh as sitting upright became too much for me. Zarak hurried to my side, catching me before I fell, his gaze turned furious.

"What?" he ground out.

"All my magic is… gone," I managed to answer, my voice slurring, and my eyes too heavy to keep open.

"Demon King!" Zarak roared, his voice booming in the small alley.

CHAPTER SEVENTEEN
ADRIK

Fear for Cali was making me careless.

I was striking faster, harder, not caring if I took a head or a hand, I just wanted these fuckers gone so I could get to my mate. I could feel her injuries, her pain, and so I knew she was badly hurt. She seemed to be holding the pain at bay though, her mind completely focused on the dying Angel at her feet and his mate who was screaming so loud I could feel her despair as if it were my own. My throat tried to close at the very real chance of losing Cali the same way. Another slice of a blade, the pain instant and rushing towards my marrow and cells. My ability to summon hellfire was waning, and that knowledge gave me pause. Hellfire was as natural as breathing to us, and now it was taking far too much energy to summon. What was going on? Was this the Angel's doing? My movements were becoming slower, so maybe the weakening of my abilities had something to do with the twelve or more Angel Blade wounds. None of them were a deep stab like Cali's, but there were enough of them that they were starting to affect me.

"I need to get to Cali!" I shouted, feeling her despair.

"We're trying. The first chance you get, you go! Tamas is on his way!" Malik shouted back, barely ducking a blow that would have taken his head from his shoulders. My brothers were suffering the same as I was, our strength waning, our hellfire dimming. All of us were alarmed at this, but we had no time to dissect why it was happening or how the Angels had found a way to weaken us so completely. We were too overwhelmed with the sheer number of Angels and Rogues before us, unprepared for the war and unable to call for reinforcements.

Tamas and Cassius had joined the fight, but they were overrun several blocks away, helping to defend the humans there. Several groups of our Demons were amongst the fray as well.

Thankfully, Tamas had thought to summon two of his Knights and their subjects to the fight before they too were injured and made incapable of telepathic speech. We needed to get a hold of whatever they were using to find a way to counteract it, but I added it to our ever-growing "to do" list.

My attention was pulled back to the fight when the edge of a blade narrowly missed my neck. The Angels and Rogues had unleashed an all-out war in their desperation to get to Cali, heedless of the carnage they'd leave in their wake and uncaring of the witnesses left behind. This disregard for everything they usually stood for was disconcerting, but it was something I'd think about later.

When the Angels began charging at us anew, the three of us summoned hellfire, the power it took from me was more than worrying now, and we created a wall between us and the Angels. Desperate, and while the fluffy fuckers were distracted, I latched onto the life forces of two Rogues, sucking them dry and using their energy to boost my own.

A deafening boom rattled the windows and shook the walls around us, and I didn't need to turn around to know who it was.

"Nephilim!" Harkyn shouted, worried.

"That's Amazarak; he's on our side," I shouted back, hoping I was right.

"Fuck, he's a big bastard," Malik called back. I refrained from replying as the Angels redoubled their efforts. How the fuck were we meant to get out of this?

Cali's injury throbbed harder, and I felt her slip a little bit. I stumbled, my eyes widening and breath catching.

No!

"I need to go!" I roared, panicking.

"Demon King!" Amazarak boomed, his voice loud enough to rattle some windows.

"Go!" Harkyn shouted as he and Malik simultaneously blew more hellfire towards the Angels before us, creating an opening for me that lasted a few seconds and allowed for me to run out of there. I reached for my brothers in my mind again, desperate now and felt an inkling of hope when the paths seemed to reforge, clear of the fog that had previously clouded the pathways. Hoping I was not sentencing my brothers to their deaths, I spun and raced for Cali, feeling her get weaker and weaker.

As I ran for my mate, my gaze caught on the droplets of blood leading from the place Cali was stabbed to where she now lay. I hesitated a moment, drawing in a deep breath, tasting the scent of her there. It was her blood, all of it.

The second shall follow her blood trail.

That familiar burning scorched my chest again, and my need to bind Cali became almost unbearable. My palm itched and ached, feeling suddenly heavy and painful, and it felt as though my soul was roaring at me, aching so much to be bound to the one it yearned for. An almighty, collective roar behind me drew my attention for a moment, and I looked over my shoulder to see Cassius and Tamas rounding a corner to box in the Angels and Demons that had been attacking Malik and Harkyn for so long, splitting their attention in two directions, forcing them to separate into two groups. The knots in my stomach loosened slightly knowing that the four of my brothers, injured or not, could handle that crowd together.

I turned my attention back to my mate, gritting my teeth as I got closer to where Cali lay with her head propped up on the bent knees of the Nephilim, her form pale and unmoving.

"Cole!" I shouted for my brother, panic overshadowing everything else as I skidded to a stop beside Cali, her strawberry red hair mussed up, her skin pale, almost translucent.

"Cali, wake up, baby. Show me those beautiful eyes," I whispered as I scooped her into my arms. I glanced down at her body and was glad I was already on the ground. The sight of all that blood coming from her would have sent me to my knees otherwise.

"No more magic," she mumbled, struggling to lift her lashes.

"Cole, I need Mika, now!"

I felt him look through my eyes and assess the situation, he knew what was going on, what we were facing.

"Bring Cali to us. I am sorry brother, but I will not risk my mate in that place, I know you understand," Cole answered, and I could hear the regret in his voice, but also his resolve. As much as I hated him for saying it, I couldn't fault his reasons.

"You need to get your mate somewhere else and find someone who can heal her," Zarak told me.

"No shit," I snapped. He raised one black eyebrow but didn't respond to my snark.

"I will stay here and deal with these Angels and Demons. Tell your brothers to take these humans somewhere they will not be harmed," he continued, as calm as ever.

"Cali would kill me if you died," I growled.

"She won't be alive much longer if you do nothing. Go. I can handle this lot, and I have friends on their way," he assured. The words had no sooner left his mouth than there were two giant claps of thunder. I glanced up to see two massive, winged creatures on the buildings above us, their forms a little intimidating.

"Malik, Harkyn! Come here to me and bring these humans to the Arrival Room. Cali needs healing and Cole will not bring Mika here. The Nephilim will take care of this lot," I ordered, standing with Cali in my arms. I winced and gritted my teeth against the pain throbbing throughout my body. I didn't care, Cali needed healing first.

"Are you ready?" I asked Zarak.

"When you are," he answered, also getting to his feet.

"What's going on?" the woman beside me asked.

"My brothers are going to come to you. They will bring you to where I am taking Cali. You both need healing, and Cali would rip me to shreds if I left you here to get hurt. Stay here, do not fight my brothers when they come for you, they will only have seconds," I warned.

The woman's eyes widened, and she looked at the Nephilim and then to Sol.

"I wasn't even meant to be here," she whispered.

"But you are. Wait here, do not fight my brothers," I ordered again, not wanting to stay any longer.

"Now, brothers," I called and then wrapped myself in shadow. I didn't wait to see if they grabbed the humans, I didn't wait to see if Zarak was overrun. My concern now was all for my mate.

I arrived in the Arrival Room and was striding towards Cole and Mika's realm when they called my name. I turned my head to see them down the hall, rushing towards me. Mika paused half-way, her hand going to her stomach where she gasped painfully.

"Help me," I begged, my voice a rasp of sound.

"To your realm, now," Mika said right away, her eyes wide and face pale. She'd be feeling Cali's pain and mine. It was still a struggle for Mika to learn to keep her barriers up at all times to prevent her feeling the pain of others.

There was the unmistakable sound of two more arrivals, and I flicked a glance behind me to see Malik and Harkyn. Both were bleeding and covered in Angel blood, dirt, and ash.

"Oh shit," the woman gasped and staggered away from Malik. She dropped down to all four and Malik pushed her head down to help steady her.

"Don't touch me, boy. I'd rather be skewered than do that again," Sol snapped at Harkyn, looking pale and unsteady on his feet.

"This way," Mika called, waiting by my door.

I didn't hesitate and moved as quickly as I could to my door, too aware of how far Cali was slipping.

"Cali?" Sol whispered, his words filled with pain and hope.

"Wait for me," the woman panted, and I heard them get to their feet and follow behind us.

"Cali, baby, stay with me," I whispered.

"Where else would I go?" Her voice was drowsy and slow.

"You are trying to slip away from me, little red. I thought we had an agreement to try out this whole relationship thing?" I added, keeping my tone light as I gently laid her out on the bed.

"Is she going to be okay?" Sol demanded as he followed us.

"What in the world..." the woman gasped, and I caught the way she looked around in wonder before her eyes fell back to Cali and all her focus stayed there.

Cali groaned and Mika rushed over. "How many times was she hurt?"

"Stabbed twice," I forced out, swallowing hard. "But she had already drained a good deal of her energy today."

Cole's hand gripped my shoulder, and he squeezed tightly as I watched on helplessly. She had already been so weak from healing, then she had made it worse by using her magic when she was already low by healing Sol again. Being stabbed with an Angel blade on top of it all?

I closed my eyes and dragged in a breath. I would never forgive myself for not getting to her sooner, for not forcing my will upon her and sending her away from that place. I'd been overrun, and they purposely kept me away from her. They stopped me from going to her when I could have protected her, left us outnumbered, poisoned us, weakened us.

Fuck!

"I do not like it when you're in distress," Cali mumbled with a tired sigh.

"Stop fading away on me and I won't be in distress," I returned sharply, pulling away from Cole to slide up onto the bed next to her, taking her hand in mine. Sol and Keira shuffled closer, and I could feel Sol's heart break from here. He was in pain too, still injured beyond what his frail body should have to handle, and yet here he stood beside Cali, his entire focus on her. I closed my mind off to him, not wanting to feel anyone else's pain. I could only focus on Cali right now.

"Did I ever tell you that the first time I saw you, I thought you were the sexiest man I had ever seen?" she recalled with a smile, letting me into her memories enough to feel how she felt. I closed my eyes and pressed her hand to my lips.

"I was so shocked to discover that you were mine, little red, but so fucking happy because you are hands down the only woman for me. You are sexy, funny, and can stand on your own two feet. You challenge me and you make me laugh," I told her, hoping to keep her talking.

"You're so powerful, Adrik. You make me laugh, your body is sinful, and you can pull off being sexily broody. I love the way your eyes change

when you get mad at me or are thinking those sinful thoughts," she continued, her voice trailing off.

"Cali, come on baby, stay with me," I urged, feeling as though she was trying to say goodbye.

"Hurry, Mika, please," I begged, wondering if my will to keep her alive would be enough.

"I'm trying, Adrik. But..." She trailed off, her dark green eyes raising to meet mine as she bit her lower lip. I shook my head, slowly at first, and then vigorously.

"No, no, you have to heal her."

"She's too damaged, Adrik. Her magic is gone, she's entirely tapped out. I'm sorry, but there's not a lot else I can do," she whispered, tears filling her eyes.

Silence fell, and I wrestled with the anger I felt, the guilt and the agony. No... no, this wasn't how it was meant to go.

"Not my girl," Sol whispered brokenly. I slowly opened my eyes to look at him and watched his pale, aged face crumble in pain. Cali was like a granddaughter to him; he'd been looking out for her since the day they'd met.

Keira was new, but she looked small and fragile standing there, her eyes wide and filled with sadness. I had no idea where she came from or what her connection to Cali was, but her regret was genuine.

Cali slipped a little further from me and I drew in a sharp breath, trying to hold her closer as if that would prevent her from dying.

"Bind her," Cole ordered, his voice low and deep.

"What?"

"Bind her soul to yours, finish the bond. Once her soul is tied to yours, she should come back."

"You know that for sure?" I asked, my mind in a state of shock. My panic at Mika's words, my fear of losing her when I'd just got her back was making it hard for me to see a way to save the woman I loved.

I couldn't lose Cali.

"The book said that by binding your souls, the Witch is basically immortal. She can die, but she will come back. It happened for Mika."

I glanced down at Cali, and the stupid thought that I wanted her to make this decision butted into my head. Fuck off, no. She was dying, and I wasn't going to let it happen. I nodded and scrubbed at my face.

"Okay," I whispered and turned more fully to face Cali.

"She might be gone for a while, Adrik. I was down for almost a week, so don't lose hope," Mika warned quickly, her lashes wet with unshed tears.

"And you'll feel it... when she goes. But she will come back," Cole warned, and I could tell by the glittering pain in his eyes that I was going to be in for my own personal Hell.

Sucking in a breath, I nodded and looked back to my mate.

"Baby... I'm going to do something else that is probably going to piss you off right now, but I don't give a flying fuck. You're going to die if I don't, and I refuse to lose you. Do you understand?" I whispered, brushing her hair back and feeling that old familiar urge build and burn within me. It no longer whispered to me to Mark her, it was bellowing, demanding it so hard my palm hurt.

"I love you," she whispered softly, her life force barely a flicker. It was now or never.

"I love you too, red. Come back to me," I pleaded and pressed a kiss to her forehead. At the same time, I gripped her wrist and encircled it with my fingers and let instinct take over. Power flooded me, an overwhelming force that stole my breath and made me grit my teeth. I pressed my forehead against Cali's as white-hot pain in

my palm seared my hand. There were those thin strands again, weaving us tightly together, their power never ending and strength unbreakable.

She gasped, even in her semi-unconscious state, and I kept my palm pressed to her wrist, merging my mind with hers to hold her close. In her mind, I kissed her and wrapped her tightly in my arms. She kissed me back, softly, her consciousness flickering in and out.

"I will wait for you, Cali. Just come back to me," I whispered to her, wishing with all my might that I could use my own will and power to keep her here, to not risk losing her. Panic was trying to well up, so harsh it overwhelmed my physical pain. I had my own injuries that needed tending, but at this point, the fear that I was too late to bind us and save her outdid everything and anything else.

"Adrik?" Cali whispered, her bright eyes raising to look at me, confused and in pain. I cupped her cheek, hating the fear I saw there. Then, all at once, her eyelids fluttered closed, and I felt her disappear. Without warning, I was thrown back into my own body, the bonds that tied us together suddenly unraveling before they faded completely.

"No." Sol's soft word of denial was broken and filled with pain. A dark, volatile rage welled up inside me at feeling her slip away and fade into nothing. A vast cavern of emptiness cracked open inside of me, the feeling of her no longer there a torment I could not have predicted. Gritting my teeth, I couldn't restrain the roar of despair that ripped from my core, and I buried my face against her neck. Pain and emptiness. That was all that was left to me. She was gone.

~

The first day after Cali stopped breathing, I did not move from her side. I laid there beside her with my eyes closed, clutching her hand in mine, and willing her back with all my might. We may not have known each other very long, and our bonds might have still been new, but their absence in my mind, my heart—my very being—were like a crater inside me. Mika had healed me as I lay there, whispering words of comfort, but I couldn't remember exactly what she said even when I tried. She'd gone on to heal Sol and Keira. Malik and Harkyn had gone back to the battlefield to help Tamas and Cassius, but the Nephilim's had done most of the work already. Zarak said something about helping to clean up the mess and come up with a cover story for the humans, something about rival gangs tearing through downtown. When my brothers had come back from the small war on the surface, Mika had healed them too.

I hadn't moved an inch in that time.

Sol stayed by Cali's side, seated in a chair, and watching her as if she'd disappear if he blinked or looked away. He asked my brothers what was happening, what the binding meant, and they'd given him the cliff notes version. I hadn't expected Keira to stay, but she insisted on waiting to make sure Cali came back. I didn't care.

By day two, they tried to get me up, but I wasn't interested in moving. Cole tried to explain that it took several days to feel her start to come back and then another day or two before she actually was back. Mika offered her comfort, but I didn't want her anywhere near us, not right now.

By day three, I was tired of the humans in my realm and insisted on taking them back. Sol fought me on it, but I won in the end with a promise to tell him if anything changed. It was hard to hold out hope and listen to Cole and Mika's request for me to have such a thing when there was this pit inside me now, this yawning cavern of emptiness that screamed at me she was never coming back. To my very core, I felt her absence and couldn't convince myself that I'd get so lucky as to have her alive and in my arms again.

We'd been too late.

I left the binding too late. I had tried to do the right thing and give her time, give her a choice. I should have done what Malik said. I should have bound her to me right away, to hell with the consequences, and get the crap out of the way immediately. We could be safe and happy right now, bound and over all the drama of the bonding process and who had what rights.

But I'd screwed up.

I felt our soul's bond right at the end, but it was obviously too late.

While I dropped Sol and Keira back to the surface, I visited the scene of the massacre and found all evidence of it cleaned up.

By day four, I was angry as all Hell and out for blood. I spent two full days ripping apart any Angel I found and decimating entire groups of Rogue Demons. There was no pity or mercy in me for any of those I found, only death and pain.

Zarak made himself known to me, but one look at my face told him all he needed to know. He expressed his condolences, but I didn't give a shit how he felt or what he wanted to say to me.

Cali was gone, it was all my fault, and I wanted to kill things. I was tempted to hurt him, to fight him and either take him down, or provoke him to the point where he succeeded in killing me. Surely the oblivion of death would be better than this endless, solitary torture. I was a King of Hell… pain was my weapon of choice; it was my job to dole it out and use it to its extremes. No pain I had ever inflicted on another being came even close to the agony I was in every second of every seemingly endless day. By day six, my brothers had begun following me around. I guess they were trying to make sure I didn't try and kill myself or get myself into a situation I couldn't get out of. I didn't care since they never interfered or spoke to me while I sought a way to vent my rage and pain.

Cali should have been back by now.

If what Cole and Mika said was true, then she should have been showing signs of coming back by now. But still, there was nothing. It only went to prove to me that I had fucked up beyond repair and waited too long to bind her to me.

"Adrik."

I turned slowly on the spot to see Corvin and Devlin standing there. Great. No one else had been able to get through to me, so they sent these two. I was amazed they'd gotten Corvin out of his realm.

"What do you want?"

"Come back home. You are drawing too much attention to yourself in your current state, and you need to come back," Devlin explained, his tone as reasonable as ever.

"I have nothing to go back for," I returned in a hiss.

"You are a King of Hell; you have responsibilities," Devlin refuted.

"Fuck it. I'm done being a King," I snapped, turning my back on them. I heard them move and I'd taken no more than a single step before they were in front of me.

"You don't get a say in the matter. We have been managing things for you, but you need to come back now," Devlin continued, his voice deepening in that way it did when he was getting mad.

"Fuck you," I snarled, stepping closer, my body aching for a fight.

I didn't care who it was, my brothers would do if they didn't get out of my way.

"You are in pain, we see that, but Mika and Cole say she will return—"

"She should have been making improvements since yesterday, but she hasn't changed at all! I waited too long, don't you see?" I snapped, clenching my fists. "I waited too long to claim her, and she is dead for good."

Both brothers remained silent as I tried to control my breathing and my self-loathing.

"She might need more time," Corvin suggested.

"What do you know? You don't know how this feels, brother, neither of you do. Now move," I growled, shoving Corvin hard in the chest. I didn't even get a chance to remove my hand before he wrenched my wrist painfully, twisted my arm, and landed me hard on the ground, his knee pressed into my back.

"Listen here, brother. I know what loss feels like, more than you know. I do not enter the outside world for a fucking good reason. I have things to do, and I don't want to be out here longer than I need to. You were in need of a serious intervention, and we weren't *fucking asking* you to come back. It was an order," Corvin growled low in my ear, the force of his impatience and rage washing over me.

"Fuck you, brother," I hissed again.

"I am giving you the option one last time to come willingly, or we will drag you back kicking and screaming and lock you up until you calm the fuck down. Make your choice, Adrik," Corvin gritted out again in a tone that reminded me why we were all wary of him.

I ground my teeth together and considered what it would take for my brothers to harm me for real, to put me down so I was out of my misery. There had to be a way for them to end me. If they didn't, I was going to go Angel hunting and let them stab me. I tensed, preparing to throw Corvin off me and start the fight that would end my life, when the most feather-like touch brushed my mind. I stilled, waited, holding my breath to see if it would happen again. Seconds ticked by that felt like hours, and then it happened again! A gentle touch that seemed to light up dead parts inside me, winding its way deeper and deeper into my core. One of those invisible strands that tied me and Cali together was slowly coming back to life, bright and hot, warming parts of me that had died along with her.

"Adrik?" Corvin asked cautiously, feeling the change in me.

"Take me back," I breathed, barely daring to believe it. I needed to see her with my own two eyes to confirm it.

"Good choice," Devlin murmured as Corvin carefully pulled me to my feet. I stumbled slightly, my attention turned inwards, watching that small glowing strand pulse and fade in and out.

"What is it?" Devlin asked.

"I need to see Cali," I muttered, unable to help the small sprout of hope inside me. I sucked in an unsteady breath and, without waiting for my brothers, I shadowed away from them and back to the Arrival Room. They were right on my tail, but I didn't wait as I ran for my door and shoved it open, slamming it closed behind me before I ran for my bed where Cali still lay. I'd bathed her and dressed her in clean clothes, and she was as still and pale as death. She wasn't breathing, there was no heartbeat. And yet... I frowned at the gently pulsing connection in my head. Was I imagining it? Was my need of her so great that my mind had chosen to betray me and give me some semblance of hope?

"Cali, baby?" I whispered aloud, gently taking her hand in mine as I sank into the chair beside the bed.

Nothing.

I sucked in a slow, steadying breath and closed my eyes, reaching for that strand in my head that was glowing and flickering in and out of existence.

"Little red? Are you there?" I rasped, hoping desperately for something to cling to.

After a few seconds, I almost staggered away from her as her chest slowly began to move. She was breathing! I stood hurriedly and leaned over her and listened intently.

There!

Her heart. It was slow, barely there, but it was starting to beat.

I closed my eyes when they began to burn and I sank to the bed beside her, pressing her hand to my lips as my body shuddered.

"I'm right here, red. Come back to me."

CHAPTER EIGHTEEN
CALI

I thought pain was supposed to stop when death came.
Groaning, I tried to figure out where I was hurt, but I could find
no wounds. The reminder that I was dead should have shocked
me, but it had been creeping up on me since that first Angel
Blade stab wound, and I had accepted it. Blinking, I tried to look
around, but was greeted with total and utter blackness.
Okay...
I frowned. There was nothing, not even the slightest glimmer of
anything but black. I was standing in a void of nothingness. It felt
as though I was standing on a floor, but when I looked down,
there was nothing but more blackness. Was this... it? Was this
the afterlife? There was just me in a giant, empty void with no
one and nothing.
"Little red? Are you there?"
Adrik's voice echoed through the void, his voice distant. I gasped
and spun around, looking for him. Could I reply? I tried finding
that pathway in my head, the one that linked me to Adrik and
allowed me to speak to him, but it wasn't there. My stomach
dropped and I breathed in sharply, feeling absolutely no
connection to the man I loved. Why? The blackness around me
creeped in until it filled my very being. We hadn't been together
long, but Adrik had filled me in a way I had not even noticed had
happened. Now that those connections were gone, it was an
aching cavern of nothingness where his absence stood out more
than ever.

I spun around again and began walking, straining my eyes to see anything else nearby, anyone.

"I'm right here, red. Come back to me."

Adrik's voice sounded again, a little brittle and broken, but louder this time. I gritted my teeth against the tears that burned my eyes and my breathing picked up. I couldn't even see myself, I had no form here, and yet I existed. How?

"Hello."

I spun quickly at the voice and gasped at the exceptionally tall man before me with wide shoulders and dark, free-flowing hair. He was classically handsome, rugged, yet somehow hauntingly beautiful dressed in a black trench coat and with an ornate sword in a scabbard at his hip. I noticed that he kept his hands clasped behind his back, as if he were attempting to appear non-threatening.

Looking at him, I couldn't help but be reminded of a warrior of old.

"Who are you?" I finally asked.

"Can you not guess?" he returned, raising an eyebrow as he walked slowly forward. My mind ticked over the facts, and I hesitated in speaking, not sure I wanted to believe it.

"Not saying it aloud won't make it any less true," the man said as if reading my mind.

"You're a Reaper," I whispered. He nodded slightly and his smile was small.

"I am here to help you transition to the other side. You are a Witch, and you have been true to your calling. You go to neither Heaven nor Hell, your soul will be recycled to create a new Witch," he explained.

"There's no way I can go back?" I whispered, taking a small step back. I didn't want to go, not yet. I didn't feel as though I had done all I was meant to do.

"I am afraid not," he replied softly, stepping forward and holding out a hand. "Come with me."

"I don't want to."

"I am sorry, but there is nowhere to run, and nowhere to hide. This is what happens."

"But I wasn't ready to go," I stressed, backing up even though I didn't feel my legs move. I didn't have a body here, and yet I felt like I was moving.

"I understand you feel that way, but it is inevitable that you will pass on," the Reaper told me, and he did genuinely look understanding.

"I don't want to go," I repeated, holding out my hand to ward him off. I think I was, anyway, it was what I wanted to do. The Reaper opened his mouth to speak, but his gaze snapped to my arm. I gasped when I saw it, when it finally came back into being. He frowned and stalked towards me. I moved to back up again, but he waved a hand and curled his fingers into a fist before jerking his hand towards himself. I was frozen in place and then dragged forward until I was a foot away from him. With my mouth gaping, I realized he had allowed me the freedom of movement so as not to scare me before. He gripped my arm and I swallowed hard, trying to keep calm.

He sighed as he studied my wrist. "You have got to be kidding me."

"What?"

The Reaper drew in a long breath and then let it out slowly before he released my hand.

"I cannot take you. You have to go back."

I blinked stupidly and then frowned.

"But you said—"

"I know what I said, and ordinarily I would be correct, but this Mark prevents your soul from crossing over," he interrupted.

Mark?

I pulled my arm toward me and looked at my inner wrist. There, as clear as day, was what appeared to be a tattoo. It was a large circle with eight evenly spaced, smaller circles dotted the inside edge of it, another in the center. The circle at the top and the next circle to the right were shaded while the other seven remained empty. Beneath the large circle that encompassed the smaller ones were a series of smaller symbols. I was sure they meant something, although their meaning was not clear to me.

"What does that mean?" I decided to ask.

The Reaper shook his head. "Some humans would call it Aramaic, but it is a language that far exceeds it in age. It is the original language of the Demons."

"Do you know what it says?"

"Bound to the Second."

I considered his words and knew what they must mean. Adrik had bound me to him, he had completed the final step and bound my soul to his. Was this why I could not cross over? Was this how I would remain in his life and by his side for all eternity when I had been mortal and he immortal?

"You are bound to the second King of Hell, and I have a feeling there will be seven other mortals I will not be able to claim if this pattern continues," the Reaper explained.

"The mates of The Nine cannot die?" I asked slowly.

"Not permanently," the Reaper replied drily.

"And the Kings... can they ever truly die?" I asked. I wasn't sure I wanted to go back to a life where Adrik might die, leaving me alone for all eternity.

"The Kings can die, yes, and their souls would go somewhere

else."

"Where?"

The Reaper raised another imperious eyebrow and shook his head. "That is not for you to know."

"But I—"

"Little red, I need you to come back to me. Come back, I need you."

Adrik's voice was stronger now, and my heart hurt at the pain in his voice.

"Your mate is calling, Witch. You need to go back to him," the Reaper explained.

"If I die again... will I end up back here?"

"Yes."

"Can I ask a favor then?"

"What is it?"

"Can you put a chair here? Or a mat with some plants? A deck of cards... something?" I asked. The Reaper blinked in confusion several times and the look of astonishment on his face was priceless.

"Why?"

"So it's not so terrifying? There is nothing but darkness here," I replied.

"Cali, come back."

"Your mate needs you," the Reaper repeated, shaking his head slightly.

"Wait!" I called when he turned to leave.

"Yes?" he asked in a tone of barely concealed patience.

"What's your name?"

"Reaper."

"You must have a real name. What is it?"

"I do not have a name," he returned, but I could tell he was lying.

"If you don't tell me, I'm going to make one up."

"Goodbye, Witch," he said softly with a small, amused smile.

"See ya around, Mervyn," I called.

"Mervyn?" he returned, looking mortified.

"You wouldn't give me a name, so I named you." I shrugged and started walking backwards, smiling.

"Leave now, Witch," he ordered with a somewhat exasperated tone.

"Later, Mervyn!"

"Cali, my love... come back," Adrik whispered.

"Adrik?" I tried finding that string in my head.

"Cali! You're there, thank fuck."

"It's a little dark here, and I don't know how I'm supposed to find you exactly," I answered, loving that I could hear him again and that he could hear me. His relief filled me, warmed me.

"Follow my voice. Feel me," Adrik instructed. I felt his hands cup my face and I sighed, sinking into his touch. I imagined running my hands up his chest to link behind his neck.

"That's it, red. Come back to me. I need to punish you for defying my orders, and then spend days fucking you into submission," he whispered with a growl in his voice.

"Just knowing I'll see you again is incentive enough, no need to shower me with the rest of your promises," I teased, feeling tears sting my eyes at the thought of holding him again, tasting him, drawing his scent into my lungs. I missed him so much.

"I mean it, red. You've taken years off my life, and your punishment will be great."

"It's a good thing you're immortal then, hey big guy?"

"Cali." Adrik made a low, grumbling sound in his throat.

"Hey, I'm the one who should be mad. You Marked me. I thought you said I'd get to choose when to do that?"

"If I left it any longer, we would not be having this conversation, would

we?"

"Oh believe me, we will be having a big *conversation about it when I figure out how to come back, mister. Just you wait,"* I replied, grinning. I was scared, and this place went on forever. How was I ever meant to get back?

"You can try to kick my ass when you come back if it will make you feel better. I just need you to come back first," Adrik whispered, and he brushed his fingers over my cheek again.

I stopped walking and closed my eyes on the tears that threatened to escape and drew in a shaky breath. As if sensing my need for him, Adrik wrapped me in his arms and I buried my face in his chest, wanting to be back in my own body, in his bed, in his real, physical arms. I sank into him, willing myself to be back, not wanting to be here anymore in this cold, dark—

I gasped, dragging a lungful of air into my lungs as my eyes snapped open. I was staring at a stone ceiling, the stone awash with the reflection of flickering, orange flames. My body hurt a little, but nothing like I thought it would. I was lying on something comfortable, something stupidly soft.

"Cali?"

I slowly turned towards the sound of that voice, not daring to hope I was back. I was no longer in the world of blackness and nothingness... I was back.

As my gaze fell back on Adrik, my vision went blurry, and he moved. Strong arms wrapped around me, strength and love pouring into me, filling me up so that I no longer felt shaky or cold.

"You're back," he rasped, and it was only then I felt the relentless pounding of relief from him, the echoes of soul-searing pain and guilt buried in his mind. I wrapped my arms around him, and cry laughed as he hauled me up into a sitting position.

"I'm back," I whispered brokenly. Neither of us spoke or moved for the longest time, and I shook off the loneliness of that place, the eerie way I couldn't even see my own body until the Reaper had allowed me to.

I was back here, in Adrik's arms, where I was meant to be.

~

ADRIK

Like a man possessed, I pulled back from her and fused my mouth with hers. She didn't resist in the slightest and I devoured her. I'd missed her so *fucking* much.

I poured my misery into that kiss, my hopelessness, rage, and self-hatred. I tried to shake off that empty feeling that had taken up space inside me, sliding my hands into her hair and pressing her back into the bed. Cali wrapped her arms and legs around me and kissed me just as hard. I was in her mind, touching her, whispering words to her I never thought I'd say to another soul. I was overwhelmed with the need to take her, to make her mine in every sense of the word.

"I love you," I whispered against her lips before kissing her harder, deeper. Cali pulled back and panted, her pale green eyes shiny with tears.

"I love you," she returned, and with those words, that golden, burning tie that bound us together strengthened more than ever, bringing us closer and closer. The pleasure in being bound to her, in feeling those bonds rebuild and restrengthen was more than I was expecting.

"I need you," I murmured breathlessly against her lips, grinding my pelvis between her legs. Cali moaned and the sound sent all the blood in my head straight to my cock.

"I'm here, Adrik. Take me; I need you too," she whimpered, clawing at my shirt. I wished away our clothes so that we were both naked and she sighed happily, running her hands across my shoulders and down my biceps.

I merged our minds, more than happy to sink into her consciousness and rest there for a century, simply appreciating the feel of having her take up space in my head again. She fit here, she was perfect, and I never wanted to lose her again.

My pleasure became hers, and her pleasure was mine. I kissed her hard, my fingers stroking her breasts and further down between her legs. She moaned against my mouth and in her mind, I suckled strongly on her nipples.

"Adrik," she whispered breathily, her head tilting back and her mouth falling open in pleasure. I dipped my head and nipped at her stomach before kissing my way down to her wet pussy. I inhaled and groaned. Fuck, I'd missed her. Without any further stalling, I buried my face between her legs and ate at her like a man starved, sucking, and flicking my tongue rapidly, sliding two fingers inside her hot sheath.

"Adrik!" she cried out, the sound like music to my ears. She was fucking kryptonite, and I didn't care. As long as I had her in my life, everything else would be fine.

I couldn't wait any longer, I needed her. Raising myself up, I notched my cock at her wet entrance. Her eyes fluttered open, her cheeks pink and eyes hazy with desire.

"Mine," I growled and surged forward.

"Yes!" she cried out, her back arching as I sank fully into her. She was my heaven, my paradise, my everything. Pulling out, I surged forward again, dragging another cry from her as her hands clawed at my arms. I pushed her legs up higher, inching deeper inside her. Her inner muscles dragged along my cock, clenching, and rippling as I rocked my hips, making sure to tease her clit with every stroke.

Her mewls of pleasure only went to enhance my own. I could feel how close she was getting already; how tight she was getting. "Adrik, more," she whimpered.

"Yes," I gritted out, rasping, my cock aching to come, my blood on fire with the power of taking my woman again. Our bonds grew hot and bright in our chests, those imperceptible ties between us growing stronger, binding us closer.

"Your pussy feels so fucking good," I gasped, gritting my teeth, holding off.

"So close… oh, fuck me," she cried out, her brow creasing and her back arching.

I took both her hands and slammed them into the mattress by her head and fucked her harder, my cock drilling in and out of her tight, wet, pussy; her sheath tightening, strangling every inch of my hard length.

"Come for me, red. Be my good girl and fucking come on my cock," I groaned, possessed with some indefinable, primitive need to come inside her, to claim her and mark her deep inside with my seed.

She gasped, her body twisting as her pussy pulsed and throbbed, rippling around my cock and milking me as I came hard with her. I shouted wordlessly to the ceiling, my body shivering and shaking as I poured myself into her.

"Yes!" Cali screamed.

CHAPTER NINETEEN
ADRIK

"Not this fucking thing again," I groaned, turning to look around the windowless, doorless room.

"You say the sweetest things," Cali's Aunt Penny greeted with a sarcastic smile.

"How can I help you, Penny?"

"I was originally going to drag you into this dream and cause you pain you didn't know was possible. I felt my niece die, felt her lifeforce fade away, and I was powerless to help her," she began.

"Why couldn't you help her? I know Witches—either those in the same Coven or those who share blood—can share power across great distances. Why didn't you help her?" I demanded, unable to hide the bite in my voice.

"I did help her," Penny shot back, her tone cold as ice. "I was with her as she healed her friend, the old man. I gave her my power when she needed it to defend herself against the Angels. I gave her so much that I almost drained myself. I was laying helpless on the floor for almost a day before one of the village Healers found me."

I felt the power in her words, the honesty. I tried to imagine what she must have gone through; the exhaustion would have been enough. But to then lie there helpless, and feel your only family member get weaker and weaker, in pain and suffering, and then disappear completely? All the while she would have been stuck on the ground, too weak to even call out for help.

"I am sorry for what you went through," I finally said. Her eyes widened in surprise before they narrowed, and she studied me intently.

"I don't trust you, Demon King."

"The feeling is mutual."

"I felt Cali come back, felt her come alive again. I have not been to see her yet, I wanted to confront you first. How is it she is back?"

"You're *really* not going to like me," I muttered and smirked sheepishly, rubbing the back of my neck.

"Tell me."

"I bound her soul to mine."

Silence fell, heavy and tense, and it stretched on for minutes as I watched her battle with whatever inner war raged within her.

"You bound the soul of a Witch to a Demon King?" she whispered, almost as if she was worried that saying it aloud would make it true.

"Yes. And before you think I did this to trap her, you should hear of the prophecy," I continued. I flicked my hand and two comfy chairs appeared and then waved Penny towards the one closest to her and took my seat. I never bothered to explain myself to others before, I couldn't give a shit what their opinions were, but AP was Cali's only living relative... I needed to at least make an effort.

And so, with a heavy sigh, I went on to recite the prophecy and what it meant to each of my brothers. I explained in as little detail as possible what had happened with Mika and Cole, and explained what we'd learned about the prophecy. I paused and let her take in the information before I went on to explain that completing the binding is inevitable, but that I tried to do the right thing, and it almost cost us Cali's life. I refused to apologize for finishing it without her permission.

More silence fell between us, and I waited a moment to give her some space.

"You won't ever harm her?" Penny asked after a moment, looking less than happy about the binding.

"I never want to. And I don't think it's physically possible for me to hurt her," I answered honestly, knowing she would be looking for the slightest of doubts. After another silence, I got to my feet.

"Where are you going?"

"I have my mate to get back to, and I do not want to spend more time here than I need to. I have done you the courtesy of explaining myself where I would not do the same for others. You are Cali's aunt, I would like for us to get along as much as possible."

AP sat back in her chair, and I could see she appreciated my honesty.

"You may be a mighty King of Hell... but I will find a way to take you down if you ever do wrong by my Cali. Death will not prevent it," she warned.

"Noted." I grinned.

With a stiff nod and a flash of amusement in her eyes, she dismissed me from the dream.

I opened my eyes and blinked at the ceiling and then groaned at the pleasure that rolled through me. I glanced down to see Cali with my shaft in her mouth and her eyes sparkling with humor. "Fuck, you look beautiful with your lips wrapped around my cock."

Her answer was to take me deeper and I hissed out a breath, tangling her hair in my hands as my hips rocked forward gently. I felt my cock slide down her throat and she swallowed around it. "Fucking hell!"

She hummed her pleasure at my reaction, and I groaned, feeling a tingle start in my spine.

"Yes. Fuck, I'm gonna come," I warned, tightening my grip on her hair. Cali took me deeper, sucking harder. I shouted wordlessly as I came down her throat, gritting my teeth as I forced myself not to thrust hard and fast into her mouth.

Cali took her time licking me clean before she kissed my inner thighs and worked her way up my abdomen, licking at my abs and tracing tattoos with her tongue.

"You're fucking perfect," I murmured, my voice a little deeper and raspier than before.

"Perfect for you, perhaps," she conceded with a grin. I gripped her chin tightly in my hand and pulled her closer, kissing her hard and deep. She moaned against me and straddled me while we kissed. I was hard again already—perks of being a Demon King. I could go all night... literally.

We'd already spent several hours fucking each other's brains out since she woke up. We hadn't even talked yet about what had happened or how everyone else was. It was just constant, one session after another, neither of us able to get enough.

"Was that my aunt in your dream?" Cali whispered as she pulled away from me.

"Yep. She wanted to kick my ass for letting you die but wanted to know how I got you back."

Cali grimaced. "Did you tell her?"

"I thought she should know." I shrugged.

Cali glanced down at her wrist, and I looked too, tracing the little circles there. Some deep, primitive part of me felt full satisfaction at seeing that Mark, at seeing her branded as mine. It didn't take a genius to guess that each circle represented a mate, and that as each one was bound, the newest Mate would have one more circle filled than the others. It was a beautiful mark, a deep gold, shaded with bits of black.

"Can you explain some things to me? I'm a little fuzzy," she asked, sliding down beside me, and twisting her arm away. I dragged one of her legs across my thighs and tucked her in close to my body, still not over the fact that she was back here in my arms, alive and well.

~

CALI

"What do you need me to explain?" Adrik asked, tracing fingers up and down my bare arm.

"Why didn't you reach out to your brothers when you were hurt in the beginning?" I asked, deciding to go all the way back.

"One of the Angels stabbed me with an Angel Blade. I didn't want you to feel the pain, so I cut off our connection. The blade was coated with something the Angels have made that prevents us from calling to our brothers, I don't know how it works. It fades away after some time, but it leaves me vulnerable and without backup," he explained.

"What happened to Sol? And Keira? Are they okay? Did Mika help heal Sol the rest of the way?" I fired off.

"Sol and Keira are fine. They were here for the first two days, but I needed space, and they were frustrating me with their presence and their emotions. Sol didn't want to go, but I didn't give him a chance. He's pissed, but he'll get over it."

"And Keira?"

"Mika healed them both perfectly. Keira wants to see you again, to thank you and maybe keep in touch. She seems alright."

"What about my people? How many of them... died?" I asked, dreading the answer. Adrik's arm wrapped around me tightly and he sighed.

"A lot. At least twelve, plus two volunteers."

I gasped and pulled back to look at him. "The Angels killed that many?"

"And the Rogues, yes. They went easy on the mortals, actually."

I digested that news and sighed. "How is Zarak?"

"Alive," Adrik answered, his jaw tight.

"What happened?"

Adrik rolled his eyes and pulled me close again, brushing a kiss over my head.

"You were out for a week, Cali. Seven days, this is day eight now," he began.

"What?!" I gasped. It had *never* taken me that long to heal before.

"This happened to Mika. She died, but it only took her five days to come back. By day six, I was... unhinged and looking for a fight that would end me," he continued, looking uncomfortable. "He found me, and we talked. I wanted to provoke him into a fight, but he didn't want a bar of it and fucked off."

"And you're still mad he didn't kill you?" I asked with a sardonic smile.

"No," he answered immediately. "Just annoyed he didn't take me seriously."

"My turn," Adrik added, tipping my head up to look at him. "Why did you go to help Hariel? Why didn't you just stay hidden?"

"Really?" I raised an eyebrow. "He saved me, Sol, and Keira. He protected us, killed his own kind and did it all because he believed that what the Angels had become was abhorrent and wrong.

"Your life isn't worth anyone else's. We've talked about this," he reminded.

"And I need you to understand that the woman you want me to be in those situations is not, and never will be, me. It is at my core that I help others, that I heal and protect. Especially those who put themselves at risk for me."

"Calixta—"

"No," I interrupted, shifting so that I could straddle him. "You need to understand this, Adrik, because no matter how much you wish I would, I won't change. I'm sorry if that doesn't make me your ideal woman, but it's how I'm built."

Adrik's hand shot up to bunch in my hair and he dragged my face down so that he could kiss me roughly. I kissed him back, feeling a sting of pain in my scalp and a shot of arousal between my legs at his harsh grip.

"You," he started, pulling away and breathing heavily. "Are. Perfect. In every way. Never doubt that."

I smiled gently, and he released my hair. Sucking in a deep breath I let it out slowly.

"Hariel had a mate, Adrik. I felt her there, in his head. I felt her despair when he was injured, her cries of agony are trapped in my mind. I felt how awful it was for her to lose her mate, to say goodbye, to not be able to reach him in time. Hariel risked *everything* to save me. I was not going to cower in a corner and let him die," I explained. Adrik's blue eyes scanned my face and he finally sighed and nodded. He understood.

"Speaking of Hariel and his mate… you and I need to find a way to break into Heaven and save her."

Adrik stilled beneath me and then he laughed. I waited, crossing my arms over my bare stomach while he laughed and laughed, tears leaking from his eyes. I rolled my eyes and waited impatiently for him to finish.

"It's not funny," I snapped.

"Oh, but it is. It's about as easy for a Demon to break into Heaven as it is for an Angel to break into Hell. I'm sorry, red, but there's no way to do it," he explained, shaking his head.

"We need to find a way. I don't care how we do it, Adrik, but I gave my word to Hariel that I would rescue his mate. It was his dying wish, and I don't give my word lightly. She needs us. She's a prisoner in Heaven," I explained.

Adrik sighed and shook his head.

"Cali..." He trailed off.

"Just... say yes. I'm not suggesting we charge in right now. I just want you to help me try, and I mean really try," I asked, tracing the tattoos on his chest.

"I don't want you in any danger," he grumbled.

"I am a Witch; I was born into danger. Now, I am a Witch bound to a Demon King. The bounty on my head has never been higher. No matter what I do I'm in danger. Just... help me do some good here, Adrik. Please?"

"Fuck." He sighed and scrubbed a hand over his face.

"Fine, we'll try. But if I say there is no way in, or it is too dangerous for me to risk you, then you need to drop it. Understood?"

I chewed on that for a moment but slowly nodded. I would do my best, and I would make sure Adrik did his best to save that Witch. She was one of my kind, and she had lost her mate. I would get her back.

"Adrik... how many more Witches do you think the Angels have up there?" I asked.

He frowned. "Did you see others?"

I shook my head. "No... but they have one Witch up there,

chained and trapped, it's not so out of the realm of possibilities that they have more," I pointed out. Adrik thought about it a moment and nodded slowly, although I could tell the idea didn't sit well with him. Maybe the Angels had discovered Witches long ago, and had been keeping it secret, quietly collecting an army of Witches before the Demons had even clued on that they were not extinct.

After a long moment of silence, I turned to him and grinned. "I want to go see Sol and everyone."

"Now? It's the middle of the night."

"So?"

"So… I had plans to ravish you first," Adrik answered, spinning us so that I was pinned beneath him, his teeth nipping at my throat. I moaned and tilted my head back to give him better access.

"I supposed we can do this first," I said on a sigh.

"Like I said… You are perfect, red."

EPILOGUE
CALI

It was with great reluctance that Adrik agreed to leave his realm… or *our* realm as he told me. I still had a life on the surface, one I had no intention of giving up. The animals at the shelter needed me, but so did the community of homeless people I'd worked tirelessly with to gain their trust and heal them. Adrik and I agreed I'd live in Hell with him, but that I would keep my home to keep up appearances. After much debate, he had agreed to let me go to the surface to work, as long as I kept one of his Knights with me. I agreed, not having realized that where one Knight went, so did five of his soldiers. It was decided that the Knight would stay in the building with me while I worked, cloaked if need be, but that the others would remain outside the building, hiding and watching for a potential attack.

I was tired, and achy, but felt oh-so-alive! As much as I would have loved to have spent another day in bed with him, I wanted to check on my friends and meet Mika properly. Adrik told me she was eager to meet me when he'd filled his family in on my progress. I had known other Witches during my life, sure, but none besides my aunt that were close to me. Besides, Mika was the only other Witch mated to a King of Hell. She would be able to relate to things no one else could.

My AP had visited me in my dreams and we'd spoken and hugged. It was so good to see her again, and she was feeling calmer now that she could see for herself that I was happy and healthy.

"And they live! I was worried Adrik was going to fuck you to death."

"Or keep you locked in his realm forever."

I lifted my head as we exited Adrik's realm and grinned at Malik and Harkyn as they sauntered forward. I laughed and rushed for Malik, throwing my arms around his neck. I was so glad they were okay. He hugged me hard and then I was yanked away. I sighed and glared up at Adrik who was glowering at the two of us.

"No touching," he snapped.

"Oh, hush you," I returned before stepping away to hug Harkyn. Harkyn grinned against my neck and let his hand slide down my back towards my backside. I zapped him and he yelped and let me go.

"What was that for?"

"You know what that was for," I glared. Harkyn grinned and shook his head.

"I think we're going to get along just fine," another voice called with a laugh. I turned to see Tomika head towards me, and I smiled and nodded.

"I hope so. Thank you... for everything. For healing my friends, and Adrik and trying to help me," I said quickly Mika shrugged and leaned back into Cole.

"It's what we do, isn't it?"

I smiled and nodded. "We're just on our way out, but can we catch up later?"

"Sure. We have some more stuff to explain to you that you might not know about. Babies and the like," Mika answered, waving her hand like it was no big deal. I froze.

"Sorry... Did you say babies?" I gaped.

Mika elbowed Cole in the stomach and glared up at him. "I told you he wouldn't tell her," she hissed.

I whirled on Adrik who had the grace to look ashamed. "Babies?"

"You're not opposed to them I assume?" he answered.

"No, but I'd like a damn choice on when they happen. Oh God," I groaned, thinking of all the times we'd had sex without protection…

"That was pretty much my reaction," Mika sympathized.

"Okay… yeah. You and I can talk later… without the guys," I promised. Mika grinned and Cole glared.

"There are no secrets," Cole warned darkly.

"Says the guy holding onto the baby bombshell," I muttered.

"It wasn't my secret to tell," Cole implored.

"So, there *can* be secrets?"

"No," he answered darkly

"Maybe not when there was one Witch… now there's two of us," I returned, grinning at Mika. I felt Adrik come up behind me and wrap an arm around my waist.

"Come on, let's go. While it's fun to watch you piss off my brother, we have people to see," Adrik reminded, but I could hear the humor in his voice.

"We'll see you when you get back," Mika replied with a laugh, patting Cole's chest.

I waved to everyone, and Adrik shadowed us out of there.

~

"Sunshine?"

I grinned and spun on the spot, searching until I found Sol among the tens of other people in the brightly lit area.

"Sol!" I cried and hurried forward. The old man stood there with his hand pressed to his chest and his eyes shiny with tears. I didn't stop and hurried to him, wrapping him in my arms. Sol's arms were slower to wrap around me, but shockingly strong. Neither of us broke away for a moment, and I could feel his relief at seeing me alive and his guilt that I was even hurt.

"It wasn't your fault," I whispered.

"It was a trap, sunshine. They took me and they hurt me to lure you out. If it weren't for me, those Angels would have left you alone," he explained, shaking his head.

"Not to make you think less of our relationship, Sol, but I would have come for anyone they hurt. The fact that it was you just made me all the more motivated."

"It still don't sit right with me. I'm just so glad you're up and about again," he answered, touching my cheek gently. I smiled and watched as Sol's gaze slid over my shoulder and his eyes turned hard.

"Boy."

"Sol," Adrik greeted with a nod.

"Glad you finally got her back," Sol grumbled.

"So am I," Adrik agreed. Silence fell and I sighed.

"Sol... as much as I know you would have liked to have been there when I woke up, it was safer you weren't. Adrik was untethered; he could have hurt you," I tried to explain.

"Yeah, well... if he had done his damn job in the first place, you never woulda been hurt, sunshine."

"Sol," I warned.

"Cali?" someone called brightly, and I turned to see Keira headed our way with a big smile.

"Hey," I greeted and stepped past Sol to hug her.

"I am so glad you're okay," she whispered, her voice breaking.

"Me too."

"We watched you die and... and seeing how much it hurt Adrik... I wasn't sure we'd see you again," she confided. My heart constricted at knowing my death hurt Adrik, and at once, he was there in my mind, soothing me.

"I'm sorry you were distressed, Keira. I'm glad you're here though, I wanted to make sure you were okay."

"Thanks to you, I am. My father would have been devastated to lose me… we're all each other has in the whole world and I shudder to think about him left here all alone," she answered.

I stood and talked to Sol and Keira for a while longer and made sure Sol knew I was giving him another healing in a week. Mika had gone a bit above in her healing of Sol and he was feeling better than ever. I noted he was still wearing the amulet and smiled.

"You still have it," I pointed out. Sol wrapped his fingers around it and smiled softly.

"You gave it to me. Call me crazy, but I feel better when I wear it," he answered.

"Good, it means it's still working. It's… special. I made it especially for you, it's meant to keep healing you, to keep you healthy," I explained, deciding not to tell him it was tied directly to me.

"I'll never take it off," he decreed strongly, his eyes suspiciously bright. Honestly, I barely noticed the small flow of power the amulet took from me now that I was at full strength again.

We stopped by to see Sara and Sky as well before we went home, and I organized to heal Sky again the day after Sol. I was disheartened to see just how many of my people had died. A lot of them who had survived thought it was a gang war and were trying to move on. Adrik was glued to my side the entire time, and I made sure three times that my protections were in place. Hopefully, the Angels thought I was dead, but you never could be too careful.

When we made it back to Hell—a sentence I never thought I'd consider happily—I was tired but determined to talk to Mika. It took half an hour to convince the guys to go somewhere else and allow Mika and I to speak in peace. We compared Marks and stories. I was at a loss to how Mika had kept her cool with Cole for so long, but I think it helped that she didn't have full control of her magic at that point. It also explained why Adrik had tried to get me to fall for him first—he knew I could use all my magic. I explained my meeting with the Reaper, and she told me about hers. It took her a good minute or two to stop laughing when I told her I'd named him Mervyn. Mika was very interested to know that I'd found out what my inscription meant, and that hers likely meant *Bound to the First*. I explained the prophecy and how it wasn't until he was going to Mark me that Adrik found my blood trail, so we surmised that the prophecy wasn't in regard to when or how the Kings would find their mates, but rather when they would Mark them. When we finally got down to baby-talk, I was petrified but relieved that I hadn't had any kind of sign that it was that time of the century and could have a baby. Tomika then went on to explain about her heritage, how it tied in with Nova and that he was currently looking for her twin. I offered to help locate her if I could and she agreed it would be welcome.

We were still talking about our families when Cole and Adrik came in.

"Alright, girl time is over," Cole announced.

"The Hell it is. You guys have guy-time all the time. I finally have a woman to talk to. Go away," Mika snapped.

"Nope. Say goodnight," Cole said. Without missing a beat, he leaned down and scooped Mika up and tossed her over his shoulder.

"Put me down, you big Neanderthal," Mika snapped, but I could hear the laughter in her voice.

"Nope. I'm a caveman, remember? And you are the woman I want. Bye, Cali!"

I laughed at the disappearing couple and turned to face Adrik.

"You know I'd stun you if you did that to me," I warned, raising my hand as if I would do it.

"I'm well aware," he answered with a grin. I lowered my hand and he lunged. I gasped, not having enough time before he tossed me backward onto the bed and was on top of me in an instant. I raised my hands, but he grabbed them and held them down above my head with one hand.

"Shithead!" I laughed.

"With words of endearment like that, how can I resist?" Adrik laughed before he tore my shirt open with one hand. The rest of my protest turned into a moan of satisfaction, followed by a few hours of mind-numbing pleasure.

~

ADRIK

Happiness is a funny thing.

Before Cali, I could have sworn I was happy, but now that I knew what true happiness was, I was aware of how empty my life had been before. Knowing the kind of joy I had, I wished it for all my brothers.

Cali insisted on hugging my brothers, and they enjoyed pissing me off and letting her. I gritted my teeth through it, but I always punished Cali for it to the point where she was walking funny the next day. She never really complained about her punishments, though. I swear she did things just to piss me off, so I'd put her over my knee or tie her up.

"My AP will be here in three hours," Cali announced.

"What?"

She frowned. "Don't tell me you forgot. I told you she was on her way because she wanted to meet you in person."

"Right. Nope... I didn't forget," I lied. Honestly, I'd tried to erase the information from my mind, but I guess it was going to happen sooner or later.

I opened my mouth to say something funny when there was a screech from outside. Cali froze and I frowned. What the hell was that?

Without pause, we both started towards the door, and I opened it in time to see Malik stride past our door, a woman over his shoulder beating at his back.

"What the—" I gaped. Malik turned and grinned at me.

"I found my mate!" he announced.

"I'm not your mate, you psychotic, overgrown, ingrate," the woman shouted, using her fist to hit him again.

"Malik!" Cali reprimanded, moving to step towards them. I held an arm out to keep her back and she frowned.

"You are my mate, human, and now that I've marked you, there's no escaping me," he answered, slapping her backside. She gasped and dug her nails into his back.

"Put me down at once, Malik! I am *engaged,* you moron!"

"Oh shit," I muttered.

"Malik, this really isn't the way—"

"I'll deal with my mate my way, you guys had your story. We'll see you in a few days," Malik interrupted with a wink. "Come along, mate," he added, sauntering towards his realm again.

"I am going to make you pay, Malik. There will be pain unlike anything—" the woman shrieked before her voice was cut off as his door shut behind him.

"Well… that's interesting," I mused.

"Adrik, we have to help her. That poor woman." Cali gasped.

"She's more than safe, red. Malik would never hurt her or force her into anything. She's safe with him," I reminded.

"He's forcing her to stay in his realm. She must be scared."

"Did you feel fear coming from her? Because all I felt was outrage and anger," I countered. Cali gnawed on her lower lip and said nothing, but I could feel how she knew I was right.

Things were about to get interesting.

"What do you want to do while we wait for your AP?" I asked, waggling my eyebrows. Cali grinned and shook her head, her shoulders relaxing as she let the issue of Malik and his mate go.

"Actually, I was thinking about that problem I brought up to you the other day, and I want to know if you can take me to Zarak?" Cali asked.

"Why?"

"Can you just trust me?" she asked.

"With my life, absolutely. With your own, not a chance."

Cali laughed and pressed a kiss to my cheek. With a reluctant sigh, I searched the surface for a sign that Zarak was around and was disappointed when I found a sure sign.

"Fine. But if I order you to leave, Cali, you do as I say. Promise."

"I promise if I am in danger and you tell me to go, then we'll go."

I frowned at her rewording but took it. It was as good as I was going to get.

We shadowed to the surface, and I watched as Zarak finished dispatching a Rogue Demon. He raised his head slowly to look at us, his black eyes sliding to Cali, and they lit briefly.

"Calixta," he greeted, his voice warming slightly.

"Zarak," she returned and stepped forward quickly. I tugged on her hand, slowing her down. She wasn't allowed to hug this one.

"It is good to see you alive and well. I worried when I found no sign of you," he admitted.

"It's taken some time, but I'm back," she assured with a grin.

"What can I do for you?"

"Well… I have this idea and I wondered if you would be open to it," Cali began and laid out the whole idea. The Nephilim listened attentively without interrupting.

"So, what do you think?" Cali asked. "You can do it, right?"

"I could." Zarak nodded slowly. "But I do not know what right I have."

"Well, I don't see why not. Everyone dies eventually, but it seems unfair that the humans either go to Heaven where they're turned into asshole Angels, or to Hell where they're tortured to become Demons. I have so many human friends who deserve neither option. You created a whole other realm for Hariel. Can you maybe make some room for others?" Cali asked in that voice that got her almost anything.

"I do not know if that is a good idea," he finally answered. Cali looked distraught and I drew her closer to me. I knew she was worried about Sol and her AP and a few of her other friends, and I couldn't blame her.

"Let me think about it, okay?" Zarak finally relented, and I noted the discomfort on his face at seeing Cali so upset.

"Oh, thank you, Zarak!" Cali cried and threw her arms around him. I growled and Zarak raised an eyebrow at me.

"Your mate is growling."

"He doesn't like me hugging other males, but he'll get over it," she answered and pulled back.

"I won't promise that I will do this thing, Calixta, but I will consider it," he agreed. Cali nodded and beamed at him.

"Have you spoken to your friends, Sol and Keira?"

"Yes, both are doing well. Keira and her father are kind of alone in the world, so she was very grateful for everything we did," Cali answered. I frowned at the interest the Nephilim showed in the human Keira when he asked a few more questions about her and swallowed my smile. The mixed breed had the hots for a human.

Interesting. Zarak was unlike any Nephilim I had known over the years, although to be honest, I'd never actually *known* any of them, just *of* them.

"Zarak... how is it you are able to see into the shadows when we have cloaked ourselves?" I asked during a lull.

Zarak turned his attention to me, his dark eyes considering.

"When we first met, Cali was hiding, but you sensed her there. No Nephilim in the past has ever been able to do that. Your wings are also a different color, and a lot bigger," I pointed out.

Zarak remained infuriatingly silent and I sighed.

"You're not going to explain it to me... are you?"

"If ever there is a time where it becomes necessary for you to know, then you will. My kind are far too rare to be telling anyone things about us, even if they are allies," he explained calmly, his face annoyingly void of expression. I wanted to be annoyed at him for his answer, curiosity was a frustrating thing when you were denied answers, but I could understand.

When we finally left Zarak to clean up the Demon mess he'd made, I wrapped Cali in my arms and shadowed us back to our realm.

"What do you think about having kids?"

Cali turned to look at me with wide eyes.

"Uh… I don't know. At some point, maybe?" she stammered.

"Not anytime soon?"

"Why?"

I shrugged and grinned. "Because I've decided I want to have children with you, and the sooner the better. Wouldn't you like your AP to get to meet some of them?" I asked.

She glared. "That's just mean."

I grinned again and shrugged. "But it's the truth. Think of Sol getting to hold at least one of your children?"

"Adrik," she warned as I stalked closer.

"A little girl with your eyes and hair," I added until the backs of her legs hit the bed.

"Stop it," she breathed, but I felt the way her heart twinged at the image I put there.

"A boy with my smile and eyes?" I added, knowing she loved those two things about me. She sat back on the bed, her heart pounding and breathing sharp.

"We need more time together first," she pointed out. I shrugged. "We have all the time in the world."

"Exactly," she agreed. "So, let's take some of that time and be together, alone, for a while before we bring what I assume will be immortal children into the world."

I grinned and leaned over her until she was laying back on the bed.

"Fine, but I want to get started in the next five years."

"Five years?" she repeated, astounded.

"Yes. I can't wait for you to be carrying a life we created together, and I will give you five years."

"Uh… Isn't there some kind of… you know… universe birth control?" she asked.

"I'm sure there's a way to bend it in our favor," I assured.

"Adrik." She sighed as my lips brushed hers, her body coming to life beneath my touch.

"Yes, red?"

"Forget about kids right now and make me come."

I grinned.

"I am at your service, mate."

Cali laughed as I lunged for her, and I wasted little time getting us naked and sweating. I didn't stop touching her and tasting her until I had her crying out her release more than once before I allowed myself the same pleasure.

She was fucking perfection.

THE END OF BOOK TWO

THANK YOU FOR READING

THE KINGS OF HELL
ADRIK

If you loved Cali & Adrik's story, I hope you'll come find me on Facebook and Instagram to stay in touch and up to date.
There will be a story for each of the Kings of Hell!

Want to know what happened two hundred years ago when Donovan earned his name, Nova? Stay in touch because a prequel is coming soon!

Did you find yourself curious about the Nephilim? I hope so! Because a Nephilim spin-off series is in the works!

Thanks again for reading, and I hope to hear from you soon!
As always, please do not forget to leave a review. You have no idea how powerful your words are, or how much authors rely on reviews to keep on writing.

DID YOU KNOW...
I HAVE TWO OTHER PEN NAMES?

I know that seems like overkill, but there is a method to my madness.

Books under the name **Alexis Maree** are for paranormal romances. Not everyone likes to read this genre, so I like to keep them separate.

Likewise, not everyone likes contemporary romances, so I have another pen name for those...**T. Maree.**

Then last, but certainly not least, are my sinfully sexy romances, the ones that border on the line of "*should she really put that down in print?*"
Some people don't like those kinds of spicy scenes, and so I decided to keep those separate from the rest under the name **Luna Maree.**

So, if you'd like to check out what else I've written, go onto my website.

Happy reading!

Alexis | Luna | T.

www.ingramcontent.com/pod-product-compliance
Lightning Source LLC
Chambersburg PA
CBHW021053030726
47496CB00006B/1818